PRAISE FOR THE NOVELS OF MADELINE HUNTER

SECRETS OF SURRENDER

"With each new book, Hunter displays more of her unique ability to draw readers into a heated romance that speaks to the body, mind and heart. . . . Her exceptional storytelling is mesmerizing." —*Romantic Times*

"Beautifully written and containing a cast of characters that provide a solid backdrop to this interesting and emotional story, *Secrets of Surrender* is a page-turner."
—*Romance Reviews Today*

"[A] captivating, compelling story of two people succeeding against all odds." —*Booklist*

THE RULES OF SEDUCTION

"Hunter is masterful at drawing readers in and creating realistic characters and powerful emotions so that each of her romances both satisfies readers and leaves them anxious for the next book." —*Booklist*

"Rich in plot and characters, rich in wit and emotion, and rich in satisfaction for any reader."
—*Romance Reviews Today*

"A carefully crafted, riveting romance showcasing Hunter's talent for both great storytelling and unforgettable romance. Her strong hero and equally fascinating heroine make this an irresistible read. . . . Hunter finds herself in the enviable position of being a writer whose novels every reader will adore." —*Romantic Times*

LORD OF SIN

"Snappily paced and bone-deep satisfying, Hunter's books are so addictive they should come with a surgeon general's warning. [Hunter] doesn't neglect the absorbing historical details that set her apart from most of her counterparts, engaging the reader's mind even as she deftly captures the heart." —*Publishers Weekly*

THE ROMANTIC

"Every woman dreams of being the object of some man's secret passion, and readers will be swept away by Hunter's hero and her latest captivating romance." —*Booklist*

THE SINNER

"Packed with sensuality and foreboding undertones, this book boasts rich historical details and characters possessing unusual depth and vitality, traits that propel it beyond the standard historical romance fare." —*Publishers Weekly*

"Sensual, intriguing, and absorbing, prolific Hunter scores again." —*Booklist*

"There are books you finish with a sigh because they are so rich, so tender, so near to the heart that they will stay with you for a long, long time. Madeline Hunter's historical romance *The Sinner* is such a book." —*Oakland Press*

THE CHARMER

"With its rich historical texture, steamy love scenes, and indelible protagonists, this book embodies the best of the genre." —*Publishers Weekly* (starred review)

"In yet another excellent offering from Hunter, her intriguing characters elicit both fascination and sympathy." —*Booklist*

THE SAINT

"[An] unassuming, witty, and intriguing account of how love helps, not hinders, the achievement of dreams." —*Booklist*

THE SEDUCER

"Hunter . . . sweeps both her readers and her characters up in the embrace of history. Lush in detail and thrumming with sensuality, this offering will thrill those looking for a tale as rich and satisfying as a multi course gourmet meal."

—*Publishers Weekly*

"*The Seducer* is a well-crafted novel . . . characteristically intense and frankly sexual." —*Contra Costa Times*

"[An] intriguing and redemptive tale." —*Booklist*

"Angst and passion battle it out in this very sensual story."

—*Oakland Press*

LORD OF A THOUSAND NIGHTS

"Hunter's fresh, singular voice and firm grasp of history set this lively 14th-century romance apart. An electrifying blend of history, romance, and intrigue, this fast-paced tale is a testament to Hunter's considerable narrative prowess."

—*Publishers Weekly*

"I have enjoyed every novel Ms. Hunter has penned to date, and it's difficult to say, but each one seems better than the one before. *Lord of a Thousand Nights* is no exception; it's a masterpiece of storytelling, one that stands alone as a superb read, as one I very highly recommend."

—*Romance Reviews Today*

THE PROTECTOR

"Hunter is at home with this medieval setting, and her talent for portraying intelligent, compelling characters seems to develop with each book. This feisty tale is likely to win her the broader readership she deserves." —*Publishers Weekly*

"Madeline Hunter has restored my faith in historicals and in the medieval romance especially. *The Protector* is definitely a wonderful read." —*All About Romance*

BY DESIGN

"Realistic details that make the reader feel they are truly living in the 13th century enhance a story of love that knows no bounds, not social, political, or economic barriers. Ms. Hunter's knowledge of the period and her ability to create three-dimensional characters who interact with history makes her an author medievalists will adore."

—*Romantic Times*

"I'd heard a lot about the previous two books in this trilogy, *By Arrangement* and *By Possession,* but little did that prepare me for the experience that was reading this book. Whether you've already enjoyed Ms. Hunter's books or she is a new-to-you author, this is a wonderful, sensual, masterfully written tale of love overcoming odds, and one I heartily recommend."

—*All About Romance*

"With each of the books in this series, Ms. Hunter's skill shines like a beacon." —*Rendevous*

"Ms. Hunter has raised the bar, adding depth and texture to the medieval setting. With well-crafted characters and a delightful love story, *By Design* is well-plotted and well-timed without the contrived plot twists so often used in romances. I highly recommend *By Design* to not only lovers of medieval romance but to all readers." —*Romance Reviews Today*

BY POSSESSION

"With the release of this new volume, [Madeline Hunter] cements her position as one of the brightest new writers in the genre. Brimming with intelligent writing, historical detail, and passionate, complex protagonists . . . Hunter makes 14th-century England come alive—from the details of its sights, sounds, and smells to the political context of this rebellious and dangerous time, when alliances and treason went hand in hand. For all the historical richness of the story, the romantic aspect is never lost, and the poignancy of the characters' seemingly untamable love is truly touching." —*Publishers Weekly*

"Madeline Hunter's tale is a pleasant read with scenes that show the writer's brilliance. *By Possession* is rich in description and details that readers of romance will savor."
—*Oakland Press*

"Ms. Hunter skillfully weaves historical details into a captivating love story that resounds with sights, sounds, and more of the Middle Ages. This is another breathtaking romance from a talented storyteller." —*Romantic Times*

"With elegance and intelligence, Ms. Hunter consolidates her position as one of the best new voices in romantic fiction. I'm waiting on tenterhooks to see what is in store for readers in her next book, *By Design*." —*Romance Journal*

BY ARRANGEMENT

"Debut author Hunter begins this new series with a thoroughly satisfying launch that leaves the reader eager for the next episode in the lives of her engaging characters."

—*Publishers Weekly*

"Romance author Madeline Hunter makes a dazzling debut into the genre with her medieval *By Arrangement,* a rich historical with unforgettable characters. . . . Layered with intrigue, history, passion, multidimensional characters, this book has it all. Quite simply, it's one of the best books I've read this year." —*Oakland Press*

"The first in a marvelous trilogy by a fresh voice in the genre, *By Arrangement* combines historical depth and riveting romance in a manner reminiscent of Roberta Gellis. Ms. Hunter has a true gift for bringing both history and her characters to life, making readers feel a part of the danger and pageantry of the era." —*Romantic Times*

"*By Arrangement* is richly textured, historically fascinating, and filled with surprises." —*All About Romance*

"Splendid in every way." —*Rendezvous*

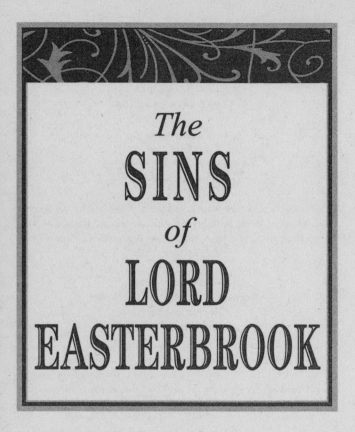

The
SINS
of
LORD
EASTERBROOK

Madeline Hunter

A DELL BOOK

THE SINS OF LORD EASTERBROOK
A Dell Book / February 2009

Published by
Bantam Dell
A Division of Random House, Inc.
New York, New York

Dell is a registered trademark of Random House, Inc., and the colophon is
a trademark of Random House, Inc.

ISBN 978-0-440-24396-0

Printed in the United States of America
Published simultaneously in Canada

www.bantamdell.com

OPM 10 9 8 7 6 5 4 3 2 1

The

SINS

of

LORD
EASTERBROOK

CHAPTER ONE

Silence. A dark, calm center absorbing chaos into its stillness.

The peaceful rhythm of inhales and exhales.

A pulse. The fundamental beat of nature extending into infinity. Awareness of everything and nothing. No thoughts. No dreams. No hungers. Pure existence. Primeval knowing.

Floating in the center now. Finally. Singular but also transcendent. Only the pulse in the darkness. Alone, but unified with a larger rhythm, the—

A disturbance. A small, silent shout of caution and worry intruding into the perfect void.

"Why are you creeping around, Phippen?"

"My apologies, my lord. I thought—you appeared to be sleeping and I just thought to come in and remove the tray—"

A louder shout. Fear now. Always fear. The world roared with it.

"I will go at once, sir."

"Take the tray, Phippen. Let us make the disturbance worthwhile, at least."

Chaos. Dismay. Thumps and bumps and the brittle cacophony of metal and crockery crashing.

"My abject apologies, sir. The footstool—I will have this cleaned off the carpet in a thrice. I will be gone faster than you can say Phippen is a fool."

"Phippen is a fool. I'll be damned, you are still here."

Noise. Sounds both audible and spiritual. Desperation amid clinks and sighs. The dark center shrinking, shrinking . . .

Christian, Marquess of Easterbrook, opened his eyes to view the servant whose intrusion had destroyed his meditation. Phippen, his new valet, tried to pick up the tray's contents without making any noise. Impossible, of course. A person's mere existence made noise.

Flushed and on his hands and knees, Phippen gingerly placed the cup on the tray, cringing at its tiny sound. He took out his handkerchief to mop up the puddle of coffee threatening to stain the carpet.

Fear. Worry. Anger too. Pique at himself as well as the new master whose habits made his job too hard.

Phippen would not be staying long. Valets never did.

Christian rose from his chair and walked over to Phippen. "Give me the tray. I will hold it while you gather the pieces."

"Very good, sir. Thank you, sir. That is too kind of you, my lord."

You are an ass, sir. An eccentric, erratic, incomprehensible—

Another disturbance. An odd shaking within the remnants of the fading center.

Christian closed his eyes and focused on that tremble. Distant but distinct, it had interfered with his meditations too often of late. Today it had taken forever to overcome its effects.

He walked to the north windows. No one was in the garden. He paced down the length of his bedchamber to look out the south windows. The kneeling Phippen waved a saucer as he neared. Christian took it, put it on the tray, shoved the tray into Phippen's empty hand, and strode on. The sound of china tumbling again reached him just as he neared the window.

In the street below a carriage waited outside the door of his house. A figure swept toward it, dodging the drizzle that so often accompanied spring weather in London. A woman of middling height and quick step, wearing a deep green dress, hopped into the carriage's twilight.

A delicate nose. An elegant jaw.

A melodic sigh from the past. He was sure that he heard it despite the distance and the closed window.

His mind shed the last mists of his meditation. His blood reacted, violently. A different pulse now. Hard. Aggressive. He peered with total focus at that carriage.

The woman's face was hidden by the angle of his high view and by her bonnet and the dim light. Her footman closed the door and her fingers reached to pull the curtain.

A hand. *Her* hand. Impossible. . . .

The footman moved toward the back of the carriage, to take his position in the rain. Only then did Christian notice the man. His attention had been so intent on the woman that he had not even seen the footman's eastern garments and long queue.

"A coat, Phippen. Boots."

His valet rose with painful care, balancing the pile of china on the tray. "Very good, sir. I'll just set this outside the door and—"

Christian grabbed the tray and slammed it down on a table so hard that the cup jumped. "*Boots,* man. *Now.*"

Even getting barely dressed took too long. Christian admitted that by the time he descended to the house's public rooms.

Common sense caught up with him at the top of the last flight of stairs. That carriage would be long gone, even with the crush around Grosvenor Square. Whether on foot or horse, he would never be able to follow it.

He pivoted, strode to the drawing room, and entered.

His aunt Henrietta and his young cousin Caroline sat together on a settee near one of the tall windows. Blond head to blond head, they gossiped about something. The progress of Caroline's second season most likely. Anxiety about Caroline's social life soaked the public rooms with its unceasing rain. It pattered down on him as soon as he opened the chamber's door.

Henrietta greeted him with glistening, vague eyes and an artificial, blank smile. She sought to hide her irritation with his intrusion, which he knew as clearly as if she spoke it. Henrietta and her daughter lived here only because he had agreed to allow it in a rare fit of generosity a year ago. Now Hen wanted everyone to accept her as the mistress of the house, not a guest. Since he accepted nothing of the kind, his company was never welcomed.

"Easterbrook, you are up and about early today." Henrietta's gaze noted his boots with relief, but her eyes reflected her eternal vexation at the lack of a cravat and his unruly hair.

"Is that inconvenient for you, Aunt Hen?"

"Far be it for me to presume inconvenience. It is your home."

"I thought that perhaps you were still receiving callers. I noticed a carriage from my window, and hesitated to come down until your visitor had left."

"You should have joined us," Caroline said. "You might have enjoyed her company more than Mama did. Our visitor is quite an original. I am surprised Mama did not send her away."

"I almost did," Hen said. "However, one can never know how it will go with such people. She has both questionable fortune and background, but there is the chance that hostesses will overlook that because she is entertaining. Then where would I be if I had cut her when she made overtures?" She shook her head with perplexed exasperation. "It is always difficult to judge the odd ones. Nor is she truly odd. Not like Phaedra. More exotic than truly odd. There is a difference, Caroline, and one must be alert and careful to—"

"What is her name?" Christian asked.

His aunt blinked, startled. He never cared to know anything about her callers.

"Her name is Miss Montgomery," Caroline said. "Mama and I met her at a party last week. Her father was a merchant trader in the Far East but she claims a connection to Portuguese nobility through her mother. Miss Montgomery is visiting London for the first time in her life. She journeyed all the way from Macao."

"What did she want?"

His aunt peered his way curiously. "It was a social call, Easterbrook. She only hoped to form a friendship that would help her make her way in town this season."

"I think that she is very interesting," Caroline added.

"Too interesting for a young girl to befriend," Henrietta said. "She is too worldly for your association, Caroline. I suspect that she is an adventuress. Quite likely a charlatan too, in her story about her mother's blood."

"I do not think so," Caroline said. "I also found her far more stimulating than most of the people who call."

Christian left the drawing room while his aunt and cousin bickered about Miss Montgomery. He sent for the butler, to learn the address that the recent visitor's calling card had borne.

Leona Montgomery stepped around Tong Wei and angled her head toward the looking glass. She gave her reflection a critical gaze while she tied on her bonnet.

Young, but not really young. Pretty, but not really pretty. English, but not really English.

She sensed people itemizing the qualifications of her countenance and identity when they met her here in

London. It had been different in Macao. Everyone there was "not really" something.

Tong Wei finally rose from his knees. Leona glanced to the statue of Buddha that had occupied his attention. She was a Christian, but she understood her guard's devotion very well. Asian religious views affected everything in China, even among the European community.

"I should come with you," Tong Wei said. His expression remained impassive but she knew that he worried about her safety in this noisy, crowded city of so many strangers. "Your brother would expect me to."

"I want to be inconspicuous." She gazed down at her gray promenade dress. Very English, it had been retrieved from a modiste yesterday. "Since you refuse to dress as a proper English footman, you cannot accompany me."

They both knew that even English garments would not make Tong Wei into a proper-looking footman. His shaved brow and long queue, his round face and distinctive eyes, marked him as Chinese even more than the beautifully embroidered shafts of garnet-toned cloth that composed his exotic clothing today.

"Take Isabella with you," he said. "It is not common to see women alone. Not ones of a high station."

Isabella looked up. Her brush froze, poised over the paper on which she drew elegant images from her adventures. "I do not mind wearing my English clothes," she said. "Tong Wei may think them barbaric, but I am not so pure."

Isabella referred not only to her opinions. Half Chinese and half Portuguese, she was a hybrid of East and West. If Isabella now wore a loose *qipao,* it was for comfort as much as preference.

"I will only be at the Royal Exchange for a short while. I am merely going to see how this big trading house is organized, so that I can walk in with confidence another time. If it is similar to the factories in Canton, it will be so busy that no one will notice me." Leona trusted it would happen that way. Her ensemble had been chosen to be subdued. There were times when she did not want to turn heads for any reason.

"What if you see Edmund there?" Isabella asked.

A little shiver of foreboding and excitement intruded on Leona's composure. The ambivalent reaction happened whenever Edmund was mentioned during this journey.

"I will not see him there. He was a gentleman, and they do not engage in trade." She had realized, since coming to London, that Edmund had been a gentleman in the true English meaning of the word. She now comprehended fully what that meant in this world of her father.

Of course, a man could be a gentleman and still be what Edmund had claimed, a naturalist and adventurer. A gentleman could even still be a thief.

"Then maybe you will eventually see him again in one of the drawing rooms that you visit," Isabella said.

It would be useful if she did. She suspected that one of her missions in London might be accomplished much more quickly if she and Edmund faced each other again. *By the by, Edmund, just how big a scoundrel are you?*

She checked her reflection again. Not really English, but English enough for today's purpose. The not-really-young and not-really-pretty parts should help her be invisible.

"I doubt that I will be gone more than two hours," she said. "While I am away, Isabella, please see if you can encourage that cook that I hired to make a dinner that is not so bland."

Bury Street was quieter than nearby St. James's Square. Much less expensive too. Leona still fretted that she had not chosen a good enough address, but she could afford nothing better.

The view in front of her door caught her up short when she stepped out of her house. She frowned and looked right and left.

Where was the carriage? It had been waiting here just a few minutes ago, before she put on her bonnet.

An impressive coach blocked her view of the southern end of the street. She rose on her toes and angled her head to see past it. Down near the next crossroad she spied her own carriage. She recognized Mr. Hubson, the coachman who had been supplied by the establishment where she had hired this conveyance for her stay.

Perhaps the arrival of this much richer equipage had required her own to move. She was not yet familiar with all the nuances of rank and protocol in this city.

She waved to Mr. Hubson and walked toward him. As she came abreast of the big coach, a man stepped into her path.

"Miss Montgomery?"

His address startled her. Young and blond-haired, he wore an expression of deference even as he interfered with her. A footman, she guessed, but he did not wear the livery of the other footmen accompanying this large vehicle. Those other two sidled away, taking stances out of view and far behind her back.

"Yes, I am Miss Montgomery. Who are you and what do you want?"

He gestured toward the coach's door. It bore an insignia. A crest. This presumptuous young man was in the employ of one of the lords of the realm.

"My lord requests your attendance," he said. "We will bring you to his house, and return you here afterward."

"Would not a written invitation have been more polite than having you accost me on the street?"

"Lord Easterbrook is somewhat unusual in his habits and impulsive in his invitations. No offense is intended, I assure you."

Leona absorbed this revelation of the coach's owner. She had visited Easterbrook's house two days ago to call on his widowed aunt, Lady Wallingford. Most likely the marquess intended to remind the trader's daughter that she was not fit for his aunt's company. He could have communicated that in a letter, too, and not staged this little drama of power.

She would regret losing Lady Wallingford's connection before harvesting what fruit it might bear. That likelihood did not endear her to this Easterbrook any more than being summoned like a slave.

"I know the location of Lord Easterbrook's house. I will go in my own carriage, thank you. Please return to your master and inform him that I will call in due time."

She tried to walk around the young man. He prevented that with a smooth side step.

"My lord commanded me to bring you, Miss Montgomery. I dare not disobey him. Please—" He held out his arm toward the carriage door, blocking her path all the more.

She looked past him, down the street. Her own coachman had disappeared, abandoning his equipage and her. She judged how far back her house was, and whether Tong Wei would hear if she called out.

She tried to hide her growing wariness. "Please give the marquess my regrets, but I have another invitation that will occupy me this afternoon. I will call on him tomorrow. Please move aside now."

The young man glanced past her, to the two footmen. His expression caused the hairs on her nape to prickle.

A vise suddenly closed on her waist.

Alarm flashed through her. A shout rushed into her throat but panic stole her breath away. The street and houses spun and blurred.

She shook the confusion out of her head. She sat inside the coach now, with the young blond man. They sped down the street.

Her blood boiled. "How dare you! I demand that you stop this carriage and allow me to leave. If you do not I will report you to the magistrate."

The young man lifted his finger to his mouth, telling her to be silent. Something in his eyes said that it would be wise to heed that advice.

———

The foils sliced the air with sharp whistling breaths. Christian parried the lithe moves of the fencing expert, Angelo, while testing his own ability to concentrate on the duel.

He had been fencing a lot of late. During the last year he had extended his apartment to take up the house's entire second story, above the public rooms. He had emptied the mistress's bedchamber to create this private room for exercise and sport.

Angelo's blunted foil made two swift feints, then lunged. The tip poked at Christian's chest directly at his heart. Satisfied, the fencing master stepped back, raised his weapon in salute, and bowed.

"Your expertise has grown significantly the last few months, Lord Easterbrook. I have rarely seen the likes of such rapid improvement."

"I have been practicing."

Angelo took a towel from the attending footman and wiped his brow. "It is not technique or practice that makes this difference, but something not easily named. A new alertness, perhaps."

Christian did not supply the invited explanation. There was no way to do so without sounding mad, and the world suspected he was half that already. Nor would Angelo comprehend the watershed that had been passed three months ago.

The focus and silence achieved in meditation had finally been transferred to physical acts. He no longer required the dark center to find peace. For a short while, when fencing with Angelo or running in a field or rowing on a river, a different breathing and a thoroughly physical absorption built walls that kept out the world's sad, silent noise.

This new control represented a freedom that Christian had worked a long time to attain. Years.

"Why don't you come to the academy, Lord Easterbrook?" Angelo helped himself to some of the punch waiting on the bare chamber's one small table. "There will be an exhibition next week. A contest. You could win. Do you not want to show your skill? No one knows of it except me and this footman, but you are almost my equal and that is most rare."

"I have no interest in contests. I do not care if anyone knows I am your equal."

"That is unusual. Most men take pride in accomplishments, and seek the fame of them."

Angelo did not mean unusual. He meant suspicious. Odd. Eccentric. Christian knew that all those words were attached to his name. Angelo, like most people, used both caution and care with him as a result.

Angelo picked up his coats and quickly dressed, preparing to depart. Not quickly enough, however. Already the intentions and calculations of the man were vibrating through the air with their unwelcome revelations.

Angelo left the chamber with the footman. Immediately another man entered. He bolted the door, then strode across the bare wooden floor to where Christian stood.

"We have her. She finally left her house without the Chinaman."

Christian poured himself some of the punch. "Did you avoid a public spectacle, Miller?"

"Barely. It was wise to bring the other two with me. She was getting suspicious so we had to move fast before she bolted or screamed."

"She was not harmed, I trust. I will have to kill you if she was."

Miller treated the warning as a joke, but his overweening confidence dimmed just enough to indicate he was not entirely certain it had not been a real threat. Since Christian was not certain either, he let Miller sweat a little.

"Only her pride suffered, I promise."

Miller could not be blamed if he "moved fast." His orders had been to fetch Miss Montgomery, and fetch her he had. Miller was useful that way.

Young, ambitious, smart, and not too encumbered by concerns for legal niceties, he served his current master much as he had served his senior officers while in the army during a brief commission—without questions. He did not execute his normal duties of a secretary nearly as well as the less traditional ones that he periodically received.

"She accused us of abduction," Miller said.

"That is because you abducted her."

"She spoke of going to the magistrate."

"Where is she?"

"In the green bedchamber. We escorted her up the servant stairs, so Lady Wallingford is none the wiser."

Christian would know if that were true as soon as he stepped out of this chamber. If his aunt was suspicious, that disturbance would resonate through the house.

He dismissed Miller. He glanced down at his shirt, breeches, and boots. He should probably make himself more presentable before greeting Miss Montgomery. He debated doing so for five seconds, then strode in the direction of the green bedchamber.

Leona paced back and forth in her opulent prison, simmering with vexation.

It was difficult to maintain one's dignity when one has been hauled off the street like so much lost baggage. Leona hoped that she had managed anyway.

She had spent the short ride to Grosvenor Square ignoring her captor and treating him like the lackey he was. Only once did she almost lose her temper, when she perceived that her young abductor found her pose of hauteur amusing.

A seed of worry sent out a vine to wind through her anger. While scathing scolds formed in half her mind, the other half assessed the implications of this insult. The Marquess of Easterbrook's treatment of her reflected his view of her lowly status. He had concluded that she deserved no better.

When others learned about this lack of courtesy they would imitate it. Nothing, not her mother's blood nor her letters of introduction, would help her cause now. Her plans here in London would be more difficult after today, and some of them might be nigh impossible.

She stopped walking. Her gaze took in the apple green silk bed hangings and drapes, and the elegant, fine-boned mahogany furniture. She noted the exquisite watercolor paintings lending rainbow hues to the cream-colored walls. Then she saw nothing at all of her surroundings, but only the mental image of her brother,

Gaspar, smiling as his boat pulled away after he had transferred her to the ship at Whampao.

Gaspar had appeared so young to her that day—far younger than his twenty-two years. Perhaps his unquestioning trust caused him to look juvenile. He had agreed to risk everything on this journey. His patrimony and his future were at stake, but he had handed the fate of both to her.

His image faded and she again saw the luxury surrounding her. Her heart still beat heavily, but no longer due to insulted pride. Calm determination had replaced anger.

Her father had taught her that if one viewed adversity from a different angle, one could often see an opportunity hidden within it.

If one looked at this development from a different angle, one might see that she had just obtained an audience with one of the highest titles in the realm. A man of such consequence could be very useful. She might want to slap Easterbrook's face, but it would be wiser to win him over.

She walked to the dressing table and bent to see her reflection in the looking glass. Not really pretty, but hopefully pretty enough.

She removed her bonnet and set it on the table. She pinched her cheeks to make them flush.

"Primping for me, Miss Montgomery?"

The voice startled her. Her gaze shifted from her own reflection to that of the room behind her.

She saw high black boots and snug breeches in the shadows near the door. She dipped her head until the white billows of a shirt came into view, then the ends of very dark hair. The man who had intruded appeared to be a servant, and a lowly one at that if he worked in such informal garb.

Only he wasn't a servant. His confidence clothed him in nobility more than any garments could. His body stood in lithe relaxation, exuding assumptions regarding his rights in this chamber, and in the world outside its walls.

She straightened, and sought the kind of poise that might impress such a man. She turned to greet him with calm grace.

"Are you Lord Easterbrook?"

"I am."

"Your invitation was unexpected, Lord Easterbrook, but I am delighted to meet you all the same." She made a little curtsy.

He appeared to be waiting for something more. She could not imagine what it might be. Her smile began to feel odd and stretched.

Goodness, he looked for all the world like a pirate now that she saw him from head to toe. The boots were high quality but his general appearance was not fashionable. His hair fell in long lazy waves to well past his shoulders. They framed a face that, from what she could see, was younger than she had expected, and handsome enough to make his lack of coats and cravat romantic rather than crude. His dishabille was an insult, as had been her abduction and her entry up the servant's stairs, but she could not afford to dwell on that now.

He finally made a bow. "Please forgive the rude way that you were brought here. My only excuse was my impatience to see you alone."

He walked toward her and the light from the windows found him. It made the black boots blacker and the white shirt whiter. His face also became distinct. Dark eyes appeared hawkish in their intense focus on her. An unexpected elegance softened the strong bones of his face. His wide mouth curved into a vague smile that could easily turn hard.

A strange sensation stirred in her. It carried dark, deep caution, but not without a thrilling note. The way his body moved in his stride . . . the tone of his voice . . . those eyes . . .

Suddenly her mind saw him with short hair and more proper garments and a younger, less severe face. Her confusion crystallized into shock. She squinted at him, peering hard.

"Edmund?"

CHAPTER TWO

He enjoyed her astonishment. It amused him.
Maybe she would slap Easterbrook after all.
Just how big a scoundrel are you?
A very big one, it seemed.

"I always guessed that you had deceived us. I did
not realize the depths of it, however." Her voice
snapped with her anger. She felt a fool in more ways
than she could list. Humiliation almost buried her girlish elation at seeing him again. Almost.

His amusement disappeared. "You know why I
could not reveal that I was Easterbrook when I arrived
in Macao."

She knew, but there might be more to his deception
than what he alluded to.

The potential implications of his true identity, to the
past and future, to her plans here in England, jumbled
together in her mind. They evoked a chaos of emotions,
but nostalgia threatened to submerge every other reaction. She struggled to hold it at bay.

An awkwardness settled between them, one created

by distance and time and the questions shouting in her mind. The silence made it worse. His proximity made it excruciating.

What a sight he was, with that long hair. The years had hardened him in all kinds of ways too. Echoes of his youthful brooding still spoke to her, but Easterbrook exuded none of the soulful pain that Edmund had carried.

"You have changed," she said.

"So have you." His appreciative gaze indicated that he found her changes pleasing.

He had always been too obvious about that. He had never had the courtesy seven years ago to pretend there was no attraction between them. He had deliberately made her blush and fluster. He still did, even if she refused to show her reactions. She warmed all over, as if he caressed her body with his gaze.

Her heart beat rapidly. The memories broke free. They flowed and an old, secret wistfulness soaked her.

It all came back. All of it, as if she were nineteen again and her womanhood was blossoming under the wayward traveler's seductive attention. Only she was not nineteen now, and the traveler had not been what he claimed, but a marquess. That changed everything about their friendship back then. It meant that he had toyed with her most ignobly.

Fury spiked fast and hot and she surrendered to it. "You unforgivable bastard."

He reached out and rested two fingertips on her lips. "Such language. What would Branca say?"

Her lips pulsed beneath his touch. A terrible, wonderful shiver slid down to her heart.

She turned her head to break the contact. "Branca is dead," she said. "Two years now."

"I am sorry. She was a good *duenna,* even if I found her inconvenient."

She could not believe that he referred to his cynical pursuit so casually. "My father is also deceased. He died the year after you left Macao."

"I know. Word came to me through the Company."

"Yes, I imagine a marquess can get whatever he wants from them. Is that how you traveled back then? Other men might have to pay their way or work for their berth. I expect a marquess need merely present himself to the captain of an East India Company ship to obtain passage."

He shrugged, as if such privileges were of little account. "I was surprised to hear that you are using the name Montgomery. You did not marry Pedro after all."

"When the financial condition of my father's trading house became apparent upon his death, Pedro withdrew the proposal. Everyone understood."

"You must have been disappointed."

"Saving the business from total failure occupied me. I was able to preserve it for my brother. After he reached his majority and was allowed into Canton, it improved significantly."

He smiled. For that brief moment he looked much like Edmund, whose rare smiles made her heart rise with both joy and relief. "I think, Leona, that the trading house improved under your own hand. Your father relied on you, and I suspect that your brother does too."

"My brother has proven most capable. I do help him when I can, of course. In fact, that is why I am in

London. I intend to meet with shippers and traders based here, and convince them to forge associations with Montgomery and Tavares for their intracoastal trade in the East."

He assessed her again, with a gaze both curious and admiring. She clung to her pose of friendly but casual interest.

His dark, deep-set eyes showed humor and warmth and disconcerting familiarity. His countenance subtly shifted from handsome to beautiful as his thoughts allowed the softening elegance to have its way.

Her instincts reacted the same way that they had when he watched her in Macao. She sensed something emanating from him, something both dark and dangerously alluring. His aura became possessively invasive. His attention tried to compel her to explore a mystery that would be her undoing.

Her inexperience had sent her running seven years ago, whenever that power sought to absorb her. Now here she was, a grown woman who had seen the world, who had bargained with Muslims and faced down pirates, and she still wanted to hide.

Instead she retreated within herself. She pulled walls around her soul so that it would be safe.

Immediately his softness disappeared. His gaze turned searching, as if he tried to see through that barrier.

"So you traveled all the way to England to serve as your brother's agent? You came for no other reason?"

He was very close to her. Too close. She had to look up to see his face. "There was no other reason to come."

"Wasn't there?"

"None at all."

"I think that there was."

"Goodness—Do you think I journeyed all this way to find *you*?" She feigned astonishment. "Of course, if I had known your true identity I would have. I daresay you can arrange introductions in a day that it will take me weeks to obtain. If I had known that Edmund was really Easterbrook, I would have sought you out immediately upon arriving in London."

He responded with a lazy smile. She could feel his aura sliding around her in a curious caress, seeking any gaps in her defenses. "You would have done no such thing. Whether I was Edmund or Easterbrook, you would have run away and hidden from me, no matter what benefit I might bring to your missions here."

"Hidden from you? Why would I do that?"

"Because I frighten you. I terrified the girl, and I still alarm the woman."

He guessed her reaction so confidently that it irritated her. She squared her shoulders. "You are a little peculiar, and you are somewhat rude, and you have been insulting today, and you were too brooding then, but you have never been frightening."

He abruptly stepped closer. She almost jumped out of her skin.

He laughed quietly. "See?"

She stood her ground, facing him down almost nose to nose. "Startled is not the same as frightened, Lord Easterbrook."

"You were relieved that I had to leave Macao. You could not get me on that ship fast enough."

"There was no choice but to get you on that ship, or have you forgotten that?"

"There was unfinished business between us and you were not sorry to escape the reckoning. You were too innocent and unawake to understand that you wanted me as much as I wanted you."

"You are wrong, but that is all in the past anyway. I am no longer an ignorant girl and you are no longer Edmund. Those two differences change everything."

"Actually, Leona, I have learned since entering this chamber that time, place, and names change some things not at all."

No, they did not. Damn it. Damn *him*.

He loomed over her, close enough to subtly dominate her. Near enough that he might hear the stunning way her heart beat.

The hard curve of his mouth matched the arrogant confidence in his eyes. He could tell that she was too much affected by him. He knew that he could still turn her into the nineteen-year-old girl promised to a fiancé who did not excite her nearly as much as the handsome stranger taking hospitality in her father's home.

However, one thing *had* changed. As a woman she understood his appeal in ways the girl had not. She recognized her response to his mysterious allure for the sexual arousal that it was. She worried that he knew that too.

She tried to move away. He caught her arm, stopping her. He pulled her toward him. His boldness stunned her.

His hand touched her face, commanding her to be still. His gaze demanded obedience. Her thoughts spun into incoherent objections when he tilted her head back.

His warm, dry lips touched hers and lingered, then began proving that he could still mesmerize her.

Warmth. Intimacy so immediate and deep that it seemed unnatural. Sly, sensual shivers and expanding wonder and astonishment.

The years fell away and she was being kissed for the first time ever by a reckless young man with a dark, chaotic spirit—a dangerous man who offered adventures of the body and heart that she dared not accept.

The kiss banished suspicions while it lasted. Youthful emotions refreshed her like a coastal breeze. Arousal tingled at her breasts and tightened her womb and teased one devilish spot very low in her body.

She restrained herself from showing how powerfully he stirred her. One sigh or gasp and they would probably end up on that apple green bed. She did not fight him, however. The sensations so stimulated her that she lacked the strength for that.

"You are an enigma, Leona," he muttered. His hand remained on her cheek and his breath warmed her ear. "You always were. Perhaps that is the fascination."

"We all are enigmas to each other, I suppose."

"Very few people are to me."

She gently lifted his hand off her arm. She stepped away and pulled her composure together.

"Lord Easterbrook, since you arranged this unexpected reunion, perhaps you will agree to aid me in my mission. Out of sentiment for our old friendship in Macao, that is."

He scowled at the way she picked up the threads of

their conversation, as if nothing of note had just happened. "That depends on the kind of aid that you request, Leona."

"I would like to be introduced to your brother, Lord Hayden Rothwell."

"What do you want with Hayden?"

"I have been told that he is likely to know the traders and investors whom I came to London to meet."

He appeared bored by such a simple petition. "I will arrange for you to meet him if you wish."

"That is kind of you. I am very grateful. Now, while seeing old friends is always pleasant, this unexpected visit has delayed my day's plans. Am I allowed to leave? Are we done?"

His attention sharpened on her. He did not care for the way she dismissed the meeting, and him. "We are nowhere near done, Leona."

"To my mind we are entirely done, Lord Easterbrook. Please accept my decision about that."

A tense silence passed, no more than ten seconds she guessed. In that brief span he appeared to be making a decision. Their intimate surroundings, the bed and pillows and sensual fabrics, ceased being mere background and turned into visual arguments for why it would be pleasant not to be entirely done after all.

She wished that she could summon anger or outrage or pride to shore up her defenses. She wished she could claim that kiss had not tempted her. In truth a little whirlwind spun in her heart now, and her body ached from the intense desire pulling between them with tantalizing tugs.

"You were always allowed to leave," he said. "There is no guard outside the door."

"I will continue with my afternoon's excursion, then. Good day to you, Lord Easterbrook."

She grabbed her bonnet and strode to the door on legs that barely allowed her to walk.

"Leona."

His quiet address stopped her after she had opened the door. The resonance of his tone sent a treacherous thrill down the center of her body.

"Leona, it appears that you are no longer so innocent and unawake."

She looked back at him. He appeared far too dashing in his shirtsleeves and open collar and high boots. Stronger than she remembered. More arrogant too. There had been poignant moments when Edmund was vulnerable in ways that she suspected Easterbrook never was.

"That is a peculiar farewell, Lord Easterbrook. Maybe I will run and hide just as you predicted."

"I am not worried about that. Your missions will keep you nearby. And this time, Leona, before any ship takes one of us away, I will have you."

CHAPTER
THREE

P lease explain what you require, Lord Easterbrook. Describe it while we examine your reflection in the looking glass together."

Christian looked into the glass. A round face peered back from atop his shoulder.

"I require you to cut it. That is what you do, is it not?"

The moon face smiled with feigned modesty. "I do not merely cut, Lord Easterbrook. Your manservant could do that. I dress. I style. I am an artist. Much as a sculptor does not merely carve, I—"

"Yes, yes. Well, be an artist. Do not overdo it, though."

The face disappeared. Two pudgy hands lifted hair, weighed it, debated it, judged it.

Shears appeared. "We will let your hair have its way with these restless waves, just do a bit of taming and bring the length to here." The shears touched Christian's shoulder.

Christian closed his eyes, not to avoid seeing the

locks fall but to block the peculiar intensity that the artist exuded while he sculpted.

The center would not form now, but his own thoughts could provide a misty retreat that diffused his sensibility. He had been practicing the last few days at finding that respite more easily. He would need it in the weeks ahead.

He pictured Leona's departure from their reunion while he watched her from his bedchamber's window.

She had paused before entering the coach. She had glanced up the façade of the house, toward the window where he stood. She had not seen him, he was certain. She would never allow her face to show so much if she knew that he watched.

Her anger had been obvious. And her indignation. Other than that, what had he seen? Embarrassment? Probably so. Something else showed in her eyes too. Worry? Suspicion? Sorrow?

He was never really sure with Leona. She possessed a remarkable ability to deflect his odd perceptions of other people's emotions. Very few people in his life had demonstrated an immunity, but with Leona he was as ignorant as anyone regarding what she truly felt.

Except when it came to desire. A man needed no special gift to sense that in a woman, or to feel her response when he kissed her.

Nothing had changed there, for all of her attempts to pretend otherwise. As soon as he entered that room the attraction had pulled between them, as intensely as ever. The reality had been far more powerful than the memory, and the memory had dimmed very little. After seven years, it was a wonder he had not ravished her on sight.

It would be preferable if she just accepted the way it was between them, and what that meant. How it had to be. It appeared that instead she was going to make him pursue her, which meant altering his habits for a while.

So be it.

Hands moved around his face like big, irritating insects. Snipping intruded on his memories of that revealing kiss. Suddenly all sounds stopped. Christian opened his eyes. A round face again beamed atop his shoulder in the looking glass.

"Do you like it, Lord Easterbrook? I believe it came out well. Very well indeed."

His hair looked much like it had an hour ago, just somewhat shorter and less unruly. If the artist considered it fashionable enough, it probably was.

He pulled off the cloth that protected his garments. "It will do."

The hairdresser retreated, carrying his case of shears and pomades. Christian called for his valet.

"My lord?"

"Send for the tailor."

Confusion. Worry. Poor Phippen. The morning's parade of messengers, tradesmen, and other visitors distressed him. The abrupt, uncharacteristic activity suggested that the worst rumors about his new master's sanity were true. "May I inquire, my lord—which tailor? Weston? Stulze?"

"Send for Davidson," a voice commanded.

Phippen startled and glanced at the man who had

just entered the dressing room. "Should I indeed send for Mr. Davidson as Lord Hayden recommends?"

"Our family has used Davidson for years. If Lord Easterbrook speaks of the tailor, that is the one he means," Hayden said. "Christian, since when do you actually meet with him before the first fitting? He has your measure, and you normally order and let him decide the cut and fabric. Since you rarely leave this house, there is little reason to fuss with either."

"Phippen, send word to Davidson that I want him here this afternoon," Christian said.

Hayden threw himself into a chair. His attention wandered around the dressing room, but eventually settled on its only other occupant.

His blue eyes narrowed on Christian's hair. *Curious now. Deeply so.*

"You seem to be commanding a lot of people to attend on you today, Christian. Tailors. Hairdressers too, unless I am mistaken. *Me.*"

Christian settled into another upholstered chair. The dressing room held five of them, all somewhat worse for wear now that he noticed. "Did my request inconvenience you?"

"*See me before noon* is not a request."

"Is that what I wrote? I intended to pen *Please call before noon if your dear wife can spare you.* How is Alexia?"

"It will be soon. A fortnight at most." *Pride. Love. Fear too.* The last emotion, so rare in Hayden, could be understood of a man whose wife was about to give birth.

"What is it you want?"

"I would like to introduce you to someone."

Hayden again narrowed his eyes on Christian's hair, then glanced to the door as if remembering Phippen's sartorial errand. "Is this someone a woman?"

"Yes."

"I hope that you are not going to ask us to receive your mistress. I have heard rumors that you have taken up with Mrs. Napier. Under the circumstances, what with Alexia's cousin Rose and the resultant delicate situation regarding society, I would prefer to wait until—"

"Not a mistress. Not Mrs. Napier, to be sure. This is an old friend. She has asked to meet you and I agreed to make the introduction."

"I assumed that you did not have any friends, old or new, male or female."

"Then you assumed too much, which you are apt to do sometimes. This friend is visiting from Macao, and seeks an introduction for business purposes."

Hayden stood. He wandered over to the dressing table. He absently fingered the brushes there, then turned and folded his arms. "Macao?"

"Her father was a Country Trader. That is what they call traders licensed by the East India Company to conduct trade between the Indian ports. Like many others, he expanded into trade between India and some other Asian countries."

"I know what a Country Trader is, Christian. I do manage our family finances."

"Forgive me. Well, Montgomery befriended me when

I visited there. He had married into a Portuguese family in Macao. He was able to establish himself through that connection, and participate in Chinese trade via Canton, in addition to his Indian coastal trading. Now his daughter has come to London and—"

"*You* were *in Macao*?" Hayden's pique crystallized the atmosphere. "Was this during those years when you disappeared and no one knew where the hell you were?"

"Did I never mention Macao?"

"No, damn it. You have never revealed a single thing about that time when you abandoned us, your duties— *everything*."

"I had no idea I had never discussed it."

"Hell, you ignored every inquiry. If you are not aware of it, that is because of your overwhelming self-absorption and—"

"It appears that I am satisfying your curiosity at last. I met Miss Montgomery while I was in Macao. Her brother has now inherited the father's business. It had suffered a series of misfortunes under her father, from which I doubt it has completely recovered. She is in London to form associations that might benefit her brother's business, and she specifically asked to meet you."

"Where else were you? Besides Macao?"

"India. Tibet. China itself for two weeks, although I nearly got caught. Russia—"

"*Tibet?*"

"All kinds of places, Hayden, but you have diverted this conversation from my intentions."

"Damn your intentions."

Hayden's anger crackled out of him. Christian suffered it as he rarely tolerated such intrusions from anyone except his two brothers. A person cannot live in the dark center all the time, and in the end knowing his brothers' joys more than balanced knowing their pains.

He waited until Hayden's little storm quieted. His brother was the most reasonable of men. The winds would disperse soon.

"I trust Miss Montgomery will be in town for at least a fortnight or so." Hayden spoke with a bland ease that matched a renewed but tenuous calm. "My mind is not on finance and trade right now."

"This introduction can wait until after the birth of your child, if that is what you mean."

"Then send another of your imperial summons at that time, Christian, and we will arrange it." He strode to the door. "Russia and Tibet. Hell."

With Hayden's departure, the memory of Leona's visit returned. Again Christian saw her face before she entered the carriage to go about her afternoon plans.

He wondered what those plans were. He did not question that she was in London to further her brother's business. He just doubted that she had truly forgotten or forgiven the way that business had almost been destroyed seven years ago.

He wandered to the fencing chamber, and into its dressing room. This space served as storage now, a place where he deposited personal items no longer in use. While he moved wooden boxes and trunks, his gaze lit on a wall covered with frames displaying insects, ferns, and seeds.

You waste too much time on that collection, Christian.

Better if you read books or practiced with your pistols. I'll not have a son who turns into one of those peculiar fellows who chases butterflies.

He had read plenty of books and practiced many hours with his pistol. Books and guns, like collecting, could be done privately. Alone.

Nor had he truly been interested in insects and seeds. They had been an excuse to go out in the woods and fields, where he would be spared the awkward and often painful awareness of another person's unhappiness. There had been a lot of misery in the home of his youth.

He pulled a trunk forward and threw it open. Full of the flotsam of two years of travel, it offered few memories that mattered. The real goal of that journey had been escape, not discovery. It had been an accident that it resulted in discovery after all.

He shoved aside statuettes and odd weavings. Down at the bottom lay a half-folio-sized journal, thick with pages. He reached for it, then stopped with his hand poised above its brown leather cover.

He had never read the notes inside it. He had reasons not to want to know what they would reveal. He had cause to think these notes might shed light on the darker corners of his father's life. They might expose secrets that still remained buried by place and time.

The last marquess had committed his share of sins, and Christian had long ago decided that he did not want to learn about them. Ignorance had been a path to liberation. He did not want to reenter that morass of inherited guilt and obligations again.

Now, however, it might be wise to open this notebook.

Leona had lied during their reunion. He needed no special sensibility to her emotions to know it.

He was almost certain that she had not come to London merely to help her brother. She had also come to finish her father's crusade. If her father had even been half right in his theories, she could be headed for trouble.

She surely suspected Edmund had taken these notes that her father had made while he worked through his suspicions and conducted his investigations. When a man and an item disappear at the same time, only an idiot would not see the possible connection.

She might have asked Edmund to give the notebook back. She probably would not trust a marquess about anything regarding this second mission, however.

He contemplated the journal for a good while. Then he closed the trunk. He would read it if he had to, but he doubted it would come to that. He intended to keep Leona very close to him. He would divert her from this particular path, if she had ventured down it.

He returned to his dressing room. There was one more chore to complete. He sent for Miller.

"Bring this to Mrs. Napier. Give her my regrets that I will not be calling on her tonight."

Miller weighed the little box in his hand. Its contents had been purchased from one of the visiting tradesmen this morning. "No note?"

"That necklace is all the explanation that is required."

Miller eyed the box distastefully. "I hope there will not be a scene. Women can get dramatic when they are thrown over."

"There will be no drama. Mrs. Napier has only two strong emotions, lust and greed. She is smart enough to know that satisfaction of the first is fleeting, while that of the latter lasts forever."

"Not to speak out of turn, sir, but she sounds a little ruthless."

"No more than most people, unfortunately. No more than you and I, that is certain."

Miller smiled, rather pleased to be included in the same circle as a marquess, even if it was a ruthless one.

Miller wandered off to deliver the parting gift. Christian assumed that a good deal of his recent physical comfort walked out the door too.

Dealing with women was the hardest part of his life. Romance was impossible if one sensed not only the desire and the joys of one's beloved but also her disappointments, her flashing moments of hatred and her grudging accommodations.

The erotic and ruthlessly practical Mrs. Napier had been, he had to admit, the perfect mistress for the cursed Marquess of Easterbrook.

CHAPTER
FOUR

Griffin Winterside, the manager of the East India Company, charged with coddling and cajoling Parliament, watched Mr. Hubson eye the ten-pound note lying on the mahogany table. It was a lot of money for a coachman hired out like the team of horses he drove.

"Describe the carriage that took her away, Mr. Hubson."

"Big one. Town coach. Two footmen and another one, young, who wasn't in livery. Secretary perhaps. A lord's coach, I'd say, but I didn't see the door."

Winterside doubted this opinion. Leona Montgomery was a mere Country Trader's sister. What would a lord want with her?

"Has she often had congress with such elevated society?"

"I took her to two such addresses. Stayed a respectable time at both. She was received, that is certain." Hubson gazed at the note again.

Winterside set the note aside. "All in good time, Mr. Hubson. All in good time. Which two?"

Hubson leaned forward, as if he worried someone might overhear his indiscretion. The pose made his rotund chest threaten the security of the buttons of his waistcoat.

"There was a party at the house of Lady Barraclough a fortnight ago. Quite smug she was at having that invitation. Dressed herself very fine, she did. Then, let me see . . ." He cocked his head and thought hard. "Six days ago it was, she had me take her to Grosvenor Square. To Lord Easterbrook's house. She called on his aunt, Lady Wallingford."

Hubson described a thin social schedule for Miss Montgomery, and not one of much interest. Lady Barraclough was a harmless woman with a stupid husband. Easterbrook was an eccentric recluse and his aunt a vapid harpy.

It sounded as if Miss Montgomery was pounding on the weakest links of the chains that barred society's doors. None of her movements presented any cause for worry.

"Did you see this coach return her to her house?"

Hubson shook his head. "I'd dealt with the carriage and horses, and was settling in for a good nap by then."

Too bad. This story of the coach nudged at Winterside. It might belong to some man who had developed a *tendre* for Miss Montgomery. He hoped so. A love affair would ensure that Miss Montgomery occupied her time in London on the most ordinary matters.

Winterside was quite sure that ordinary matters

were all she intended here. Others did not agree. It was not so much who Miss Montgomery was that provoked their interest, but who her father had been.

He sighed inwardly. What nonsense over ancient history. As if a woman would know or give a damn about Reginald Montgomery's bizarre accusations. Nonetheless, important men wanted reassurance that she had not picked up her father's standard.

Hubson must have thought the silence reflected displeasure at his answer, because he tried again. "I didn't see her return, but I did see her later that day. She went out again."

"Did she now?"

"There I was, settling in, and she sent the Chinaman to tell me to bring the carriage around. It did not please me, mind you. I'd made everything ready once, and to start all over again—"

"Where did you take her?"

"To the Royal Exchange."

"The Royal Exchange? You are quite sure? No doubt she sought a shop nearby."

"It was the Exchange itself that she wanted. I saw her go in. She did not stay long. No more than a quarter hour. I thought it odd. A woman going to the Exchange."

Not so odd. She was a trader's daughter and sister. The Royal Exchange was the center of trading in London. She may have just been curious.

"Tell me, Mr. Hubson. Have you taken her anywhere else that you considered odd?"

Hubson thought so hard that his fleshy face creased at brow and mouth. "Not really."

Of course not. Winterside checked the tip of his pen. He would write to his contact among those important men and explain that Miss Montgomery had engaged in no activities to cause the slightest interest—

"Except that day she went to Mincing Lane."

"Mincing Lane, you say?"

"Actually to the crossroad. She bade me walk the horses and return in a half hour. But as I moved on I looked back and she was walking down Mincing Lane."

"You are very sure it was Mincing Lane?"

"I've been a coachman in London for twenty-two years, sir. I think I know the City streets well enough, thank you."

Winterside sat back in his chair and contemplated this last tidbit. The coachman looked longingly at the ten-pound note.

"Take it, Mr. Hubson. We are done and you have been most forthcoming."

Hubson swiped up the note and took his leave. Winterside moved his ink within reach. He had been too optimistic in hoping he could end this matter today.

There was only one reason for Miss Montgomery to go to Mincing Lane.

"It is good to see you preparing to go out," Isabella said. "You have been so quiet the last few days that I feared you were ill."

Leona bent her head while Isabella stroked the brush down her scalp and back. "I have not been ill. I have been thinking."

"Good things, I hope."

Not entirely.

The reunion with Edmun—*Easterbrook*—demanded a reassessment of many matters. She had been reexamining her past with him. She had been mourning for her innocent memories, preserved carefully over the years even while maturity taught her more skepticism.

Her heart cringed as she saw it all with newly opened eyes. She had thought they had shared a special intimacy of souls and minds, and an unfulfilled passion of bodies and hearts. In the years since, she had even convinced herself that she had been a fool not to grab the excitement he offered instead of being so good. She had come to curse her girlish fears, and cherish her nostalgia for the young man who had thrilled her blood.

Now her mind saw every slow smile and every dark gaze, every stolen kiss and every private confidence, from a different perspective. She had merely been a convenient plaything to amuse the marquess when he was not busy addressing other, more important matters.

Those other matters occupied her mind now. This morning she had put the past behind her and turned her attention to the present and the immediate future. She had begun considering how this shocking discovery might affect her plans in England.

Easterbrook had been suspicious about her reasons for coming to London. Despite her insistence that she intended only to aid her brother, he had not believed her. Even at the end he referred to her missions. Plural.

That implied that he knew what other reasons might draw her here. Which in turn probably meant that her suspicions about him were correct.

Had he done it? Stolen her father's papers? Fled Macao with all that evidence that her father had accumulated while he investigated the attacks on his business?

The timing of the notebook's disappearance had always made her wonder, even if her heart had argued against her mind most forcefully. After all, what use would their guest have for those notes and letters? They had no value to a naturalist and adventurer.

Her father had not been distressed by the notebook's loss, but then his sharp mind could recall its contents with little effort. She, however, had almost no information at all after he died. She wanted that notebook and the evidence it contained.

Easterbrook knew that. She was almost sure that he did. He guessed that she had hoped to find him so she could ask for the papers. Now she dared not even let him know that she suspected he had them.

His identity changed so much. Everything. For the Marquess of Easterbrook, that theft could have been the reason he was in Macao to begin with. He might have learned that her father had traced the source of his oppression back to England, and believed that some members of the House of Lords were behind it.

Easterbrook probably arrived in Macao seeking a way to protect his wealthy friends, his family, or even himself. He had lied about his identity so he could learn what her father knew and interfere with her father's attempts to expose them all.

Isabella finished dressing her hair. Leona felt the topknot and dangling curls. "Where is Tong Wei?"

"He is in the library studying his English reading."

"Let us go to him. I want to tell you both something."

They found him there, bent over a child's book. As a boy, Tong Wei had traded language lessons with an English clerk in Macao. It was illegal to teach foreigners Chinese, but Tong Wei had risked it. In turn he had learned English far purer than the fractured dialect spoken by the official interpreters, and he had perfected it in her father's service. However, he had never learned to read English.

"I saw Edmund," Leona announced once she had Tong Wei's attention. "The day I went to the Royal Exchange."

"So that is why you have been so quiet and thoughtful," Isabella said. "Is he much the same?"

"He is not at all the same. He is not even Edmund. That is not his name. That traveler who accepted my father's hospitality was actually one of the highest-ranking noblemen here, the Marquess of Easterbrook. He lied to all of us."

"It is good news, is it not? That he is this marquess?" Isabella asked. "He had much affection for you. If he still does—" She raised her eyebrows at the possibilities.

Isabella's allusion revived the memory of Easterbrook's recent kiss. And his touch. And his confidence in his advantage. Leona's heart trembled softly, an echo of her reactions in the green bedchamber.

"Affection is not the correct word for his interest back then," she said.

"He is a powerful man merely by his birth," Tong

Wei said. "I hope that you did nothing to anger or insult him when you learned of his old deception."

"I do not think that I did, but I was unable to hide my shock. He agreed to aid me."

"That will be very useful."

It would be. If she could trust herself, she might even try to obtain more of Easterbrook's aid. Not to her private plans, but to the ones that touched on her brother.

His parting words, however, indicated that she dare not have too much congress with the marquess. *I will have you.*

Leona was not above using a man's interest to her own purposes, but she knew better than to play with fire—especially when the flames were in herself as well as him. He had already proven that they were. Even her suspicions about his betrayal did not change that, to her dismay.

"You will require a better wardrobe if you will consort with such a man," Isabella said. "We will have to sell some of the jade."

"I will not be consorting. He will provide one introduction, nothing more. I thought that you should both know his true identity, however." Leona sat at the writing table and thumbed through the letters of introduction stored there. "Do not sell the jade yet. We may need it later, and for more important things than my wardrobe. We may be here longer than I anticipated."

She hoped not. Coming to England had meant leaving her brother for over a year. She had taken pains to prepare him and the business for her absence, but she could not stay away indefinitely. Gaspar might be the titular head of their company now, but he was still very inexperienced.

She found the letter written by another Country Trader to provide an introduction to his sister in London. She would call on this woman today. Although she did not expect the visit to yield any direct benefit, one never knew who knew whom. She would be grateful for the most tenuous connection to the people she needed to see.

With the recent setback to her plans, even a small step forward would be helpful.

Leona entered her house, contemplating her meeting with Mrs. Fines. It had been more useful than she had anticipated.

Mrs. Fines might be a trader's sister, but she had married above her family. Her husband was a barrister, and related through his mother to a baron. By the time the visit ended, Mrs. Fines was insisting on obtaining good invitations and introductions for her new dear friend.

While Leona untied her bonnet, Isabella hurried into the reception hall.

"He is here," she said with excitement.

"Who is here?"

"Edmund. You are correct. He is much changed. I did not recognize him at first."

"I saw no coach. No horse. And his name is not Edmund."

"Maybe he flew. He is above, in the library with Tong Wei."

Leona struggled to maintain a bland countenance, but this surprise had her heart racing. She had not expected Easterbrook to come *here*.

"He asked to be told when you returned—Easterbrook did. I think that he came to see you, not Tong Wei," Isabella said.

"I am not sure that I want to see *him,* however."

"I do not see how you can avoid it, unless you want to insult him. That would not be wise."

No, it wouldn't be. A little annoyed and more excited than she wanted, Leona went up to the library.

No sounds greeted her when she opened the door. The chamber held a stillness that she recognized.

Tong Wei sat on the floor, his legs crossed before him and his back so straight that his queue dangled. Easterbrook lounged in a chair. Like Tong Wei his eyes were closed. Nothing about him moved, not even an eyelash.

Leona did not move either, but she sensed the disruption that her mere presence caused. She became a tiny pebble dropped into a serene lake. Little eddies wobbled across the surface.

They emerged from their reveries together. Easterbrook's lids rose and he gazed at her with eyes not yet entirely in the world again. Tong Wei rose with a fluid movement that reflected both strength and agility.

Tong Wei bowed to Easterbrook, then walked over to her. "He never stopped. All this time he has continued."

"He does not do it the same as you, though. He does not sit as you do and as you taught him."

Easterbrook had emerged completely and risen from his chair, but he allowed the conversation to continue and remained out of hearing.

"Nor does he believe. He uses the truth, but does not accept it as truth. All the same—" Tong Wei bowed to their guest again, and retreated from the library.

Leona faced Easterbrook alone. "He says that you have mastered the methods, but do not accept the truths."

"It is not my faith. Do I insult him by showing the methods do not depend on believing?"

"You disconcert him, not insult him. He is also pleased, I believe, to see that you continued your efforts and that you find peace in the results. He is flattered that you visited today."

"I would have sought him out in any case if I knew he was in London. However, I did not visit today just to see him."

No, he had not. God help her. She sought some calm by focusing on the many ways that his appearance had altered from their last meeting.

No one would mistake him for a servant now. He appeared the lord he was. His frock coat avoided the exaggerated nipped waist that was fashionable, but still revealed his form. His waistcoat was quite conservative. His hair looked shorter by a hand's breadth, and it more neatly framed his handsome face.

"I did not acquit myself well when last we met, Leona. I should have accounted for your shock at seeing me again. The manner in which I had you brought to me—I apologize. I should have found a better way."

She doubted Easterbrook apologized often, to

anyone. She allowed him to dwell in the vague discomfort this little speech appeared to cause him.

"Perhaps I did not acquit myself well either, due to the shock."

"I would say that you handled me splendidly. But then you always did."

Not always. Not completely. It was kind of him to pretend she had never been a fool, though.

He meandered through the library, taking in its cases and appointments. "Have you let this house for long?"

"Three months."

"How long have you been in London?"

"One month tomorrow."

"I assume that you brought letters of introduction."

"Quite a few."

"Yet you only recently made it into my aunt's company, and she is more approachable than most, and not too strict in whom she receives. It is going slower than you expected."

"Regrettably, yes."

His path had brought him close to her. "I have taken steps for you that you did not request. I trust you will not mind."

"What kind of steps?"

"I have told my aunt that it would please me if you were invited to more assemblies. Those of good society. She will open a few doors. I have also told the family solicitor that it would please me if you received invitations to parties of less elevated society. Traders, financiers, and such."

"That is good of you. However, I have learned a

thing or two in the last few weeks. You are well known, of course, and the object of some gossip. It is said that you do not partake of social events yourself. A recluse, you are called. Why do you think your stated pleasure will produce invitations for me?"

"Because I am Easterbrook."

His answer did not even sound arrogant. He merely stated a reality that explained everything.

An insight came to her, one that she suspected was important. He announced his identity not only with calm confidence, but also with utter acceptance.

Being Easterbrook would not only be about influence and wealth. It would not only mean that people bowed to you, and sought to please you. There would be bad along with the good, and obligations along with the prestige.

This was how he had changed, she realized. His appearance was the least of it. The young man in Macao had exuded dark chaos. The darkness still existed, but it did not rule anymore, and the chaos had been tamed. She wondered whether the calm way he said *I am Easterbrook* was the reason for this essential change, or the result of it.

He checked his pocket watch. "My carriage should return soon. You will accompany me to the park."

"That is kind of you, but I have had a full day already."

"You will join me, Leona. It will reinforce my patronage of your efforts. Society will see you in my company, and the invitations will come no matter what your birth and history."

"If I am in your carriage, alone in your company, won't society misunderstand?"

That gave him pause, but not for the reasons it should. His soft smile implied that to his mind they would misunderstand nothing if they drew conclusions, but that he would indulge her hesitation for now.

"Isabella will come too," he said. "That should make it proper enough."

While it might make it proper enough for his intentions, she doubted that Isabella's presence would prevent gossip. However, only a fool would refuse the influence of a marquess who had decided to aid her plans, no matter what his motives and no matter what her suspicions.

And Leona was not a fool.

CHAPTER FIVE

Christian suspected that when he finally went to hell, perdition would bear an uncanny resemblance to the fashionable hour in Hyde Park.

The crush itself did not oppress him. He could tolerate crowds, and even sought them out for brief periods of time. Markets could be stimulating, for example. They were so full of variety in the people assembled that the good balanced the bad. Much like a symphony could invigorate with its contrasts and multiple instruments, a good crowd, experienced sparingly, could actually be enjoyed.

The fashionable hour, unfortunately, was no symphony. Rather it consisted of innumerable horns bleating the same weak note, over and over. Even interesting people became tedious and shallow in Hyde Park at five o'clock. Being assaulted by the overwhelming vapidity exhausted him.

All the same, he instructed the coachman to plow into the thick of it. He centered his thoughts on the woman who graced him with her company in the open carriage, until the horns became muted wails in the background.

Leona chatted with Isabella, pointing out hats and coaches and other things of a woman's interest. Isabella had dressed in English clothes, but her Oriental heritage showed in her soft, round face, distinctive eyes and simply coiffed black hair.

He remembered Isabella as a girl adrift between two worlds when he was in Macao. The unacknowledged daughter of a Portuguese official who had made her mother his mistress, she had been barely tolerated by the Europeans, despite her mother giving her a European name in hopes it would help. The Chinese for their part had completely ignored the child of mixed blood.

Leona had befriended the outcast Isabella back then. As best Christian could tell, Isabella was Leona's lady's maid and companion now.

Isabella had dressed her mistress's hair in a fashionable style that took advantage of Leona's mane of chestnut curls. He had seen those locks flowing wildly and sensually a few times, rather than primped into the knots and tendrils that fit so neatly beneath her straw bonnet today.

One time had been the night she helped him to flee Macao. Another time had been earlier in his visit, when she found him at his worst, then became the mirror in which he saw the coward he was.

Leona tried not to look at him while she enjoyed the park. Eventually she acknowledged his attention, however. Her dark, expressive eyes met his and lingered just enough to reveal her caution regarding him. She was still inclined to run and hide, he guessed.

"You are talking to Isabella too much," he said.

"Are you telling me that these fine people think it wrong to converse with one's servants?"

"I am saying that you should be talking to me instead. You will have to eventually, Leona."

She leveled a direct gaze at him. She had no idea how much passion could be seen in her eyes when her temper was prodded, and how that could arouse a man.

"Fine, we will speak. Will you choose a topic, or should I? Mine would be a simple one and a product of the curiosity of the moment."

"Now the curiosity is mine, so the choice must be yours."

She glanced at the horses and carriages so close one could touch them. "Since we arrived, many of these people have tried to catch your eye and greet you, but you have cut every single one. Are you always so rude? Or does your title and station mean that the word rude does not even apply to you?"

It was more a scold than a challenge. He had no option except to turn his attention to the many bodies pressing past them. He nodded a few greetings as addresses were paid.

Since this was hell, a reminder of his sins was inevitable. No sooner had he unmuffled the horns than two of them blared right in his ear. Mrs. Napier approached from the other direction, displaying her blond beauty from her perch on a•white horse. Seeing his carriage, she aimed toward him.

Around her neck she displayed a diamond necklace,

one most inappropriate for the hour. It served as proof to society that being thrown over by her recent lover had left her with more profit than enjoying his constancy ever would.

She smiled down while her cool eyes scrutinized Leona from the shadows beneath the brim of her violet hat. An unkind merriment communicated that she thought he had made a far worse bargain than she in the affair's final accounting.

As if one demon were not enough, another horse pulled up alongside Mrs. Napier's during the time it took Christian's carriage to pass her. Another of his sins joined the examination of the carriage's occupants, then the two women paced their mounts away, enjoying a private joke.

"For a recluse, it appears that you are not without friends," Leona said dryly.

"I am not a recluse. That is a baseless rumor."

"Obviously. I trust that the other rumor is baseless as well. The one that says you are mad."

"Actually it says that I am half mad, and that is at worst an exaggeration."

She laughed. It was a throaty, sensual sound, and the first memory he had of her. That laugh, coming from the back of her father's house, intruding on the quiet study where Reginald Montgomery received the traveler who had arrived at his door.

Nostalgia invaded him, for that moment and the next, when the girl suddenly appeared in that study with her vivacious black eyes. He had known two things in that moment, known them so essentially that they required no thoughts. He knew that she was immune to his curse, and he knew that he wanted her.

He bore the passing crowd for a few more minutes, then shut them all out. "I had not noticed the attention paid me because I was intent on enjoying your company, Leona. And, I confess, I was picturing your hair down the way I saw it in Macao, and wishing to see it thus again."

"It is unlikely that you will, even if you are Easterbrook and expect the world to conform to your pleasure. I am a mature woman now, and must look like one."

He would soon see it however he chose, but he let it pass. "Tell me how your brother fares. You spoke of his capability with trade but nothing else."

She settled back, perhaps relieved by such an easy topic. "He looks much like my father now that he is grown. There is little of my mother in him."

"You said that he goes to Canton now. That means he has to leave you alone in Macao during the trading season. It must be lonely for you."

From October to May, the European traders lived at Canton, outside its walls in the trading houses—or factories—maintained by each country on the narrow strip of land designated by the emperor. Their movements were strictly regulated by the Mandarins who executed the imperial will.

Even their visits to their families in the Portuguese enclave of Macao involved an elaborate protocol and the payment of high fees. Since Canton was the only portal for legal trade with China, the restrictive system was tolerated even though it was strongly resented.

"Not so lonely. There are other women who wait as I do. I have Isabella, and Tong Wei remains as a guard."

"Does your mother's family aid with the business? There was no need to be involved while your father lived, but your brother is young still."

Her expression turned cool. "Although our company still bears their name, the Tavares family chose to sign away their rights to their share when my father died. They calculated it would fall into ruin, and did not want any debts to make their way back to them."

"Since it did not fall into ruin, they calculated wrong."

"It appears so."

The better calculations had been hers. She knew her own abilities and worth as her mother's family never would. Christian could picture her, the grieving daughter, perhaps dramatic in her desolation at her loss, silently weighing the risks and profits if the Tavares family handed over their share.

"Pedro broke the engagement at the same time, I assume." He watched her closely, left with nothing more than normal instincts to ascertain just how sly she had been.

"Yes, it all happened at the same time."

A little disturbance trembled toward him. Not from Leona, but from Isabella. *Sadness. Sympathy.* The companion remembered Leona's distress back then, even if Leona masked it completely.

Not so distressed that she did not play her cards shrewdly, though. Whether the Tavareses wanted to distance themselves from a failing business or from a

woman insulted by a fiancé, Leona had secured whatever remained for her brother, in total.

Leona made a display of gazing along the path, announcing with her distraction that this particular topic
was finished. He occupied himself with admiring the
fine bones of her face and the unfashionable, erotic
fullness of her lips.

Maturity favored her unusual beauty. That mouth
and her eyes reflected her Portuguese blood, but the rest
of her face was English. The combination resulted in
the familiar tinged by the exotic, and her dark eyes con-
trasted starkly with the translucent paleness of her skin.

"Lord Easterbrook, you are still summoning a good
deal of attention," she observed. "There is a man over
there by those trees who just stares at you, much as if
he is seeing a ghost."

He noticed the man in question. Handsome, dark-
haired, and elegant, he accompanied a woman far less
fashionable in dress but lovely in her Celtic way. Right
now the beauty was noticing her companion's interest
in the Easterbrook carriage and expressing her own
gape-mouthed astonishment.

"If you mean that man with the woman whose red
tresses are flowing the way I would like to see yours,
that is my youngest brother Elliot. The woman is his
wife, Phaedra."

"Why is he looking so stunned?"

"He is surprised to see me here. I do not partake of
this social ritual often." He told his coachman to pull
aside and stop. "I should introduce you, I suppose."

"If you only suppose, perhaps you should not."

"The goal of this outing was to encourage introductions for you. We may as well start with my family."

She accepted his hand and stepped down beside him. "Just how infrequently do you partake of this ritual?"

"Rarely."

"When was the last time?"

He tucked her hand around his arm and strolled toward Elliot. "Let me think. I believe it was five—no, six—years ago."

Lord Elliot Rothwell had swallowed his shock by the time Easterbrook hailed him. He bowed to Leona and listened with interest to the introduction.

"Macao, you say. How interesting." Lord Elliot gave his older brother a deep, curious look. A peculiar awkwardness settled between the two men.

Lady Phaedra rushed to ease the moment. "More than interesting. I daresay fortuitous, for me at least. Let us take a turn together, Miss Montgomery, while I pepper you with some questions that I have about your experiences in the Far East."

Lady Phaedra guided Leona away, leaving the two brothers alone under the tree. Lady Phaedra's strides caused her dress to flow around her body, revealing that she was with child.

Leona glanced back at Easterbrook and his brother. "Are they angry with each other?"

"The marquess is too peculiar to incite anger. Perplexity, yes. Confusion, often. Annoyance, daily. But not anger."

"I have heard some rumors that agree with you."

"People spin theories when they are not handed a story that explains what they see. In truth no one knows much about him. Not even his family. He shuns society and rarely leaves his house, or so we think. But we don't really know, do we? He does not suffer fools kindly, and can be autocratic, but any man of his station is like that. The fact is, even we do not know what he is about, or how he spends his time, or what he thinks about, or whether he thinks about anything at all." She grinned mischievously. "Except *now* we know that he once visited China."

Leona snuck another look at the brothers. Their conversation did not appear contentious, but it did not look convivial either.

"Enough about Easterbrook," Lady Phaedra said. "I would much prefer to talk about you. I find it interesting that you journeyed here to act as an agent for your brother."

Leona briefly told her story. She sensed that Lady Phaedra's mind was as unconventional as her appearance, and that the tale was received differently than it was by other women.

"What adventures you must have had," Lady Phaedra said. "Just your journey here is remarkable, but your description of visiting India and the Far Eastern islands to secure trade while your brother was a minor is astonishing."

"There was no choice except to do it."

"There is always a choice, and most women would have made a different one."

The only different one would have been total dependency on her mother's family. However, she understood what Lady Phaedra meant. She had embraced the fate given her, and not sought too hard to alter it.

She was proud that she had succeeded more often than not. Necessity had forced her to conquer any fears, and be bolder than even her father would have expected. Nor had her duties truly ended when Gaspar reached his majority. Her father had taught her much of his business without really planning to, but Gaspar had been too young to absorb such lessons before their father's death. Her brother would probably manage this year while she was away, but he could not yet run that business on his own forever.

Lady Phaedra brought them up short in a patch of sunlight. "Do you have any talent with the pen?"

"An average amount. I do not write poetry, if that is what you mean."

"I would guess that you probably write a good letter, though. I ask for a reason. I have a small publishing house that I inherited from my father. I have decided to publish a lady's journal. I intend to have it be more literate than the others. It occurs to me that you might describe these distant lands as you saw them, and educate my readers in the customs and important matters of these places."

It was a novel notion, and one that captivated Leona's interest. "Would you only want descriptions of clothing and food and such?"

"It could be about anything you choose. Events that you witnessed. Problems that you perceived. Of course you should not ignore fashion and society totally. That will always be of interest to most women."

Not so much to the woman who would publish that journal, Leona thought. Lady Phaedra was lovely, but unusual in the simplicity of her pale green dress and her unbound hair. No other woman in Hyde Park looked like that.

"Say that you will consider it," Lady Phaedra urged. "Your letters will make the first issues of this journal distinctive."

"I will see if I can write one that you find acceptable. If you like it, we can talk further."

Easterbrook approached with his brother by his side. "It appears that you have formed an alliance, Miss Montgomery."

"One that promises to be beneficial to us both, I hope," Lady Phaedra said. "Please call on me soon, Miss Montgomery."

Easterbrook watched Lady Phaedra stroll away with her husband. "She is not the wife I would have chosen for him, and the story surrounding their marriage caused a scandal, but he is more than content." He spoke as if Leona had invited his opinion.

"I found her very amiable and interesting. Why would you not have chosen her?"

He began escorting her back to the carriage. "Amiable to be sure. And interesting. But also willfully peculiar and deliberately unconventional. That did not recommend her initially." He looked over at her. "I have said something that amuses you."

"Not at all, Lord Easterbrook. It was generous that you reconciled yourself to her willful peculiarity. What an open mind you have."

Upon returning to her house, Easterbrook accompanied her and Isabella to the door. Then he entered it behind them.

"Leave us," he said.

Isabella bowed and scurried away.

Leona refused to invite him into one of the other chambers. Whatever he had to say could be communicated in this reception hall.

He regarded her a long while, as if he expected her to speak first. It unnerved her, to suffer his gaze like this. The chamber seemed to shrink, bringing him closer even though neither of them moved.

"This plan, to make introductions and such," he said. "It will be much more effective if you move to Grosvenor Square."

She had not expected such a blunt overture so soon. "I am content here, and I would never impose on your aunt."

"She would not consider it an imposition, I guarantee."

"All the same, joining your household would be too much intimacy with a woman I barely know."

"There would be no intimacies that you did not agree to. It is a very big house."

"I must decline your generous offer."

He took it well enough. He paced aimlessly around the shrinking chamber. "The introduction to my brother Hayden will have to be delayed a week or so. His first child will be born any day now."

"I am sorry that you even raised the matter with him under that circumstance."

"He did not mind. In the meantime, invitations will begin arriving for you tomorrow—more than you can accept. If you have any questions regarding which should take precedence, I will gladly help you with that."

"Thank you."

"Do you have the necessary wardrobe? If not, I will—"

"I cannot allow that, so please do not offer."

He took the second rejection very well too. Leona stood her ground and tried to ignore how he managed to dominate what had become a tiny space now, one where she stood in the center and his casual stroll arched around her.

"You are nervous, being alone with me," he observed. "There is no reason to be afraid."

"No? You declared your intentions explicitly when we met in your house, and they are not honorable. Now you are proposing things that are intended to lure me."

"Does that matter so much? Whether they are honorable or not?"

"Of course it matters. A marquess may sin with frequency and impunity, but I am not so privileged."

"As a woman of the world you know that these arrangements are so normal and so accepted in every society that calling it a sin is a joke. If I am luring you, it is to more than a casual seduction, in case you do not understand that."

"I have lived in China. I know what a concubine is. An English mistress does not have even that security. I was not born or raised for what you offer, no matter how comfortable and lucrative the situation may temporarily prove to be."

She spoke with more determination than she felt, and not only because he made her stupid heart jump the way he always had. As Easterbrook's mistress she might accomplish all that she had come to do here in London, and in very little time.

Even if he tried to thwart her, even if her worst suspicions about him were correct, she would be better placed to learn it all if she were in his house and his bed. She might even find that notebook if she could move freely in his home.

Her own ruthless calculations shocked her. But the insidious arousal that he inspired urged her to grab the excuse.

She trusted that he had heard the finality in her voice. She assumed that he would take his leave.

He did not. Instead he contemplated her with that direct examination, much as he had during their last meeting.

"Why did you not marry? I do not believe Pedro ended the engagement as you said."

"Oh, he ended it. Thoroughly." The sudden turn in topic vexed her. He had a talent for throwing her off balance.

"But you did not mind so much. Just as you do not mind my lures so much now."

Her temper cracked like a whip. "How dare you presume to know my mind? Now or then? I was a young woman alone, orphaned, with no fortune and no security, and I was not so stupid as to ignore that Pedro offered both."

"That is not the same thing as wanting to marry him. It may have frightened you to be left to your own devices, but you were not heartbroken to be free of him."

"You are an insufferably arrogant, conceited man. You think that your birth gives you the power to read the hearts of others like a god. My father taught me the value of pride, but my mother taught me about the sins it breeds, and your presumption of omniscience is close to blasphemous."

"I do not claim to know your mind. Your story does not ring true, that is all. Pedro might have ended the engagement because of your father's failing business. However, he could not use that excuse because that would not be enough reason to end it with honor."

She could barely maintain her composure, and she proved incapable of holding her polite stance. She paced out her growing anger, back and forth, in strides too long and fast.

He had no right to pick and probe at this. He had no right to interfere with the past as well as the present, and demand answers from her as if he had a divine right to hear them.

"How wasteful that you have turned your brilliant mind to my story, Lord Easterbrook. Surely there are more pressing matters to occupy you. Of course, you are correct. Pedro did not admit the true reason. He found a better one to give the world. If you must know, that reason was *you*. He accused me of more than a silly flirtation, and he was believed."

Christian watched her furious words pour out. He

cocked his head and made a small frown. "Pedro had no proof, however. There was none to have."

"Do you think anyone cared, after they heard his tale? Do you think he was so stupid that he could not tell that *something* had happened between us? Do you think Branca could stand against him when he browbeat her to learn what he needed? You sought me out alone again and again, and were careless with my reputation. There was evidence enough for his purpose, and with my father dead there was no one to defend my honor."

He caught her arm as she strode by, stopping her. She did not fight his hold, but she refused to look at him.

"If you were held up to scorn, I apologize, Leona. If you wanted that marriage, I am sorry." His fingers cupped her chin and turned her face to his own. "Did you want it?"

Saints, but the man was impossible. "And if I say no, not really, does that mean your guilt is gone?"

"First sin, now guilt. I do not think that way. Nor do you."

"You have no idea how I think. Now, please, the day has tired me and this conversation has me too vexed to be hospitable. Show some kindness and leave me to compose myself."

He did not release her at once. She sensed that invasive attention sliding around her, as if he sought to truly know her mind. She protected herself as she always had. His expression hardened in response, as though a wordless battle had just been fought to a draw. Finally he let her go and stepped away.

Severe now, he strode to the door. He faced her again before he crossed the threshold.

"I may not know your mind, but I know enough and I'll be damned if I will pretend that I do not. I know that you also sought *me* out. I know that desire binds us so powerfully it affects every word and every motion and even the air we breathe. I know that I'm glad that pompous ass did not get you. And I know that the only sin I committed with you in Macao was not taking you when I could have."

CHAPTER
SIX

Silence. Calm. His breaths matching a larger rhythm in the darkness. No turmoil. No cravings. A state of suspended self trying to form and grow . . .

The center would not hold. Instead a memory intruded, more vivid than was natural. Images moved in the darkness of his mind. Suddenly he was back in Macao on a perfect night . . .

Colors shimmering with silver moonlight. Scents of lotus from the nearby pond. Lamps glimmering in homes beyond the stucco wall. Silent noise finding him, mixing with the sounds of night.

The garden's beauty and peace mocked him. The tranquility made the storm inside him all the less bearable. Hungers and doubts and resentments rumbled in his head. He lifted his face to the salty breeze, so it might cool the anger burning from an unknown source.

He could not live like this. The anger would lead him to violence or madness. The storm would break someday and drench him with despair. He had come too close already. He had found solace in the worst ways . . .

A sound. Not a silent one. A human noise of the normal kind. Footsteps and breathing and a low feminine hum.

She was there suddenly, on the path in front of him. She saw him and stopped. Her white nightdress glowed beneath the dark swath of her long silk shawl. Her dark hair veiled her. Her skin appeared radiant in the moon's light.

Desire ruled him at once, as it always did with her. Seeing her was all the spark needed to make his arousal flame wildly. She was innocent and erotic, shy and vivacious, girlish and worldly, all at the same time. He wanted her, constantly, and he did not dream of sweet, gentle love play either.

This was not the night to face this temptation.

"You should not be out here," he said. "Branca will whip you if she learns of it."

"Branca is asleep, and I am too old to whip. I am not a child, Edmund."

No, she wasn't, despite her innocence and ignorance.

"Why did you leave the house, Leona?"

She shrugged. "I could not sleep. I was restless. The day bored me. I would walk on the quay, but it is too late."

She bent to smell a flower on a nearby bush. Her hair fell forward while she leaned and her eyes closed as she inhaled the fragrance.

He had to go to her, of course. The storm had

retreated, as it always did in her presence. The heat in him had a reason now.

She straightened as he neared. He plucked the flower and held it, beckoning her to sniff again.

She leaned toward it. Toward him. Her own perfume mixed with that of the bloom. She looked up at him, over the petals. She knew what was in him. She always had.

He stroked the soft petals down her cheek. "I think you were restless for a reason, Leona. I think that you came into this garden looking for something." The flower fell away, and his fingertips replaced it on the path up and down her soft skin.

She trembled. She pulled her shawl tighter but it had not been the breeze. Her lids lowered and her lips parted from the sensation of his caress.

"You should go back to the house." His words warned her but his touch lured her. He wanted her. Right now he wanted her desperately. He could have her tonight. He did not doubt that.

"Maybe you are the one who should go back to the house," she said. "It is my garden."

He had to smile. He did that a lot with her. He could not remember smiling much in his life before Macao.

"That would be rude. You came looking for me tonight, after all."

"Why would I do that?"

He slid the caress down her neck. "For this." He cupped her nape and eased her toward his kiss. "And this."

Damnation.

Christian opened his eyes. Memories like this had

intruded for three days now. This one left him as hard as that kiss had that night, and as agitated as the mood that had sent him into the garden in the first place.

He stood, to walk off both effects.

It was Leona's fault. All of it. The retreat into meditation was because of her, and the distractions that made it impossible were too.

Marry Pedro, hell. What a waste that would have been. If she did not like men who thought they were gods, she would have been miserable.

That bastard had accused her of an affair with Edmund. The coward. The liar. *Edmund* had been too damned noble to take advantage of Leona. He had let her run away that night, even though it had near killed him to do it.

Still, he had sought her out often enough, just as she had sought him. He had displayed an impulsive lack of discretion with her, and made her vulnerable to Pedro's accusation. That it had saved her from marriage to that fool pleased him, but he did not like to imagine her under the cloud of scandal.

It had given her freedom, though. Freedom to now come to England. Freedom to sail the Eastern seas. Freedom, perhaps, to have love affairs if she chose to.

She had lived in a world of men ever since her father's death, a lovely young woman with dark eyes that revealed her passionate nature and lack of reserve. Sea captains, traders, even members of the Company and the naval service—she had sat at many dinners with men who would want her.

An aggressive, primitive heat entered his head,

bringing a mood so black that he found himself glaring at nothing.

He calmed the storm before lightning flashed. How like Leona to inspire emotions so long unknown that he had lost the ability to sense them coming.

He needed to find distraction from these constant thoughts of her or he truly would turn half mad.

London never fell silent at night. Even in winter an invisible energy flowed through the dark, the echoes of the yearnings and fears, the hopes and joys pulsing in its buildings behind shutters and drapes.

In spring the forces of life spoke more clearly, especially on a clear, cool night such as the one that Christian traversed.

He found the nights peaceful. He even welcomed the life whispering around him. The worst part of his curse had always been the isolation it encouraged. Not only was it unhealthy to retreat totally from the world, but also he had long ago admitted that he did not want to. As long as the dark center waited with its respite and its peace, he could indulge in human congress a little.

Leona had given him that. She did not even know the value of the gift. When she asked Tong Wei to teach the young Englishman about meditation, the reason had been unrelated to Christian's ability to sense the emotions of others.

He had never explained it. Not to her. Not to anyone. It was the sort of thing that sounded insane. For a long time, he had been sure it would eventually make him deranged. A man cannot live like that, invaded at every turn by instincts regarding others' private selves. Worse, the temptation to use the curse to his own ends was almost unbearable, and he still occasionally succumbed.

He tested himself as he walked, blocking the vague energies first with concentration on his thoughts, then with a rigorous pace that provided the peace found in sport.

All of the strategies derived from the first, however. If he had never found the utter silence of the selfless center, he would have never known what to strive for in experiments that required less oblivion.

His path eventually brought him to a fine house on the edge of Mayfair, near the park. Like many others it still showed the glow of lamps through its windows. London did not fall silent at night, and Mayfair during the season did not sleep until close to dawn.

A footman escorted him to the library. The men assembled there looked over when he entered.

A table of four went back to their game of cards. Christian walked over to another group occupied only with glasses of spirits.

"What ho, Easterbrook. Did not think you would show this time. We are in need of a fourth tonight too. Been left with naught to do but drink and gossip until now."

Drink and gossip were the real purpose of these informal meetings, and games of whist mere filler, so the absence or presence of one or another person really did not matter.

Christian had inherited this circle along with his title. An invitation to join them had come as soon as his father died. For generations, it was explained to him, Easterbrooks had been members of this very small, very private club.

Six peers and four bishops comprised the circle, all with titles and sees among the oldest in the realm. The club's origins were shrouded in political plots so dangerous that each member was also known by one of the face cards in a playing deck, in the event secret communication were necessary.

As Easterbrook, Christian was the King of Hearts. The bishops had taken the aces for themselves. Sometimes members still made use of those designations in their reference to each other, but the club's function now was mostly social.

Mostly. They still swapped political favors. On a few rare occasions the members decided how to privately punish a peer for crimes that would be too embarrassing to the peerage if he were publicly tried in the House of Lords.

"I rearranged my plans just for you, Denningham," Christian said to the tawny-haired, corpulent man who greeted him. The Earl of Denningham was the only member of this club whom he occasionally saw outside these nights. He and Denningham had been friends at school, in part because Denningham was so amiable, so lacking in guile or ulterior motives, that his only emotions were the ones written on his face for all to see.

"You have had a change of habit. Out and about quite a lot these days, or that is the *on-dit*. Would it have anything to do with the handsome woman seen with you yesterday in the park?" Rallingport said.

Viscount Rallingport was a regular at these card parties and had been for five years, since he inherited his title. His attendance was so predictable that the meetings now took place in his home. He was basically a good man, just too fond of brandy.

"Miss Montgomery is an old friend," Christian said.

"I wish my old friends looked like that. I am stuck with Meadowsun here, and he resembles an old apple."

Meadowsun did resemble an old apple. An older man, his face possessed a pattern of wrinkles much like fruit develops as it begins to dry. Since he was slight of build and sparse of hair, that face was really all one noticed about him.

It would be easy for a person to dismiss frail, pale-eyed Meadowsun as inconsequential. That would be a mistake. He was a favored cleric in the Archbishop of Canterbury's court. He had the ear of one of the most powerful men in the realm, and through the archbishop exerted influence throughout the church and the House of Lords.

In the oldest days the archbishop himself had attended these meetings, but for generations now archbishops had sent proxies. That proxy had been Meadowsun as long as Christian could remember.

Meadowsun's sobriety lent little to the convivial mood in the library. He observed most nights, not participating. The necessity of discretion to his position meant Meadowsun buried his emotions so deeply below the surface that only bland indifference emanated from him in public.

"Say, I spoke with the King of Spades today,"

Rallingport said. He referred to the Duke of Ashford, a senior member of their group who rarely attended during the season. "He begged off tonight, but mentioned that he has heard from our friend in Kent. The fellow is most unhappy."

"Pity," Christian said. Rallingport referred to the subject of one of their private judgments. The peer had been offered a choice between permanent house confinement in the country or ruinous scandal and insurmountable disgrace at a trial.

"He was petitioning for relief. Wants to come up to town. Wants to be rid of that housekeeper he was given. Wants to have a party."

"That is not possible," Christian said. "Not this season. Not next season. I would say not for twenty seasons to come."

"I expect so. Of course."

"It would displease the archbishop most grievously if your friend left his estate in Kent," Meadowsun said blandly. "I will explain that to His Grace if you prefer not to."

"I did not say Ashford thought otherwise, did I? No need to explain anything, either of us."

"Denningham, you should write to our friend and recommend he find an interest to occupy his time," Christian said. "Gardening, for example. You could share with him the restful delights that you enjoy in your horticultural experiments."

Denningham took the suggestion seriously. He nodded to reassure everyone that he would deal with the problem in Kent.

Christian strolled over to the bookcases to choose a

cigar from Rallingport's selection. Denningham followed to fetch one too.

"So, how did you come to know Miss Montgomery? Not like you to cavort in public with a woman." Denningham's grin was that of one young blood goading another, even though he had never qualified for the role even when of age to do so. "I see that you are also looking less barbaric these days. Her influence?"

"It was only a ride through the park."

"Your first in memory. Everyone says you threw over Mrs. Napier too. Everyone is curious about your new interest. Lots of questions buzzing around."

"What kind of questions?"

"Who is she, why is she here, what is her history with you. There are suggestions that she is other than she says, and here for purposes other than she claims." He wiggled his eyebrows. "A lady of mystery, and there are those collecting the clues."

"Where did you hear all of this?"

"Why, right here. Before you came."

"From whom?"

Denningham lit his cigar and glanced at their company while he puffed. "Damned if I can remember. It was just there, before the cards started, the way talk is. How you were seen with this woman from China, and someone wondering who she is and what she is doing here, and in your company no less. That sort of talk. I can't really say who raised the matter."

But someone had. Here, among the men who probably knew him as well as any men other than his brothers. It might have just been talk. The speculations about Leona were probably just curiosity.

Christian took his place at the table across from Denningham. To his right sat Meadowsun the Obscure.

That evened things out. Denningham's cards might as well be printed on his face, after all. Whatever advantage Christian had with the fourth person at the table was balanced by the advantage that both of his opponents had with his partner.

Dear Readers,

Allow me to introduce myself. I am the daughter of three countries. My mother was Portuguese and my father was English, but I have lived my life in China.

Leona read her salutation three times before deciding it would do. She dipped her pen.

She spent a half hour describing Macao. She visited her home in her mind while she wrote about the white houses rising in terraces and the promenade along the quay. Giving an accurate picture of the Cathedral of St. Paul and the famous Camoen's Cave required some thought.

She turned to the residents, the Chinese who comprised half the population, and the Portuguese families with their women so often garbed in black. She introduced the English, who included eccentrics like Mr. Beale who had an aviary in his gardens, and dozens of caged birds on his veranda. She ended with a glimpse of the walls of Canton.

She paused. This would be her first of several letters, if published. This introduction would be sufficient. She should finish now with the promise of what would come in later essays.

And yet—

She dipped her pen.

I look forward to describing this exotic land to you. Its rituals and beauty are of great interest. However, I also must tell you of matters less colorful and more serious. For great evil lurks in the waters around China, evil that the currents of time and trade will inevitably bring to your shores.

She hesitated. It might be wiser to avoid announcing her interest in this subject. However, exposing this evil was one of the reasons she had come to England. Nor was it a purpose apart from her desire to aid her brother, but intimately entwined with it.

Fate had handed her an unexpected opportunity in Lady Phaedra's request for these letters. Her father had always said to be alert to such moments and to make the most of them.

She dipped her pen and jotted two more paragraphs. Satisfied, she brought her letter to a close.

Let another correspondent restrict herself to stories about dress and manners. I promise you all of that, but also mystery and intrigue and secrets that are not even heard in your Parliament. I promise you both the exotic beauty and the terrible sorrow that is China today.

She set down her pen just as Isabella entered the library, carrying a stack of letters. "The mail has grown today."

Leona broke some seals. Easterbrook had been correct. Invitations were arriving already. She would have to exercise more judgment than she possessed in deciding which to accept.

Isabella could not read English, but she understood the contents well enough. "Do we sell some jade now?"

Leona made some quick calculations. Her current wardrobe would not last through many of these events before looking tired. "I suppose that we must. Tell Tong Wei to see what offers he can get. This evening you and I will look through the trunk of silk that we brought with us too, and choose some fabric for dinner dresses and ball gowns."

That afternoon Leona sat in Lady Phaedra's drawing room while her hostess read her letter to the journal readers. There were smiles during the first half, but a deep frown formed over the second.

"You did say that I should write about matters of importance too," Leona said.

"You took me at my word, I see."

"If it is *too* important, I could—"

"You will not change it. It is not what I expected, but it is compelling. Do you have the next one written yet?"

"I did not know if you would want a next one."

Lady Phaedra laid the page on her lap. It glowed there in sharp contrast against the black garment on which it rested. If Lady Phaedra had appeared odd in the park, she looked theatrically so today, with her black dress and flowing red hair and no jewelry or adornments.

Leona occupied herself admiring the drawing room. The furnishings comprised an odd mix of styles, but each item was exquisitely crafted in its own right. The combination of surfaces, colors, and textures created a vaguely exotic total that appeared more sumptuous than any particular item warranted.

"Does Easterbrook know that you wrote this, and plan more?" Lady Phaedra asked, her brow still furrowed over the paper.

"Why would I inform him of it?"

She received a sharp glance in response, then Lady Phaedra folded the letter. "My journal will be titled *Minerva's Banquet*. It would be appropriate if, among the fruits and sweets, there were a serving of meat. I will publish this, but only if you promise three more letters in a similar mode."

She offered a modest sum for the letters. Leona was accepting when a footman arrived, bearing a card.

Lady Phaedra examined it. Her eyebrows rose. "Surely he wants my husband," she said to the footman.

"He does, Madam. Lord Elliot, however, asks that you receive the visitor while he completes a letter that he is writing."

Lady Phaedra told the footman to bring the visitor. She handed Leona the letter. "Tuck this into your reticule for now."

The reason for doing so entered the room.

"You honor us, Easterbrook," Lady Phaedra greeted. "Another daytime excursion, and to call on our humble abode no less. Society will not know what to make of it. I do not believe you have experienced so much sunlight in years."

Easterbrook accepted her tease with smooth grace. "You are incorrect. My chambers do not block out the light. They are awash in it. Miss Montgomery, it is a pleasure to see you again."

He turned his attention to the chamber, examining its furnishings with curiosity. "I see that you are settled in."

"It has been six months, Easterbrook. I hope even a woman bad at settling in could manage it in that time. However, it was generous of you to wait to call until I was able to prepare for your visit. Permit me to have refreshment brought for you."

"There is no need. I came to see Elliot, but he is occupied and threw me off on you." He pierced them both with a sharp gaze that gave lie to his casual, distracted manner. "I sense that I have interrupted something, however."

He strolled toward them, his attention focused on Lady Phaedra. Her amusement took on a sardonic edge while she faced him down.

"Phaedra, you would not be leading Miss Montgomery astray, would you? Involving her in some scheme that will bring her no credit?"

"I am incapable of leading any woman astray. Nor is Miss Montgomery a child who requires your interference."

"Lady Phaedra is hardly leading me astray. Quite the opposite. I came here to ask her advice on which invitations to accept. She was so friendly in the park that I felt confident she would aid me."

"I said that I would be happy to give that aid," he said.

"I thought that a woman would understand nuances that a man might not."

"Phaedra does not often deign to partake of the society you seek to frequent, so her advice cannot be relied upon. You might spend the next month in the company of fools who waste your time."

"Since you do not partake of this society either, and are my only other friend in London, I must be left to my own judgment then."

"Perhaps two flawed opinions can together aid you better than one alone," Lady Phaedra said. "Easterbrook will not mind joining his to mine, for whatever they are worth in sum. Will you, Easterbrook?"

For the next half hour Leona named names and Easterbrook opined on who was a fool worth knowing and who was a fool unworthy of her time. On several occasions he pointedly said she must attend a particular ball or party.

For the most part Lady Phaedra agreed with his assessments. Leona did not know if their combined intelligence had just mapped a true path for her, or if their combined ignorance would send her to wander in circles.

Lord Elliot entered just as they finished. With the skill of a practiced courtier, he permitted a little more conversation, then removed his brother to the library.

As soon as the door had closed on the gentlemen, Lady Phaedra held out her hand for the letter. "Easterbrook has this unnerving ability to know when people are dissembling, and we raised his curiosity. Lest he decide that I am indeed leading you astray, and find a way to interfere, you had better write your other letters as quickly as possible."

"How could he interfere?"

"I think he has his ways when he chooses to use

them. It is always a mistake to underestimate that man, or to forget that he is Easterbrook."

"Your home is very pleasant. Airy." Christian offered the compliment as Elliot closed the library door.

"I find it odd that you chose today of all days to investigate just how pleasant it might be. There have been invitations aplenty that were not accepted."

"I do not mind your attempts to draw me out, Elliot. But I do not have to cooperate with them either."

Elliot accepted the fairness of that. "So what finally did draw you out?"

"I have been contemplating something, and realized that I should consult with you."

"You are full of surprises today. Are you saying that you would like my advice?"

"I feel obliged to discuss this matter with you because it bears upon you. If you are compelled to offer advice, I have no choice but to hear it."

Elliot made himself comfortable on one of the library's pale blue sofas. "You have my attention."

He certainly did. Elliot's great gift was an ability to concentrate without losing hold of reality. No doubt that accounted for his success with those history books he wrote. And also for an evenness of temperament that suggested he had escaped the worst of the bad blood coursing through the Rothwell veins.

"Elliot, I find myself wondering if you have any expectations of one day having the title."

Elliot's amazement filled the library. "You wonder

about the oddest things, Christian. Of course I have no such expectations. Third sons never do."

There was no dissembling in that astonishment. No guile or secret resentment. "I am relieved to hear it. Once Hayden's son is born, the line will bypass you, of course. My anticipation of that happy event was clouded this morning by the thought you might not share the joy."

Elliot peered over, perplexed. "It may not be a son. I trust that you will still find joy if it is not."

"Of course, but it will be a son."

"Christian, you cannot merely prefer that a son be born and it happens. I cannot believe that I am explaining that as if you would not know, but sometimes you—"

"It will be a son."

Elliot rolled his eyes.

"And when it is, I will know the line is secure for the next generation. I refuse to be owned by the expectations of my station, but there are a few obligations that I do accept and that is one," Christian explained. "In fact, I will step aside if I can arrange it. The title should have a more active man. A man like Hayden. There are responsibilities and—"

"Now you are definitely not talking sense. Your own son will secure the line, not Hayden's, for one thing. For another, if you believe there are obligations to be met, then meet them."

"I will have no heir. I dare not." The last words were out before he knew it. He shocked himself with the indiscretion. He paced away, toward the bookcases, and braced for Elliot's own shock to eddy toward him.

It never came. Instead, other emotions rolled in the

air behind his back. Worry. Maybe pity. Also surprise that the topic had been broached at all.

"You are not mad." Elliot's voice came firmly. "Nor was she. No matter what was said about Mother then, or you now."

"I know that I am not." Nor was she. Christian knew that better than anyone. But he also knew the pain she had suffered, knowing what she knew about too many people. About him. She had retreated from everyone, but especially her eldest son. She had seen herself in him, and known that she could not help him.

"Is your concern tied to Father, then? Whatever he was, whatever he did, it is not in us. He made choices you would never make." Rather more agitation flowed on Elliot's words this time. But then Elliot was still coming to terms with the fullness of that half of the legacy.

"I like to believe you are right, but sometimes I know you are wrong. However, this is not about him. For once."

Youthful memories assaulted Christian as he stared at bindings in the silent library. The horror of knowing his mother's fear of their father and her certainty of his ruthlessness. The guilt that poured off the man along with the rivers of desperate love. The misery of both as his father turned bitter and controlling and his mother gave up hope for any happiness.

Christian had never spoken of it to anyone, but here he was, on one side of an open door with his youngest brother on the other.

He turned and faced him. Elliot's expression showed little more than patience.

"I know that I am not mad. Not even half so. Nor was she. I know that better than anyone. But she and I had much in common, and that suggests that our eccentricity is carried by our blood."

"We all carry that blood. Hayden's child might too. Nothing is resolved by your conviction to have no heir."

"His child might, that is true. I think that I will know soon. If so, I can help him in ways I might not be able to help my own. But I do not think it will come to that. Hayden is very . . . normal, and Alexia is without any shadows at all."

The conversation troubled Elliot more than expected. More than intended. But then it had veered into areas not anticipated.

"Christian, you reassure me that you are not half mad, as if I ever thought you were. But you also allude to eccentricity as if it is an affliction that cannot be escaped."

"It is not an affliction." Christian had never described his condition and was at a loss to begin to do so now. "Much as Hayden and I look much like our father, I inherited this feature from our mother. Since we all also received her ability to block out the world when we tend to a task or interest, I am not without compensations."

"I do not understand."

"I do not expect you to. I misspoke in alluding to it and wish I had not. I now reassure you that it is not the makings of great drama or misery. Just a bit of oddity."

Elliot half accepted that. With time he would decide there was no cause for worry. Right now his brother's words returned him to the topic at hand. "I doubt that

Hayden will allow you to make him the marquess, even if you could find a way to arrange it. Best to put that idea out of your head. Take up the reins yourself if you believe they have been left hanging slackly."

"Are you scolding me, Elliot?"

Elliot smiled. "It appears that I am."

"Since I began the conversation, I do not get to indulge in annoyance with this presumptuous turn you have given it, I suppose."

"That would indeed be unjust."

"I can, however, simply end it, which I shall now do. I will take my leave. There is one other matter before I go."

Elliot raised his eyebrows in question.

"Your lovely wife is cooking a stew and I think she has just added Miss Montgomery to the pot. Find out what is going on, and let me know, but don't inform her that I asked."

"Christian, we do not live a marriage of mutual intrigue such as one finds in old plays. I will ask Phaedra outright, and share what I learn if she allows me to do so."

There was nothing to do except let it stand at that. Christian left the house, certain that Phaedra would never permit Elliot to report on whatever scheme she and Leona were concocting.

Nor would Elliot be conveniently indiscreet. That was what happened when men fell in love. Their loyalties centered on their beloveds, not duty and family.

Elliot would be useless. What a nuisance.

CHAPTER
SEVEN

Tong Wei took a position right in front of the carriage door. Leona rearranged her silk shawl so it dipped around the puffed short sleeves of her ivory ball gown.

"There is no need for you to stand here the whole night," she said. "The coachman will probably walk the horses, and you might as well ride along."

"I will be here."

He glanced at her bare skin showing above the low, straight neckline of her dress.

"It is the fashion," she said.

His stony expression communicated what he thought of fashions that permitted obscene glimpses of flesh that should be covered.

Leona gave up trying to placate him. Tong Wei understood that she had to enter assemblies without his protection. He just wondered about these parties that he never saw, and perhaps imagined proper formalities breaking down as people drank and men leered.

Leona approached the door, inserting herself into the

river of good society. Both Phaedra and Easterbrook had insisted she accept this invitation. A ball hosted by Lord and Lady Pennington, a baron and his wife, the sheer size of the event promised the potential for meeting many of the right people.

Their advice on the invitations had borne fruit already. The last week Leona had enjoyed a very active social life, and harvested many tidbits that gave her some encouragement about her missions. In particular, she had sat at a dinner party last night during which she discovered some astonishing information. The man seated on her left thought that he remembered a notice published upon her father's death.

She had not known such a notice had been printed. Her father had not been a notable in England, and it made no sense. Finding that obituary was now at the top of her list of things to do in London. She was eager to read it.

Her hostess approached her immediately after her announcement, and guided her through the throng to a quiet spot near a wall. "We are pleased that you agreed to join us. You have been noticed for the prestigious company that you keep and we are all eager to know you better."

Lady Pennington smiled conspiratorially, like an old friend confiding good gossip. Only she wasn't an old friend, and Leona was the subject of the gossip.

"The marquess is an acquaintance from my girlhood. He has been generous to aid me here in London."

"He is known to be most generous when he chooses to be, which is not often. And most amiable when he also chooses, which is even less common." She looked over her shoulder meaningfully.

Leona looked in the same direction. Near the opposite wall a tall man with a beautiful, severe face was being generously amiable with two elderly women who flushed like schoolgirls.

Easterbrook appeared both very lordly and vaguely dangerous. The latter she attributed to his dark garments and reckless hair and the intensity in his eyes that he could never completely hide.

He spotted her and walked across the room with a deliberate purpose. Eyes followed and heads turned even while conversations continued.

She suffered it. Nor could her annoyance stop how her pulse beat harder with each of his steps. Her hostess discreetly moved away, to permit the marquess a few private words.

"Miss Montgomery."

She curtsied. "Lord Easterbrook. I am astonished to see you here. I was told you never attended such functions. Dinners on occasion, but not crowded gatherings such as this."

"Since you would not accept the convenience of being my guest at Grosvenor Square, I am forced to pursue you through more traditional paths. In order to do so, I have had to mend my isolated ways."

She would never be able to accuse him of not giving her fair warning, that was certain. "Lady Pennington must be delighted to have her ball chosen for your first stitch. I daresay your presence alone makes the evening a success." Her pique broke through her pretense. "Did you let it be known that you would attend if I were invited?"

"I never spoke a word on the matter. If hostesses are hopeful it might work that way, it is not my doing."

Except it *had* been his doing. That ride in the park, so rare for him, had announced his pursuit to the world. He had encouraged hostesses to calculate that if they invited the object of his interest, the elusive Easterbrook might come too. The implications had been reinforced by his presence tonight.

"It would never have happened otherwise, Leona."

It irritated her even more that he had all but read her thoughts. "If I have traded my reputation for a chance to meet the best of the best, I should make good use of the opportunity. I trust that you will not be a constant escort. I will never learn anything of interest if you are."

She excused herself and plunged into the crowd. She quickly found Lady Wallingford and exchanged a few pleasantries. Lady Wallingford in turn introduced her to some other ladies. Within an hour Leona was surrounded by a little clutch of people, regaling them with stories about Asia.

"What the hell are you doing here?" Denningham advanced on Christian, looking like a man in shock. "Are you unwell?"

"Perhaps I am finally well, not unwell."

Denningham puzzled that, then gave up and smiled. "I am glad you are here no matter what your health. You can help me decide which young ladies I should petition for a dance."

"I recommend that you dance with them all, and twice with the ones who are not too impressed by your title."

"Easy for you to say. My title is all that is impressive."

"That is not true." Although it probably was, for the ladies in question. Young girls did not favor simplicity and decency, which were Denningham's notable features.

Denningham surveyed the girls in question. Christian struggled not to look at the knot of people twenty feet away. Leona stood in their midst and all attention was on her, in particular that of a young naval officer.

Suddenly laughter erupted in that group, loud enough to draw many eyes, including Denningham's. He noticed the raven-haired woman with dark eyes who clearly had told the good joke.

"Is that her? It is, isn't it?" he asked. "That is why you are here. A handsome woman, Easterbrook. Not typical, is she?"

No, not typical. Right now the handsome, atypical Leona was favoring the naval officer with too many smiles.

"Here comes the King of Spades, to scout out the fun," Denningham said. "He probably cannot bear that he is not in the thick of it."

The Duke of Ashford's attention was on Leona's group while he approached them. He would probably ask for an introduction to her, so he could indeed be in the thick of things.

If so, he could rot first. Christian did not think that young officer could be true competition, but Ashford was another story and not only because he was a duke.

For a man of at least forty-five years and with hair shot through with silver, the duke wore his age with annoyingly youthful grace. But then much about Ashford was annoying. His social skills were unsurpassed, his elegance legendary, his mind brilliant, and his political shrewdness the stuff of legends. Tall, broad, and fit, he accepted it as his right to be noticed and admired wherever he went. He fit the role of the ultimate peer, and was held up to the world as an example of the aristocracy at its best.

They greeted each other and Ashford only noted Christian's uncharacteristic presence with one raised eyebrow. Arch still in place, he looked meaningfully at Leona.

"I heard that you had a new interest, Easterbrook. I had no idea it was serious enough to get you to a ball."

"I decided to enjoy the season before it was over."

"You should stick close to her or she may be distracted. Young Crawford there is flirting hard. I could warn him off if you like. I still have friends in the Admiralty and he knows it. I got him his commission, after all."

Ashford tended to drop mention of his influence like this, another annoyance. Everyone knew the role he had played in government during the war. Reminders like this one, of his frequent consultations with the Admiralty back then, were unnecessary.

"If he requires warning off, I can manage it," Christian said. "If you want to insert yourself into a friend's affairs, help out Denningham here. Tell him which of these hopeful girls he should marry."

"Marry?" Denningham reddened. "I spoke of one dance!"

"You were born to marry if ever a man was, and it is long past time," Ashford said. "As for which one, let me see . . ." He scrutinized the ballroom, examining girls with seriously critical eyes.

Denningham obediently suffered it. Christian had to smile to himself. He was being too critical tonight, and too quick to feel jealousy if any man looked at Leona. Ashford deserved his praise. If he actually did choose a girl for Denningham, it would probably be a perfect match.

Christian turned his attention back to Leona. Beside him, Ashford exuded an exhausting amount of intrusive noise.

That was the real reason he was not fond of the man. If he welcomed the King of Spades' frequent absences from the whist tables, it really had to do with his intensity. Within the elegance and grace a tiger waited, tensed as if to pounce.

The noise remained abstract and did not translate into emotions. It was just there, an unceasing, unchanging hum. This eternal alertness had probably produced the incisive thought and shrewd analysis that made Ashford so useful and successful in government and politics.

"That one there, Denningham. Near the wall in the white gown, near the woman in cerulean. That is Miss

Elizabeth Talorsfield, third daughter of a good family in my county. She is known for her virtue, modesty, and good heart. The settlement should be at least respectable. Come with me, and I will introduce you."

Like a sheep to the slaughter, Denningham dutifully followed Ashford across the ballroom. Christian assumed his friend would have a fiancée soon.

His aunt caught his eye, something she had been attempting for some time despite his resolute avoidance. She beckoned him to join her and Caroline, and angled her head toward a nearby young, unmarried peer. Aunt Hen clearly wanted introductions to be made.

Since Hen stood close enough to Leona to keep an eye on her, Christian strolled over to do his familial duty.

Easterbrook was never far away. She saw those eyes on her when she looked in his direction. She sensed his attention even when he was out of sight, a presence charging the air like a summer storm.

His awareness settled around her, evoking a lively patter in her heart. She engaged in her conversations with more spirit in an attempt to thwart his power, but her heart ruefully admitted that his mere proximity excited her.

People joined her circle and left, but one young man remained by her side. Blond and wiry, he wore a uniform that marked him as a naval officer. He had been introduced as Lieutenant Crawford. Since he had also traveled in the Far East, he joined in her tales to the delight of their audience.

"Miss Montgomery, allow me to spirit you away to some refreshments," he whispered during a lull while the guests rearranged themselves. "Some conversation with you privately would be more charming than entertaining a crowd. I daresay we share acquaintances and similar sympathies."

She allowed him to extricate her from the circle and guide her to the dining room where a supper could be had.

"Where did your ship take you?" she asked once they had settled at the long table. "Were you in the East long?"

"My commission took me to India, and from there to the China Sea."

"Did you go to China itself?"

He nodded. "We anchored at Lintin. We had a passenger of some importance who had business in Canton, and we waited at Lintin while he disembarked and went there."

"I assume that he was someone with the Company. It is odd that he traveled upon one of His Majesty's ships and not one of the Company's own."

Lieutenant Crawford ate four full bites of food before he spoke again. "This passenger was not with the Company. Not officially at least. He represented other interests, I think."

Powerful ones, if they could gain him a berth on one of the king's ships. She itched for him to go on. When he did not, she sought to encourage him.

"I have always been interested in the other interests in the China trade. Besides the Company's, that is. Legally they are the only traders between China and

England, but there are ways around that. And, of course, there is trade between the countries in the East itself."

He noted her suggestion with a confidential, meaningful nod. "I know nothing for certain. I merely had cause to speculate. It would not do to be overheard, however." He appeared so serious that one had to assume the revelations were dangerous. He dipped his head closer. "There should be less of a crowd on the terrace. Would you honor me by taking some air with me, Miss Montgomery?"

If it meant hearing tales of secret visitors to Canton, she would. He excused himself. After a few minutes she did the same. She aimed for the terrace doors.

She did not see Lieutenant Crawford upon exiting to the terrace. Finally she spied him at its far end, deep in the shadows.

When she joined him, he took her arm. "This way, if you do not mind. It is bad for one's career to be considered indiscreet."

She allowed him to guide her down the terrace stairs and into the garden. They found a bench beneath an ivy-covered arbor. The sounds of the party came as so many muffled laughs and hums out here.

She wrapped her shawl closely and looked at the shadowed face of the man who sat beside her.

"I do not seek to force any indiscretions," she said. "I have cause to believe that there are men in England engaged in illicit trade with China, however. They operate through intermediaries. Do you think that your passenger was such an agent?"

"He might have been."

"You said that you had cause to speculate. Was that the direction that your speculations took?"

"Yes, I suppose."

"You suppose? If you speak of your speculations, should you not know what they were?"

He shifted slightly. He faced her now, and suddenly seemed very close.

"I may have exaggerated, to engage your interest," he said. "I find myself incapable of remembering if I did or not, or what those speculations were. You are even more lovely in these shadows than in the candle-light inside, and I cannot take my eyes off your ripe lips. I must . . ." He bent closer yet. "I must . . . taste . . ."

Incredulous, Leona angled away as Lieutenant Crawford's face moved closer. His arms suddenly embraced her, keeping her from falling off the bench but also imprisoning her. She struggled to free herself.

"Sir, you forget yourself." She twisted her neck so her mouth would be out of reach. "I demand that you—"

"Lieutenant Crawford, are you good with a sword?"

The question came out of nowhere.

Lieutenant Crawford froze. For a moment they stayed like that, a statue depicting a man pressing a kiss on an unwilling woman.

A sound rustled in the garden. A few footsteps could be heard. A figure emerged. A tall one, in dark garments and longish hair framing his face.

Lieutenant Crawford released her and moved away.

Leona had recognized the voice, and was relieved that Easterbrook had managed such a timely interruption.

"Does ardor make you mute, Crawford? I asked if you were good with a sword."

"More than fair."

"That is unfortunate. If I discover that you importuned Miss Montgomery, and call you out, your chance will only be more than fair if you choose swords."

Lieutenant Crawford went very still. Then he stood. "I would not choose swords."

"Ah. Well, with pistols you would stand no chance at all. None of which signifies if the lady is unmolested. Did you importune her? Doings in that arbor appeared a little ambiguous in the moonlight."

Lieutenant Crawford's discomfort was palpable. Easterbrook had just invited him to condemn himself with honesty, or to lie in vain since the lady in question sat three feet away.

Leona did not mind the marquess's interference this one time, but if this ended in a duel it would just be stupid.

"He was not importuning me, Lord Easterbrook. He was boring me."

"Boring you? Crawford, that is probably more worthy of a challenge than the other. You had best go while you can."

Lieutenant Crawford decided that was good advice. With a cursory bow to Leona, he faded into the night. Leona stood to follow him.

"Still slipping into night gardens with young men, Leona? I would have thought you learned your lesson in Macao with me."

"It was supposed to be a brief conversation. Nothing more."

"Let me guess. He dangled information about Canton, and could only tell you more if you were alone."

She turned from the path and faced him. He had guessed correctly. Too correctly. "How did you come to be here, to rescue me?"

"I was seeking some quiet in the garden. I am not accustomed to the unceasing noise of all those people."

"But you knew who he was. It is dark." She looked into the arbor, where it was darker yet. "You knew what he had dangled."

"His intentions were obvious all night. As for what he dangled, I am not surprised. Only secrets about Eastern trade would cause you to act so foolishly."

"You followed us? You listened?"

"Of course. For your protection." He walked closer and looked down at her. "It appears that I am correct in suspecting that you are tempted to dig at matters that will only bring you trouble. You followed a stranger into a night garden on the flimsiest evidence that he might provide information about illegal trade with China."

"I come from a trading family in China. Such a tid-bit would be of interest to anyone with my heritage. Listening to gossip is not digging."

She could not tell if she had convinced him, or if his thoughts merely wandered elsewhere. His attention still centered on her, however.

"You deliberately listened to our conversation before making yourself known. That is inexcusable," she said.

"I have the best excuses. I wanted him to cross a line first, so I could scare him away. I also wanted to be alone with you in this garden without a hundred people knowing about it, and here you are."

Leona glanced askance at their location. She could not even see the terrace, although the sounds of the party hummed on the breeze. Darkness enclosed them, but it was not so black that she could not see Easterbrook's expression.

The night, the scents, the delicious, dangerous expectation, reminded her of another garden, long ago and far away. She had left her chamber to take some air, drawn into the dark by a restlessness of the heart. When he found her there, she had realized that she had hoped he would.

They had faced each other in that garden much as they did now.

She did not know if it was nostalgia's doing, but she felt that she faced the same man now. For the first time since seeing him again, it seemed that he had not really changed so much. He was less a stranger suddenly, and their old intimacy poured through the night to her. She felt naked standing here, and wonderfully vulnerable to both herself and to him.

Her defenses began crumbling. No logic would save her if they fell. No suspicions would get a hearing if she yielded to the yearning ache inside her. Already her body thrilled from their isolation and from his closeness. Already she anticipated the touch that would come.

She had to leave. She could not indulge the arousal titillating her like so many tickling licks.

She found it terribly hard to take the first step away from him. With her second footfall, a drenching disappointment triumphed over a vague relief that he would be decent enough to allow her to go.

Her third stride met with resistance.

A warm hand, male and firm, settled on her shoulder above the edge of her dress. It neither grasped nor squeezed. It just held her carefully and announced that she would step no more.

She could shake off his hand and run, of course. She *should* do that. But the human warmth on her bare skin made her senses spin. The physical connection felt so good, so alluring. Her entire spirit sighed a groaning "yes" that overwhelmed her so thoroughly that she almost went limp.

"You will not leave yet." His voice sounded very near her ear, carried on a breath that sent a shiver down her neck.

"Why not? Because you command it?"

Lips smoothing over her ear, then lower to her shoulder. "Because you do not want to, and because this is destiny."

His arms embraced her from behind, his hands splaying over her midriff and hip. His hair feathered at her cheek while he pressed a line of devastating kisses along her shoulder and up her neck.

She closed her eyes and tensed her body, trying to contain what he did to her. The struggle proved futile and brief. Her body succumbed forcefully, and tingles of desire began in the worst places. Even her heart sab-

otaged her, by whispering memories and secret dreams
that had sustained her for years.

She gave in as if it truly were destiny. Perhaps her
soul believed that it was. She dully acknowledged that
she had no strength because the years had robbed her of
it. She had long ago decided that denying his excitement in Macao had been a sinful waste.

She did not resist when he turned her around and
claimed her with a kiss that reminded her so much of
the past. He had always been Easterbrook when it came
to seduction. Always confident. Always dangerous. His
kiss lured her in deep, then took possession and control.

He caressed her boldly. His hands moved in sure
paths over her dress, arousing her without mercy. His
embrace tightened. Her feet left the ground and she
floated. Then she was sitting on his lap in the arbor,
their passion hidden in its dark ivy cave.

His kiss called forth all the sweetness she had ever
known with him. All the memories and all the dreams.
Her physical responses fascinated her. She relished the
new sensitivity of her skin to the cool night air, and
welcomed the pressure of his strong thighs beneath her
bottom. Her breasts grew heavy and their tips so
aroused that she could hardly bear it.

He held her face to a harder, more demanding kiss.
His mouth claimed her completely, and insisted she
permit the stunning, sly invasion that he had taught her
in Macao. She submitted, knowing it was an acceptance of much more, and a symbolic encouragement of
his passion.

He took what she allowed, and more. His spirit

seeped into her, and she accepted it like a starving woman offered food. She pulsed against his thighs and shifted to find more pressure for that wonderful discomfort. She followed his lead when he cajoled her to kiss him back.

His caress slid along her body, against silk that offered little armor. His hand raised silent cries in her head that emerged as gasping sighs. His fingertips smoothed along the naked skin of her shoulder, to the exposed flesh above her breast. It rested there, tempting her, teasing her so badly that she almost begged him to go on, to continue, to let her feast on the wonders that she had only tasted in Macao.

The mixture of pleasure and hunger undid her. Her blood fired, making her half crazed. She embraced him and kissed him hard and sought his own body with her hands, searching and seeking beneath his coats for his form. Like a flame meeting oil, his passion flared higher until they met in a conflagration of kisses and embraces, mouths meeting and leaving, tasting and biting.

The madness retreated but the heat did not cool. Holding her to more deliberate and calculating kisses, his caress moved up silk to her breasts. The sensation, so intensely pleasurable, so directly erotic in its effects, made her consciousness spin.

His fingers found the tip through her dress and teased. Overwhelmed and breathless, she tucked her head against his neck, unable to do anything more than feel how that devilish touch made her want more.

"I have waited seven years to do this." He cupped her breast. His head lowered. "And this."

A moist breath and a gentle bite created a pleasure so stunning, so intimate, that she wished cloth did not interfere. As if hearing her silent pleas, his left hand moved to her back, to the fastenings of her dress.

Suddenly he stopped. His mouth met hers, silencing words not spoken.

A laugh. A voice. She emerged from her stupor and heard both, not far away. She also heard her own deep breaths, the remnants of the cry he had swallowed.

The voices came closer, very near. Then they drifted away.

The intrusion made her alert to the world, to the garden and the night. And to him. To how his arm cradled her shoulders, and to the masterful way he encouraged her recklessness.

His palm smoothed slowly over her breast even while they listened to the other lovers retreat. She closed her eyes and floated on the wonderful streams of arousal.

"Did he have you? Pedro?"

She opened her eyes to see him looking down at her. Even in the black night his attention made her vulnerable. "No."

"Did another man?" A soft kiss on her cheek followed the quiet question.

"No."

A brief smile formed against her cheek. He rubbed her nipple more directly, and the sweet pleasure took on darker colors. "You knew we would meet again."

She had to work hard to find a voice. "Your conceit knows no bounds. I was not saving myself, least of all for you. I just never wanted a man enough."

"I will have to make sure that you do now."

He already had. He had seven years ago, and right now she was almost lost to his power. But time and place had reasserted themselves. The hum of the party played like a spirited melody not far away, an accompaniment for their sensual dance.

She did not really want to be saved. Her baser self calculated how she might be relieved in this ivy arbor despite the risks and discomforts that the setting implied. She found little contentment in finding the strength to reject that option.

"My advanced age may be making me rash, but I am quite safe no matter what you make me want. A gentleman will not ask me to give myself in a garden arbor with a hundred people nearby."

His touch turned more gentle. The light, brushing arousal actually titillated more. She squirmed as her discomfort pitched higher, and took on a desperate edge.

"We will leave here. You will come back to Grosvenor Square with me."

A new, delicious touch tickled her. She smothered a moan in his shoulder. "If you try to take me away in your carriage, Tong Wei will have to kill you."

"Then I will return with you to your house in your carriage, so he understands you are truly willing."

"No." An especially effective stroke turned her denial into a gasp.

"I can see that I will have to do better. Here I thought I had conquered your rebellious spirit."

"If you do any better I will die, so that will avail you

nothing. A marquess may have whatever he wants, but the rest of us learn that often we cannot."

He lowered his head and kissed her breast again. His hand slid down over silk, along a body too eager to feel that caress. "I think that I will do better anyway, so that you reconsider what you can and cannot have. I promise you will not die, at least not for more than a moment."

She felt his hand on more than silk suddenly. He caressed the skin above her knees and garters, and the soft flesh of her thighs. She peered through the dark, stunned, as the skirt of her dress bunched higher. His boldness awed her. Anticipation shivered through her, so pleasurable in itself that her brief respite of rationality dissolved.

It was all darkness then, a sightless place of sensation. She rocked into his sure caresses and her thoughts fractured into senseless pleas. A terrible desire, so close to that wandering warmth, tortured her to the point of madness.

Careful touches. Wicked ones. Sweet insanity. Destiny, yes, destiny. A kiss pressed her crown and a hand cupped her mound, stunning her. Then a stroke, long and slow, created a pleasure so intense it frightened her. Out of control now, no longer with a will, she lifted her hips subtly and begged for more.

She turned her face to his chest so her groans would not sound through the night. The wonder just got better, worse, necessary. Her desperate desire grew more and more intense until the tension broke through her in a long, silent scream of release.

She turned at the end, trying to twist away from the edge of pleasure, as if she guessed she faced a passage that would change everything.

He held her limp body as the last of the climax flexed through her. Her hands still clutched his coats and her face pressed against his chest. His own relief left him motionless. He doubted she realized what she had done to him without a touch.

His hand splayed over her bottom so she would not fall off his lap in this odd pose. He would like to see the roundness beneath his hold. And the full breasts that he had finally caressed. All of that would come soon enough. Right now he just held her and waited for her to find herself, and enjoyed the contentment like a normal man.

She did not emerge slowly from her stupor. Instead she snapped alert, as if the world had smacked her back to sanity. She scrambled to right herself and her dress, but he managed to keep her on his lap. She sat upright and turned her head to the garden for a long, silent minute.

"Well," she finally said. "Now I feel a fool for being so good all these years."

"You are assuming another man could have done that. I am better at it than most."

She laughed quietly and shook her head in amazement. "You really are insufferably conceited."

"I am honest. You were smart to save yourself for me."

She smacked his chest playfully, but not entirely so.

"I did not save myself for you, and I expect there are lots of men who are as skilled as you."

"Perhaps. Not that you will find out now."

Ignoring his assumption of possession, she scrambled off his lap. "I should thank you for your restraint. I am still officially a virgin."

"Is that important to you?"

His question made her pause in whatever flight she intended. "In Macao I did not care, but then everyone there assumes I had an affair with you. If anything, I resented the unfairness of bearing the brand without knowing the sin."

"And now?"

"Now you have given me a taste of what a woman experiences in passion, but also what she relinquishes. I understand why our mothers tell us not to yield too easily." Her hands went to her head and she felt her hair. "I fear that I look totally ravished, in ways everyone at the ball will recognize."

"There will be another way out of this garden." He stood and took her hand. "Come with me."

He led her through the paths and the plantings, enjoying the feel of her soft hand in his. Right now little could interfere with his peace, but their conversation indicated he had not claimed her as thoroughly as he intended.

He found the back garden gate, and guided her down the lane to where it met the street where the carriages waited. He spied Tong Wei standing sentry.

She touched her hair again.

"It is dark," he said. "He will not notice." He pulled her into an embrace and looked down at the tiny stars visible in her eyes. "Send him away. Come back to Grosvenor Square with me."

"I cannot."

"You mean that you will not. Why?"

She caressed his face, then slid from his embrace. "Because by summer's end I will return to my real life and my true destiny. And because you are Easterbrook."

CHAPTER
EIGHT

~⌇~

Leona passed Tong Wei as she walked through the drawing room. He gazed out the window blandly, as if counting the paving stones in the street.

"What are you watching?" she asked. "You have been there an hour."

"Just now I watched nothing. When the mind thinks, the eyes often stop truly seeing."

"What thoughts blinded you?"

"Those of your brother, and his charge to me."

Leona wished she had not pried. Tong Wei had been more enigmatic than normal the last few days. It was as if he had seen what transpired in the garden at Lady Pennington's ball, even though he stood with the carriages. She had sensed criticism in his silence, and hesitation in his conversation.

Perhaps she only attributed her own emotions to Tong Wei. She had been thinking a lot since that night. When alone, in this house, she knew the intimacy had been a mistake. The questions that she had about

Easterbrook's actions and motives in Macao would not go away.

But when she saw him—the careful judgments did not sustain her. And she had seen him since then.

He had attended a dinner at his solicitor's home last night, one to which she also accepted an invitation. The presence of a marquess at the table had awed everyone so much that she had learned nothing at all about trade and finance, even though two men famous in those areas also were guests.

It had been a discomforting evening. Everyone knew that Easterbrook had come because of Miss Montgomery, but the honor of his presence demanded a liberal point of view. The hostess could not fawn enough, so delighted was she in her most unexpected catch. Her husband tried twice to arrange privacy for the lovers, as if he assumed that was his important guest's expectation.

Their own exchanges had been most proper, almost formal. But for the entire evening, whether in the drawing room or at dinner, whether sitting under his gaze or alone with the ladies, Leona had been aware of him. She was helpless against the stimulation he created.

If he only drew her with desire she would not be so confused. However, the attraction now contained all the memories. Those kisses in the garden had been too familiar. The soul behind them, within them, still had much of Edmund in it, hidden away. An ache of wistful yearning had lodged in her heart that night, and seeing him again made her painfully aware of its power over her.

"Before we left Macao, your brother spoke to me,"

Tong Wei said. "He commanded me to ensure that you came to no harm. He told me to protect you."

"You have done so."

"I protect you from thieves and criminals. I do not, and cannot, protect you from yourself."

She felt her face getting hot. "If you refer to the marquess, you do not have to concern yourself. I—"

"I do not speak of him. Your brother may want me to fight him, but I do not kill men just for taking willing women."

"You are assuming that much more has transpired between Easterbrook and me than you have good cause to."

Tong Wei expressed impatience as he rarely ever did. "I assume nothing. It is of no interest to me. I am not a nursemaid. I speak of your time abroad in this city when you refuse my protection. If you go to meet *him,* I do not care. But until you meet him, I should be with you."

His agitation surprised her. This matter had been discussed since their first week in London and her first refusal of his company. She thought that her explanations had swayed him. Apparently they had not.

His face fell into an impassive mask, as if its recent expressiveness was cause for shame. Nonetheless he faced her squarely, his posture upright and proud. "You do not accept my company because you are doing things that you do not want me to know about. I can imagine what they are. If I am correct, then I have cause to worry for your safety, and to consider what steps I must take to fulfill my duty."

"You are worried over nothing. I am not in danger when I go in the carriage without you."

"Are you not?" He turned back to the window. Immobile again. Watching. "A man on a brown horse followed the carriage yesterday for a long time. Another man watches this house from a window across the street. He stands there just as I stand here. He looks at me, and I look at him. Why does he not move?"

"Why don't *you* move?"

"I am watching him. I have cause to. He has no cause."

"Perhaps he simply finds you . . . interesting. He may have never seen people from China before. Come away from the window now, and you will see that he will leave too."

"No. I will let him know that I watch. I will let him see me, so he knows that Tong Wei is aware that there are those who are too interested in you and your movements."

"Sir?"

The interruption came quietly. Christian opened his eyes.

"What are you doing here, Miller?" He had not heard Miller enter. The young man was sly that way.

"I was sent by your aunt. Your valet was too timid and no footman would take the charge either. I apologize if I have intruded on . . ."

The sentence hung there, since Miller had no idea what the intrusion might be. In fact he had intruded on nothing besides memories and calculations regarding

Leona. They had blocked out the world more thoroughly than any meditation, it appeared.

"What crisis has my aunt bothering me? Did a modiste add too much lace to a ball gown?"

"Rather more important than that, sir." Miller nodded to the table beside Christian's chair. A salver rested there, bearing two cards. Christian shuffled through them.

"Lady Wallingford has been distraught ever since they arrived," Miller said. "They said it was not a social call, and that you must see them. They would take no refreshment or accept her company, and have been waiting a half hour in the library while she sent for me."

"All to no avail." He let the cards fall to the floor and closed his eyes again.

Cocky young Miller was suddenly much less so. Christian opened his eyes again. His gaze settled on one of the cards on the carpet. In particular, on three of its words. East India Company.

He stood. "Hell. I will go to them."

Miller looked at him. More specifically he looked at Christian's robe and bare feet. Annoyed that this nuisance had interfered with very pleasant memories of Leona's generous and soft breast, Christian strode to his dressing room, pulled on trousers and boots, and strode out again.

Someone had opened the library windows. Afternoon sun and a refreshing breeze flowed in. The two men sitting nearby did not appear aware of the glorious day.

Christian greeted them and took a chair at their head. He waited while Denningham smiled privately at the robe. Mr. Griffin Winterside of the East India Company blinked in surprise.

"My apologies, Lord Easterbrook," Mr. Winterside rushed to say. "I had no idea that you were ill. Now I am appalled at myself for requesting this meeting, and for pressing the matter."

Christian felt no need to explain himself. He allowed the apology to stand.

Denningham was more honest. "He is not ill, Winterside. My friend here does not dress unless he has an engagement. You and I do not qualify as one. He did put on boots for us, however, so we are almost important."

"You brought Mr. Winterside here for a reason, I assume," Christian said to Denningham. He did not care for Winterside. The man exuded worry and small-mindedness. He was the sort who endlessly pondered every greeting that he received, to determine if the greeter had revealed any special sympathy.

"I did indeed. Mr. Winterside is an acquaintance of mine, and well known in the House of Lords. If you ever attended sessions except for major votes, you would already know him. He represents the Company's interests and provides us with information that we need in order to make our decisions. He executes his duties with admirable skill and tact."

Winterside bowed his head with humility at the praise.

Christian settled back in his chair. "I think that I understand. If Parliament is a bank of heavy snow, and the

East India Company is a sleigh, then Winterside here is the grease on the runners."

Denningham chuckled. Mr. Winterside did not.

"What do you want with me?"

Winterside reached under his coat and removed a thin, soft book with a pale blue paper cover. He handed it over.

Christian examined it. "A journal. For women. *Minerva's Banquet*. Clever title, but a little pompous." He flipped through the front pages. "A few poems. A report from Paris. Drawings of dresses. A pretty hat here on page fourteen." He set the journal on his lap and looked at Denningham and Winterside, waiting for enlightenment.

"My lord, that journal is being published by your sister-in-law." Mr. Winterside said.

"It appears to be well done, but then I would expect nothing less from Phaedra."

Winterside wagged a finger at the journal. "If it pleases you, Lord Easterbrook, turn to page thirty-one."

Christian obliged. On page thirty-one, Phaedra had treated her readers to a letter from a woman who had sailed the China Sea and beyond. The letter gave a concise description of Macao, then veered into political matters.

He reached the paragraphs that would interest Mr. Winterside.

For great evil lurks in the waters around China, evil that the currents of time and trade will inevitably bring to your shores. With this evil comes a form of slavery that even your Mr. Wilberforce cannot fight, because it binds with chains that I have seen only a few men break. I speak of the evil of opium.

This great curse has ensnared untold numbers of poor souls in China and India, and has spread its tentacles into England. I have seen this for myself. Some might say there is a perverse justice in this latter development. For without the complicity of the English East India Company, the trade in opium would be a mere fraction of what it is today. The negro's bonds were not the only ones forged from our fathers' greed

He did not need to read the author's name at the bottom to know who she was.

"You can understand our concern, Lord Easterbrook," Winterside said. "She has impugned the Company. She implies that we are responsible for the smuggling of opium into China. We are in no way—"

"Winterside, I am not ignorant of the world. Opium bought from the Company in Calcutta is in fact smuggled into China every day."

"That is not our fault."

"Without your sales to the smugglers, there would be no reason for you to grow all those poppies in India on the Company's land."

Winterside bowed his head like a servant well scolded. "My apologies. Yes, let us speak frankly. The Company buys many tons of Chinese tea and pays the Chinese a huge amount of silver to do so. However, the Chinese are forbidden by their emperor's law from importing our goods in turn. The Company runs a huge trade deficit with China as a result."

"A balance must be found, you mean," Denningham said. "So you sell the smugglers opium. That income from the opium balances what you lay out for your tea purchases with China."

Winterside turned red. "We sell an agricultural product in Calcutta. What is done with it—"

"As you can see, you were lured into the devil's cause, Denningham," Christian said. "The Company is well aware of how that opium is smuggled, and the devastation it has brought to China. It is convenient, however, for everyone to pretend it is all out of our hands."

"There are times when economic necessity requires accepting realities that one does not like," Winterside said.

"That is what was said for generations about the slave trade," Christian said. "I see that Miss Montgomery did not miss that analogy. I ask you again, sir, what do you want with me?"

"We thought that perhaps, as a friend of Miss Montgomery, you might persuade her to avoid this topic in the future letters that she has promised. And that, perhaps, as a relative of the publisher, you might use your influence there as well."

"Miss Montgomery reveals no secrets here. It is a story told before. Why silence her when others have published freely?"

"There is gathering talk in Parliament about ending all the Company's special licenses. This is not a time for this fire to be fanned."

"She writes in a ladies' journal," Denningham said dismissively. "I think Easterbrook's point is well made, and I am regretting that I submitted to your expressions of urgency."

"The ladies can influence matters through their

husbands, through their reform activities, through their pens, and through their gossip. Better an obscure pamphlet by a vicar in Cornwall than a series of letters in a fashionable ladies' journal." Winterside turned to Christian again. "Will you at least speak with Miss Montgomery? We are told that you are old friends, and she may be amenable to any suggestion that you make."

"You are assuming my suggestion would be for her to desist in any more references to the opium trade. I do not know why you would think that."

An awkward silence ensued. A very long one.

Denningham straightened and craned his neck to see better out the window to the garden. "I say, your head gardener is down there. I think I'll slip out and speak with him. I am experimenting with a graft that is going poorly, and old Tom there is the best at that."

"Why don't we all go? The day is fair and a turn in the garden is called for."

They filed down to the terrace and out to the garden. Old Tom knew Denningham, and after a greeting they were deep in discussions of his graft.

Mr. Winterside took the opportunity to sidle close to Christian. "If I might have a private word, Lord Easterbrook?"

They left Denningham with the gardener and strolled down the path.

"You met Miss Montgomery in Macao, I have heard. Did you know her father?"

"I met him. It was a brief association while traveling widely some years ago. I found him a little bland and very sober, but welcome company since he was English." Actually he had found Montgomery suspicious and calculating and sharp as a nail.

"We know about his history, of course. We license the Country Traders and maintain information on them all."

"How resourceful of the Company."

"His trading house met with some reversals some years ago. That is always a danger in trade. A ship goes down, a cargo catches fire—it is not for the faint of heart. Mr. Montgomery, unfortunately, was one of those men who thought his misfortune must have been planned."

"Are you saying that he blamed the Company?"

"Not directly. He did blame the opium trade. There were some letters from him to the Company. Rash, accusatory ones. He insisted that the largest smugglers had formed a company of their own, and that the owners of that company included men of high standing here in England. He suggested that this secret company connived with ours, and that his efforts to expose the cabal had led to his persecution. Well, it was all preposterous, of course."

"Of course." Christian knew all about Montgomery's claims and suspicions, but he could think of no reason to inform Winterside of that.

"This first letter in *Minerva's Banquet* does not make that accusation, but I fear Miss Montgomery plans it for one of the next ones. She promises great revelations. Secrets. Intrigues. If she names names—" The mere thought agitated Mr. Winterside.

"Do you think that she has names to name?"

"Her father had become half-crazed with this mad theory. He was certain his business was being destroyed by these men because he would not cooperate with them. He may have convinced himself he knew who these so-called partners are. She may publish—"

"She will publish no names without solid proof. That much I can promise you. Since it is impossible for Miss Montgomery to obtain proof, this is all much ado about nothing."

"Impossible?"

"You called it a mad theory of a half-crazed man, Mr. Winterside. She cannot obtain proof of a conspiracy that does not exist."

Winterside squirmed in the corner where he now found himself. "Of course not."

"Go to your masters and reassure them that the application of logic to the problem resolves everything. The Company has nothing to fear from Miss Montgomery and her letters besides a bit of moral disgrace."

Their stroll had brought them around to the terrace. Denningham pulled himself away from Old Tom, and he and Winterside took their leave.

Old Tom was a simple fellow, at ease with his life in this spring garden. Christian found him restful company after the jumble of high-pitched worries pouring off Winterside. He sat on a bench not far from the gardener's pruning basket and opened *Minerva's Banquet* again.

He reread Leona's article. He wondered what she sought to achieve with it. If she hoped to arouse opposition among the English to the opium trade, good luck to her.

But if the goal had been to flush out the men in England behind the smuggling ring that she thought had targeted her father, she may have been too successful. Because while Mr. Winterside may have come here today to grease the sleigh runners for the Company, Christian did not believe it was actually the Company that had sent him.

CHAPTER NINE

Leona gave a cursory glance to her letter in *Minerva's Banquet*. Lady Phaedra had sent a copy fresh off the press, and normally Leona would have taken pride in her published words for a few minutes at least. Other matters occupied her mind, however.

She studied another bit of her writing instead. On the paper in her hands she had copied the death notice published in *The Times* of London about her father. The newspaper saved all its old issues in large bound books, and obtaining access to the year in question had not been difficult when she presented herself at the paper's offices yesterday.

Her temper had been one thread away from unraveling ever since. The words on her copy were barely legible, having been scratched by a hand tightened into a fist.

The few facts about her father's life were accurate if sparse. The last line, however, amounted to a scurrilous lie.

Mr. Montgomery passed away after a long decline

*attributed to a wasting disease well known in Asia, the
result of ingesting dangerous agricultural products na-
tive to that region.*

The notice all but said that her father had succumbed to opium. Who would have reported such a
thing? There had been no such malicious gossip in
Macao. Everyone there knew about his weakening
heart, and had seen the evidence of that illness with
their own eyes.

Her eyes narrowed on the tiny printed name at the
bottom of the notice. *C. Nichols.* There had been no Mr.
Nichols in Macao for as long as she knew. This was not
a correspondent's report. It must have been written
right here in London.

She pondered how to find this Mr. Nichols. She
needed to talk to him and discover where he had obtained this information about her father.

The old editions of *The Times* had yielded little
help. Mr. Nichols's name did not appear often as a
writer. In recent papers, however, she had found it several times below lively descriptions of proceedings in
the magistrate offices in London.

A subtle change in the air alerted her that she was
not alone. She looked up to see Tong Wei standing ten
feet away.

"A lady is here," Tong Wei said. "One of high
status."

Leona took the card with curiosity. She went to the
drawing room where her guest waited.

Lady Lynsworth wore a geranium promenade dress
and hat, and an expression of reserve badly compro-
mised by the anxious lights in her blue eyes.

She and Leona exchanged a few pleasantries while those lights burned ever more brightly. Finally the rest of her soft face could no longer maintain the mask that pretended all was well with her.

"Miss Montgomery, I read the first volume of *Minerva's Banquet*. Easterbrook's sister-in-law has created a most commendable journal."

"She will be happy to learn of your good opinion."

"Your own contribution in particular interested me. Your reference to the opium trade—I found it very educational."

"I hope others do as well. The people of England should learn about it, even if it takes place so far away. It is my hope that public opinion will force the East India Company to change its ways."

Lady Lynsworth fingered her reticule nervously. "Your letter speaks of seeing people die. Our poets and artists do not consider it poison, but an enhancement for their creative imaginations."

"I am aware that is the popular view in Europe. Please believe me that the lure is insidious and becoming an habitué almost inevitable. Once caught in the snare a person wastes away."

"You wrote of knowing a few who had not, however. Who had broken the chains."

"Very few. The vast majority—"

"But some. You did not write that only to appease the concerns of your readers, did you? You in fact do know of a few at least who—" A tear began a slow path down her cheek. She wiped it with her hand and turned her face away.

Leona went over to sit down next to her. "Yes, a few. I did not lie about that."

Lady Lynsworth dug for the handkerchief in her reticule. "Forgive me. I read that one line and could read no more. A few who broke the chains. I have been in a state of desperate hope since this morning."

She wept gently. Leona waited for her guest to compose herself.

"Who is it?" Leona asked. "A relative?"

"My younger brother. We thought he was ill. My father learned the truth of it a month ago and washed his hands of him. I have not seen Brian since. He was in a bad way when last we met. I fear that it is as you wrote, and that this is an illness from which he will not recover."

Leona wished she could offer reassurances, but she had none to give. If Brian's addiction had reached the point where his family recognized the symptoms, he was far along.

"Is there some elixir to end this? Some secret from the East? I came to see you in the hope that you knew a way for me to help him."

"You cannot help him. Forgive me, but it is the truth. There is no secret as such. No elixir. I am sorry, but it is not for you to save him. He must save himself."

Lady Lynsworth wept into her handkerchief again. Leona rested her hand on the geranium shoulder. "If he could break the chains, do you think he would? He must want to. If he does, there is some hope."

Lady Lynsworth nodded. "When we spoke he was desolate, and angry at himself. But so sad and helpless." She clutched the handkerchief in her fist. "My father's disappointment has turned him cold. My husband refuses to hear me. He sees only scandal waiting if the world knows the truth. But Brian and I have always been very close, and if you know of any chance, no matter how small, I must try."

Lady Lynsworth's determination and sorrow moved Leona. She knew just how small the chance was, but if this woman wanted to give it to her brother, then she would help her.

"Do you have a property away from London, and a good distance from any other town? It must be isolated. The servants must be those who will do your bidding."

"My family has a manor in Essex. My father never visits, and the servants will obey me."

"Then let us go to your brother. You will take him there. I will send Tong Wei with you. He is the man who brought you to this drawing room. Tong Wei will know what to do, and you must instruct the servants to obey him as well."

Lady Lynsworth looked up, relieved. Then her face fell. "Oh, dear, I do not know where Brian is! Not at his home. He has not been there in several days. I cannot bring you to him until he returns there."

"We must find him. Do you know if he is eating opium, or smoking it?"

"He began by eating it. But when we spoke last he was very emotional and cursed his weakness. 'It is as if my soul is tied to that damned pipe,' he said."

"Then I know where he might be. We will take your carriage. I trust that your coachman is prepared for an immediate journey to Essex if we are successful."

Christian rapped on the door to Leona's house. When it opened, he did not face Tong Wei as expected. Instead Isabella did the duty.

"Tell Leona that I am here and need to speak with her about an important matter."

It was time to turn the cards faceup regarding Leona's purposes in London. Christian did not give a damn if she wanted to raise the call to arms regarding the opium trade. He did care if she raised the alarm of men who could act rashly if they considered either their fortunes or their reputations at risk.

"She is not here," Isabella said. She tucked her hands into the broad sleeves of her *qipao* while she stayed in a low bow. "She has just gone."

"Is Tong Wei with her?"

Isabella nodded.

"Where did they go?"

"Into the city. Leona said Tong Wei must come. They went in the lady's carriage."

"What lady?"

"I do not know her name."

Isabella began to close the door. Christian pressed his hand against it so it could not budge.

"So a lady came here, and Leona left with her. What was said before they all left? When she sent for Tong Wei?"

"She said, 'Come, Tong Wei. With luck it will be one more who snuffs out the lantern instead of his life.'"

It was not what Christian wanted to hear. Leona was

out in the city on a mission of mercy that was bound to take her to places she should not go.

He strode back to his carriage. He gave the coachman an address and a command to make haste.

He thought that he knew where Leona had gone. If he was correct, even Tong Wei's presence might not be enough protection.

Twenty minutes later Christian entered a coffeehouse on Mincing Lane. The real business conducted here was finished for the day. Only a few patrons dotted the rustic interior.

He called over a servant. "Tell Mr. Garraway that Lord Easterbrook wants to speak with him."

Shortly, a man approached Christian's table. The proprietor looked like a character in a play set in the last century. Dressed in a silk brocade waistcoat of pale blue and breeches of a slightly darker hue, his white hair had been caught in a tail at his nape. His perfume preceded him.

He set his spectacles more precisely on his nose with his pinky. It was more a bit of stage business than an attempt to see more clearly. "Lord Easterbrook. I am honored. My humble establishment rarely sees patrons of your station."

"That is because men of my station have no need of your establishment. Their physicians and apothecaries supply the laudanum when it is called for by medical necessity."

"And even when it is not, I daresay." Garraway blandly acknowledged the alternative uses for the drug.

"Suppose a young man's physician were not so

helpful. Where would he go to obtain relief?" Christian asked.

"To another physician or an apothecary, I assume."

"And if he preferred to avoid the normal routes of sale, or sought something stronger than laudanum?"

"Why do you think I would know? My establishment is used for the auctions of opium, that is true. What my patrons choose to negotiate while drinking coffee is not my concern."

"I need the names of the opium parlors in London, and the men who come here include those who run them. In particular, I am interested in establishments that have been buying opium from the Far East, not from Turkey, and that has been prepared for smoking, not eating. You would know it from its appearance. It is sold after a special process that turns it into balls."

"Balls, you say. From the Far East?" Garraway's brow puckered theatrically. "I have been told that Oriental opium is inferior for medicinal purposes. It has lower morphine content than Turkish. The apothecaries do not want it. As for non-medicinal purposes, it would only be economically advantageous to bring it in if one could avoid the tariff." He sniffed. "I would not know about *smuggled* opium, Lord Easterbrook."

"Mincing Lane is the center of the opium trade in England, and this coffee shop is the center of the trade on Mincing Lane. I think you know whatever is to be known." Christian reached into his coat and retrieved five guineas. He threw them down on the wooden table that separated him from Garraway. He also removed a pistol and placed it beside the coins. "I do not have more time to waste. Which way shall we do this?"

Garraway blanched, then turned peevish. "I do not care to be threatened, sir. Although I confess that I prefer that the threat comes from you than from a woman."

"A woman?"

"A fortnight ago. She also had an interest in those balls. She also refused to accept that they did not find their way here for auction."

"Did she wield a pistol?"

"Worse. A visit from customs officials." He dabbed his long nose with a lace-trimmed handkerchief. "A pretty harpy. Vaguely exotic. But a harpy all the same."

"If she left you in peace, you must have given her a name or place. I want it too. Now."

Garraway swiped up the guineas. A minute later Christian was again in his carriage, aiming for the St. Giles rookery.

The house reeked even from the street. Nestled between a gin house and a decrepit grocery, its drapes shielded it from light. The man at the door discouraged any casual visitors.

"Do you think he owns it?" Lady Lynsworth asked as she and Leona alighted from her carriage. The sentry was Chinese, and dressed much as Tong Wei dressed, only in simpler fabric with no embroidery.

"I doubt it," Leona said. "I think that he is only a guard. He is also an advertisement. His figure says that mysteries from China can be had within."

Tong Wei viewed his countryman with disdain. "Describe your brother. I will find him if he is here."

"He is rather average in height and coloring. In

every way, really. There is nothing notable in his appearance. Please ask that man to allow me in. I will know at once if Brian is there. I will recognize him at a glance and we will not disturb the others."

"I think that you need to talk all of us in, Tong Wei," Leona said. "Brian may not agree to go with you, but he will acquiesce to his sister."

Tong Wei left them near the carriage and approached the door. After a ritual of greeting, he and the guard conversed with spirit in the singing language of China.

Leona had never learned much Chinese and could offer Lady Lynsworth no reassurance that Tong Wei was making progress. The guard appeared to swing between belligerent denial and groveling obeisance.

Tong Wei returned to them. "It is promised to the patrons that there is privacy within. He should not allow us to enter, but he will. We must be quick."

"How did you convince him?" Leona asked.

"He is a thief, but he is not beyond being shamed for aiding the use of this poison that our emperor has condemned."

A crate filled with large brown balls could be seen several feet inside the door. The opium the crate contained had taken a long path. Grown and processed in India, then sold in the market at Calcutta, it had eventually made the journey to England.

Tong Wei led the way as they followed the doorman to the back of the house. Shadows blanketed the space. As Leona's eyes adjusted she saw pallets on the floor, and figures stretched upon them. Beside each pallet stood an opium lantern, and a long pipe within easy reach of the victim finding a false heaven in the drug it delivered.

"It is so dark," Lady Lynsworth muttered through the handkerchief pressed to her nose. The smoke in the room resembled a heavy fog.

Leona took her hand and dragged her between the rows of pallets. "We do not have much time. You must see if he is here while you can."

Lady Lynsworth bent over face after face, peering into vacant eyes, searching for her brother. Tong Wei followed in their wake.

They had searched half the room when a man entered the chamber. A full head taller than Tong Wei and sporting a red beard to match his curly hair, he was clearly not Chinese.

He spied them and strode in their direction. His expression did not bode well for their mission.

"Keep looking," Leona urged.

Tong Wei turned and positioned himself between them and the approaching proprietor.

"You've no business here. Get out," the man said.

"The ladies seek a relative. We will leave soon," Tong Wei explained with careful clarity.

"I'll not be having no reformer types here, interfering with my business and that of my friends."

"These people are not your friends," Leona said while she shooed Lady Lynsworth on. "A man does not allow a friend to endure this."

"Don't look to me like any of 'em mind it, so the enduring must be nice." He snickered. "Now you collect that other woman there and be out of here or things may get difficult."

"I hope not," Tong Wei said. "I cannot allow difficult to happen."

"Don't much matter what you allow, does it?
Now, get."

"Here he is!" Lady Lynsworth's discovery rang off
the ceiling. "Brian! Dear heavens, he looks dead."

Tong Wei barely turned his head to glance at the
blond young man over whom Lady Lynsworth bent.
"He is not dead, but he is lost."

Leona knew what he meant. He was probably correct, but she had promised to try to help and now they
had to see it through.

"I will carry him out," Tong Wei said.

"You'll do nothing of the kind," the proprietor said.
"That one owes me a pretty penny. I've had his coat off
of him for today's portion, but he don't leave until his
arrears are met."

"He can hardly meet them if he doesn't leave,"
Leona said.

"Can't he now? Fine coat it was, and I expect his
family will honor his debt."

Lady Lynsworth was coaxing Brian to alertness, to
no avail. Tong Wei gestured for Leona to walk. They
went over to Lady Lynsworth.

Tong Wei crouched down, and rose with Brian slung
over his shoulder. Brian was taller than Tong Wei, and
might have weighed more, but Tong Wei's strength did
not only come from his body.

"We leave now," he said.

"The hell you do." The proprietor strode toward
them. Dim light from beneath a drape caught the glint
of metal.

Lady Lynsworth gasped at the sight of the knife. Tong Wei bowed and allowed Brian to fall back on the floor. He faced the proprietor with utter calm. Leona sensed the stillness of meditation claiming him.

This was hardly the time for that. She was about to say so when she saw his face. Tong Wei had not retreated into any meditative reverie. He gazed at the knife with eyes that permitted no other sight. She had never before seen him appear this hard.

He did not wait for the knife to move. Instead he floated forward while his body twisted and turned so gracefully that there came no sound.

The proprietor flew and landed on his back among his victims. He scrambled to his feet, furious. He eyed Tong Wei and came toward him with menacing steps.

"You will stop right there. One more movement that endangers these ladies, and I will kill you. Do not doubt my resolve on this."

The voice came from the shadows near the doorway, behind the proprietor. He froze, then pivoted to face the new intruder.

At first all Leona saw was the pistol. It appeared to hang in the air. Then Easterbrook took two steps into the chamber. He gave one quick scan of the pallets. She saw the expression of disgust as his gaze lit on the closest faces. Then he had eyes only for that knife.

"Who might you be?" The proprietor asked with a sneer.

"I am Easterbrook."

"Well, m'lord, I am honored." He made a mocking bow. "M'name is Harry Timble and this is my property."

"It is your heir's property unless that knife is on the floor in three seconds."

The knife clattered to the floor. Tong Wei picked it up and threw it across the chamber. It embedded itself deeply in the far wall.

"Please collect what you came for, ladies," Easterbrook ordered, his pistol still aimed directly at Harry Timble's chest.

Tong Wei reached down, grabbed Brian's arms, and had him slung across his body in a trice. He led the way from the chamber.

Once they were out of the house, Easterbrook joined them. The pistol now pointed to the ground from his dangling arm.

"Lord Easterbrook, you have my gratitude," Lady Lynsworth said.

"My pleasure to serve you. I assume that is your carriage there?" Already Tong Wei was lowering his burden through its open door.

"Miss Montgomery suggested that I take my brother to the country and remove him from the temptations here in London. She thinks it may help him."

"Tong Wei will go too," Leona said. "He will aid Brian through the initial pain of abstinence. You must command the servants to obey him, Madam. It would be better if you are not there yourself. You should return to London once all is arranged."

Easterbrook watched the preparations for departure silently. Once Tong Wei and Lady Lynsworth were in the carriage and it began to roll, he spoke.

"It is fortunate that I arrived, Leona. Had I not, you would now be alone in London's worst rookery without any protection, assuming that you were even still alive."

"Tong Wei would have stopped that man. I do thank you, however. It *was* more efficient your way."

He held out his arm toward his coach. "I will bring you back to your house, Leona."

CHAPTER
TEN

～

She kept gazing at him in the carriage. Her dark eyes tried to read his mind, much as he would have liked to read hers.

The noxious odor of the opium parlor hung on his clothing. He pulled back the carriage curtains to let in air and light.

"Did it oppress you? Being there?" she asked.

"Not at all."

"That is good. You have been so quiet that I thought that perhaps . . ." She smiled kindly, then shrugged.

"I have been quiet because I am deciding how to punish you for being so foolish as to go into that hell. There are places in London that are uncivilized, and the rookeries are among them."

"I could not refuse Lady Lynsworth."

"It was a fool's errand. Tong Wei will nurse her brother through the torture that is waiting, and after two weeks he will be on his pallet again, smoking in his death through that pipe."

"It might not happen that way. You know it might not."

Again those eyes. Those knowing eyes. Seeing too much and looking for yet more. It had always been thus, and her gaze created more intimacy than she realized.

A small, sardonic smile formed on her full lips, but her eyes remained inquisitive.

"Or do you think it was different for you because you are Easterbrook?" she asked quietly.

Her allusion called up a memory, one both cherished and hated. He was in his chamber in her father's house late at night, and the door had opened. She had been there, much as he had dreamed by night and plotted by day, with her dark curls rippling down her white nightdress and wonder and fear and determination in her eyes.

Despite her fear she had come to him, to the desire that perfumed the air between them, to the mysteries waiting. She had risked everything to come, only to find him with pipe in hand and the fog blanketing the chamber despite the open window.

Do you want to die? Because you will die, like a coward. It is a coward's escape from life that you seek with it. Whatever it is you run from is inside you, and if you will not face it at least have the courage to use a gun so you do not die in ignoble disgrace.

Her words had been furious, brutal, and so loud it was a wonder the household had not been woken. There had been no more desire in her that night, but only anger and a pity that he could not bear.

"You do not know for certain that it was different for me," he said.

"I knew at once. So did Tong Wei. I saw you in

there, and your expression of anger as you looked at the people and the pipes, and I knew even more certainly that you no longer crave that false paradise."

She was wrong there. One always craved it a little. If he did so less than most, it was because the man she had upbraided that night had been in search of a soul, and the one he was now had accepted the only soul permitted him.

"Do you assume that Lady Lynsworth's brother will have a knack for meditation, Leona?"

"I think Tong Wei will have to resort to cruder methods. Your willingness to learn the breathing techniques spared you the worst. Also, you were not enslaved yet, and Tong Wei said Brian is lost." She cocked her head, and looked at him even harder. "It is odd. I am not sure that Edmund would have survived, but it is clear that Easterbrook has and will. You are not the same person."

"Is that what you have been thinking since that afternoon I had you brought to my house? That I am not enough like Edmund? Not sad enough? Not weak enough?"

"I did not mean—"

"I assure you that I am the same person, much as a man is the same person as the boy he once was. I had to choose whether to live or die. Just facing the choice resolved many things, Leona. Making the choice settled many others."

"Then I am glad that you are no longer Edmund, Christian."

It was the first time she had addressed him by his real given name. That, as much as the warmth in her eyes, told him that she had begun to reconcile the present with the past.

He regretted it when the carriage stopped. A row waited for them inside the house, and it would spoil what had been the true reunion between them.

He handed her down, and ignored her farewell at the door. He stepped in after her and sent Isabella away with one glance. "I came looking for you today for a reason, Leona. The conversation that I sought cannot be delayed."

"I trust the topic is entertaining."

"Do not try to be clever with me. You have been abroad in this town looking for more than alliances for your brother. You have also been looking for trouble, and I have cause to think that you have found it."

There was no choice but to face what was coming. She wished that she could put this off, however. She had found a bridge to the past on this carriage ride, and to the soul-wrenching intimacy she had shared with him back then. She feared that he would once more become a stranger whom she could not trust if they broached the topics he alluded to.

She led the way into the library, and closed the door so that Isabella would not overhear. She faced her inquisitor and sought to control the way her heart warmed just being near him.

His expression said he would brook no nonsense. "Does your brother know what you are up to?"

"Of course he knows. He did send me."

"For your stated purpose, yes. I do not believe he knows about the other."

"I think he suspects that I hope to bring him back a wife, if that is what you mean, but I never told him of that plan."

"Stop it, Leona. Do not try my patience."

"Then do not try mine. What other purpose do you imagine me to have here in London? State your suspicions and perhaps I can ease whatever troubles your mind."

He looked away and rubbed his eyebrows with his thumb and finger, as if containing his exasperation took effort. "I think that you are hoping to prove what your father failed to prove before he died. That the smugglers attacking his business were the agents of powerful men here in London."

Disappointment slapped her out of her silly daze. It was as she feared. He had been one of them from the first. "How do you know what he suspected, or wanted to prove?"

"Your father told me about it."

"If he had known who you were, he would not have revealed anything. You learned what he knew and what he planned only because you deceived him."

"I think he guessed I was other than I said. He was suspicious of me. He still told me."

She dared not believe him, much as she ached to. It would be reassuring to know that her father had found cause to trust him. Her father had been good at sizing up a man.

Unfortunately, her father may not have trusted him at all. Easterbrook could have learned everything by reading her father's notebook. It disheartened her that the evidence now indicated he had it in his possession.

"What did you learn from him?"

"That for two years before I arrived in Macao, your father's business had been suffering a series of incidents that were threatening its solvency. Accidents. Lost cargo. Pirate raids. He was sure it was retribution. At first for not aiding smugglers who wanted him to help move opium into China. Later, for his efforts to expose what was happening. That fire on my last night there was more of the same."

"Not exactly. You saw Lau King among the men who set fire to that ship. That was new."

"I really saw that there was far more danger than your father suspected."

Yes, danger. Too much danger. Especially for Edmund. To have seen Lau King meant he had to flee. Lau King was the servant of the Hoppo of Canton, the Mandarin who controlled customs. Lau King's involvement in that fire meant that the smugglers who coerced her father had friends in very high places in China as well as England. The emperor might forbid the trade, but his own officials were enriching themselves with it.

The truth had disheartened her father. The strength had drained out of him. He had believed that he was protecting foreign trade in Canton, and even the Chinese people themselves, by exposing the smuggling. He had even written to the emperor, describing all he saw and knew.

The evidence that Chinese Mandarins were complicit had been a terrible blow. The fight had gone out of him, and soon the life had too.

Leona looked at Christian and saw him that night, resisting her warning that he must leave at once, denying that the men who set fire to the ship had seen him just as he had seen them.

The scents and sounds came to her, the glare of the fire and the moans of her father's despair. She smelled the smoke on the water as she and Tong Wei dragged Edmund onto a small boat and spirited him away. She remembered the last view of him before he climbed onto the ship at Whampao.

She tasted again his farewell kiss, feverish and hungry and angry, before he let her go.

Easterbrook faced her now, not Edmund. The kisses were the same, though. He was the same man during their passion. She had learned that in the garden, to her undoing.

"Are you trying to learn if your father was correct, Leona? Are you trying to discover if there are men here in London who control some of the opium smugglers in the China Sea?"

Are you trying to bring scandal and disrepute to men I know and friends I love? She pushed thoughts of the garden's thrilling pleasure out of her mind so she would not turn into a puddle. "I can't imagine why you would think that I am."

"I read *Minerva's Banquet*. You threw down a gauntlet there. You also knew your way to an opium den in London, so you have been investigating something."

"If I am curious about my father's theory, what would it matter? It is not as if I could do anything about it."

"The threat of scandal and exposure is not nothing. If you are correct, and if you get close, there may be efforts to stop you."

It could have been a warning, or a threat. Her rising emotions could not tell which, or if there was even a difference.

"As they tried to stop my father? Perhaps they will use one of their later, more subtle tactics. Maybe they will only send a man to gain my confidence and learn what I know. Maybe they will have one of their own use persuasion and seduction instead of coercion."

He strode to her. He cupped her face in both of his hands and pierced her with his angry gaze.

"Is that what you have been telling yourself since you learned who I am? That I went to Macao to stop him, or to learn what he had discovered? That I am one of the men he spun theories about? I knew nothing of this until he confided in me."

"Then why do you care if I try to expose them now?"

His hands held her more gently, but no less firmly. His thumb stroked one of her cheeks. He looked at her as if he held and studied a fascinating possession.

"If I knew who they were, I could protect you. But I do not know who they are, or how dangerous they may be."

"So you think my father was right! You believe—"

His lips brushed hers, silencing her. "You will give this up, Leona. There is nothing to be gained by it."

His touch and kiss stole her breath. Excitement began to vanquish good sense. "They killed him," she whispered. It sounded more like a plea for help than an accusation. "Little by little they destroyed him until he was broken. Even if they violate no English laws, the world should know them for what they are."

Again his lips teased at hers. The warmth of his palms on her face made her whole body flush. "He would not want you doing this. He would have charged you with this duty if he did want it, and told you everything he knew so you could carry on for him. Did he?"

She looked in his eyes, into dark depths that both thrilled and frightened her.

"Did he?" he repeated.

She barely shook her head. She barely breathed.

No victory showed in his eyes at her response. He held her to a different kiss, one that closed the door on their argument.

There was care in that kiss, as if he mostly sought to soothe the turmoil this discussion had raised in her spirit. If he also wanted to influence how she weighed the truth of what he said, he failed, because the kiss distracted her from making any judgments at all.

His embrace wrapped her with strength and support. The dark intimacy surrounded her too, both comforting and exciting this time. She did not know if he intended a seduction. She did not care. Her heart sensed kindness in him, and genuine concern. Both altered his desire and even his power to something less threatening.

He lifted her chin with the crook of his finger and stroked her lips with his thumb. He kissed her again, almost discreetly. "You believe me, don't you? That I did nothing to harm or betray your father and you?"

Right now she did believe him. His embrace had banished the anger and suspicion. The sweetest calm settled on her, a calm so complete that she could feel and note the little beats and pulses in her body that said she would not stay calm long if they remained like this.

The waters of a wave were gathering. She and he were not in a garden near a party now. It was time to run and hide again, or be swept away.

He kissed her again. He drew her deeper into the intimacy. Trickles of pleasure began a hundred trembling paths through her body.

He was good at seduction. Too good. The pleasure in the night garden had left her with fewer defenses. Delicious anticipation spoke louder than any caution.

Whatever his intentions had been with that first kiss, he had others now. There was nothing tentative in the way he held her, or in his expression as his kisses sought her neck and pulse. His caresses moved over her body. Luscious sensation flowed and crested and finally submerged her.

She gasped as his mouth sent lively heat to her blood. She arched against the firm strength of his body and turned her head so he could make it worse.

An embrace, so close and tight that she felt his heartbeat. His voice, ragged and low near her ear. "Where is your chamber?"

"Isabella . . ." she murmured.

"She will not interfere." He lifted her in his arms.

His arms cradled her above his long strides. She barely saw the doors and walls slide past. Her heart remained in her throat and her eyes on his face. She experienced the climb up the stairs in a dreamy, half-stunned state.

He found her chamber. He held her to one hot, reassuring kiss, then laid her down. He cast off his coat, then joined her immediately, boots and all, as if he knew that the shock of her position raised misgivings.

He kissed her, and all questions and thoughts retreated. She grasped him to her, for reassurance and warmth. His sure hand caressed down her body, raising delicious expectations of that stroke on her flesh. He dominated her with his body, his embrace and his power, and she surrendered.

Hunger slashed through him. Hard. Aggressive. The acceptance in her embrace, the fire in her biting kisses and clutching hands, stretched his control. It was all he could do to restrain himself, and a wonder he did not tear her skirts off and take her at once.

His hand was between her thighs and his caress sliding in her cleft before he tamed the ferocity in himself. Her hips flexed above his hand. Her cries and slickness said she was aroused enough, but it would be stupid and thoughtless to ravish her, no matter how ready her body might be.

He kissed her soundly while he bridled the ruthless drive that compelled him forward. He drew her back from her own frenzy for now. A frown of frustration said she was less than pleased.

He kissed her furrowed brow. "It will end badly for you if it continues like that, and I do not want to hurt you."

She nodded but her expression remained petulant. He rolled her to her side and worked at the dress's fastenings.

She began to roll back when she realized what he was doing. He stopped her with gentle pressure against her shoulder. "You will not stop me. There is little enough left for me to see, and I will not be denied."

She did not stop him again. He guessed her state accounted for that as much as anything. Or perhaps her resistance had been more instinct than will.

It pleased him to undress her. He slid the dress off completely and went to work on the stays. Her breaths came deeply, as if this affected her as much as love play. He rolled her onto her back.

Her dark eyes watched him from beneath lowered lids while he slipped the stays away. The full sensuality of her body was already visible beneath the filmy chemise. He slid it down until she was naked except for her hose and the pretty garters above her knees. They added a piquant erotic touch. He decided to leave them on her.

She was beautiful. More beautiful than he had imagined when his mind had stripped her in the years since they met.

Her full breasts rose, round and firm, their dark tips tight and provocative. He traced his fingers around those swells, then down along the curve of her waist to the flare of her hip. He splayed his hand over her stomach, enjoying the contrast of her glossy soft skin against his palms.

He dipped his head and kissed the side of one breast, then its hard nipple. She flexed sensually from the sensation and her gaze turned smoky.

"You are perfect," he said. He enjoyed no special advantage with her, other than the immediate connection that formed whenever their gazes met and the spiritual intimacy that sexuality created. He explored a mystery like any other man did when he gave her pleasure, and had to rely on instincts more primitive than in the past. The sheer normalcy of it fascinated him, as did the discovery that the less secure sensing could be more profound than the literal one.

Her naked body luxuriated in his caresses. An indescribable expression softened her face. He saw the pleasure in her. Felt it. And as she became more lost, more abandoned, he sensed it.

No fear. No holding back. She embraced more than his body. A deeper closeness existed in their mutual desire and warmth, in her cries and yielding. A state akin to the dark center formed, only she was in it too. It was not selfless and empty but full of need and it tremored with the ecstasy waiting.

He pulled off his clothes while he kissed her soft curves. He flicked his tongue on her nipple until she cried out. He used his mouth and hand to take her deeper into madness. He wanted her screaming from the pleasure, begging for him, so that his possession would be complete when she gave herself and she would never again question how it must be.

His own body tightened with each indication of her arousal. The darkness closed in more. He spread her legs and knelt between them and gazed down at her. She looked so erotic that his jaw clenched against the fury throbbing in him.

Her lids rose, revealing glistening, enraptured eyes. She watched as he extended his arms and smoothed his hands down her shoulders and around her breasts. They were fuller now, tighter, and extremely sensitive as she approached her climax.

She watched his hands and her breath shortened. She arched when he gently teased her nipples and she whimpered softly in her need. He caressed down her hips to where her thighs were parted near his knees. Moisture sparkled on dark hair around soft, pink flesh that her vulnerable pose made visible.

She did not try to contain her delirium at all. She gasped with his first touch, then descended into cries while he stroked in ways that he knew would make her cry even more.

A thundering pulse beat stronger and stronger and the darkness obscured every thought except the urge to have her. He made her come so any pain would not matter as much, then pressed his erection into her. He lowered his body into her arms and eased into her tight passage.

Her body resisted. Even the throes of her release did not obscure her pain. He gritted his teeth and waited for the worst to pass. He lifted one of her knees to the crook above his hip to open her and ease it for her.

Her hot breaths panted against his chest. He moved carefully, restraining the driving urge to ram deep and hard. She slowly relaxed, opened, accepted. She looked up at him, into his eyes, and captivated him with the wonder in her own.

The dark center grew then. Nothing existed in it but the sensation of her flesh against his and the howling pleasure and the awareness of two climbing to ecstasy together.

The whole world split apart. His mind disappeared

for a long, black moment of bliss. The center did not shatter, however. Instead it absorbed everything, in a fulfillment that he had been promised since the first time he had looked into her deep, dark eyes.

She did not want to return to herself. It was too pleasant floating like this, somewhere above the world, surrounded by his arms and nothing else at all.

The intimacy soothed her. It deepened as his scent and warmth entered her head. His heartbeat sounded in her ears, quieter now, no longer the escalating rhythm of hot blood seeking a conflagration.

Slowly she grew aware of her nakedness in the cool breeze of early evening. She noticed how her face pressed against his chest and the encompassing nature of his embrace. She felt small against him, but not as vulnerable as when he was in her and his power flowed unchecked, commanding surrenders that she had not expected.

She opened her eyes and looked down his body. In the heat of her sensual abandon she had not really noticed when he undressed. Nor had she been shocked to see him without clothes kneeling above her, his dark hair framing eyes that all but scorched when he looked at her. Now his nakedness made her blink, and become more aware yet. His body reminded her in very frank ways of the implications of what she had just done.

Her contentment did not permit much thought about that now. The world and its rules would not be denied, but she did not have to invite it into this chamber yet. She let her gaze meander down his flat stomach to the dark curls and soft phallus, and on to the legs, one half bent. He had very nice legs, she decided. Well formed, with dark hair covering lean, taut muscles.

She shifted, seeking more closeness to his warmth. She felt moisture on her stomach and legs. She looked at her own body, and the streak of blood on her thigh.

A memory came to her, of an instant of surprise when he withdrew from her as the climax broke in him. Her own mindless state had permitted no more than the briefest sense of loss, and the smallest relief that he had been more careful with her future than she had been.

Her head rose and fell on his inhales and exhales. They came so regularly that he might be sleeping. Or meditating. Only he wasn't. His hand kept touching her head, his fingers languidly penetrating her topknot in a charming, comforting touch.

"Do you sleep, Leona?"

She turned her body so she could see his face. Her topknot tilted, then sagged to her shoulder. She spied a stack of hairpins on her pillow. She plucked at one more that dangled near her eye. Her hair tumbled more.

"Kneel so I can see you," he said.

As she did so her hair fell around her body, a chaotic mass of curls that made Branca curse when she was a girl. She drew a corner of the sheet to her body, to cover what the hair did not.

His arm reached out. A fine arm, revealing more strength than his tall, lean form implied in garments. The same tight muscularity could be seen in his shoulders and torso. For a recluse he appeared surprisingly athletic.

He plucked at the edge of the sheet and peeled it

away. Their nakedness suddenly made her shy. It was one thing in the frenzy of desire, and another in the cool light of day when rationality returned.

"You are perfect," he said. "I always knew that you would be."

His gaze almost made her believe him, even though she knew she was not perfect. Not nearly so. She certainly was not fashionably pretty, especially here in London. Now, after what they had shared, he saw her through very kind eyes.

His words touched her, and not because of the flattery. He alluded to the past, and to the time apart. It would be nice to believe that she had not fallen from his memory all those years, only to reenter it when he saw her name on the calling card given to his aunt that day.

"You must come to Grosvenor Square, as my aunt's guest. I will send the servants to move your belongings tomorrow."

"That would not be wise. You have announced your interest in me. If I now live in that house, everyone will think—everyone will know that—"

The objection sounded silly even to her own ears. Everyone would think and know what they already thought and knew. Except it was not really silly at all.

"I do not want society's heralds to announce me as your mistress. I do not want that kind of notoriety. It would not be wise for me to be that indiscreet, or that dependent."

He did not care for her resistance. But then he was Easterbrook, and a man, and did not care what anyone thought. "So you are going to force me to slip in your door, and leave before dawn? I would much prefer if you were up the stairs or down the corridor."

"I am sure that you would. Then you could go back to your old habits, content in knowing that your pleasure could be had with little inconvenience." She bent and kissed him. "I know that attending those parties did not suit you. I am flattered that you wanted me enough to bother. I will not join you in that isolation, however. I am of the world, and have responsibilities that require I remain in it, and that I take some care with my reputation."

"That is a damned excuse." His attention sharpened on her eyes. "You do not want me sure of you, that is what you really mean. You do not want to admit that you are mine. It is not society with whom you want to dissemble. It is with me and it is with yourself."

His accusation pierced her with its truth. Rather suddenly the playful negotiations ended and more serious ones began. "I cannot be yours because you cannot be mine. Or do you assume such things only go one way?"

"I think that we are both incapable of denying how this will be."

"One afternoon of passion does not make the bonds you describe, and I am mature enough to accept that. Nor do a few months of pleasure, if we meet like this in the weeks ahead."

His expression found a severe beauty at her allusion to her eventual departure from England.

That magnetic, invasive aura flowed from him. His gaze searched, as if he tried to read her thoughts. She instantly hid them away, from him and herself.

He took her hand and tugged her into his embrace. He rolled until she was on her back and he was braced above her, looking down. "And here I thought that you had surrendered completely. It appears that I will have to do better yet, *when* we meet like this in the weeks ahead, Leona."

CHAPTER
ELEVEN

Vague sounds of London wakening entered with the
breeze. Christian listened to the distant rumble of
the first carriages and carts making their way down the
streets.

Leona slept in his arms. He derived enormous contentment in her femininity and softness. He could stay
like this all day most likely. There had been little sleep
last night and she was dead to the world.

The pleasure had been very good. Whether it was
good enough remained to be seen. He did not want any
more of her ambiguities about how it would be between
them. He would rather not propose a formal arrangement, but he would if that was what she wanted.

Perhaps it was. She had spoken of security when
they argued about Pedro. Right now her only security
came from her place in her brother's home.

He was an idiot. Of course a woman would worry
about that. Especially Leona, who had known so much
insecurity while her father's business wobbled under

the onslaught of those ruinous setbacks when she was a girl.

He looked down at her dreamy expression. Her cheek pressed his chest. He could see long, dark eyelashes and the subtle parting of her full lips. Her raven curls tumbled over his arm and shoulder.

Some birds alighted on the tree outside the open window. Their song rang in the bedchamber. A little mumble provided a base line to the music. He closed his eyes and focused on that deeper sound.

It was human, and part of it entered him inaudibly. He had experienced an absence of all such intrusions for hours now, since he entered this house.

He realized it came from the garden below the window. He eased away from Leona and rose from the bed. He went to the window and looked out.

Isabella was down there, in a simple *qipao*. Her black hair hung long and straight, an indication that she had just risen. She spoke quietly to two men, but her agitated gestures made the broad sleeves of her garment fly around her.

The three looked to be arguing. Heads together, they spoke so lowly that little more than that annoying buzz reached the window.

"What in the name of Zeus are you doing down there, Phippen?"

Shock. Alarm. Three faces turned up to him. Phippen froze, then scurried behind Miller and peered at the window from behind his shield.

Miller smiled, being a young man too callow to know when he was about to die. "We are sorry if we woke you, my lord. But it may be just as well. The maid here refused to intrude."

"That is because she knows how very grievously it would displease me if she did. Being a proper servant, she knows the importance of discretion and the value of being invisible."

Phippen's eyes grew wide. Miller's smile trembled just enough. "Nothing short of a serious matter would ever cause us to be here, sir. Last night word for you came from your brother, Lord Hayden."

Hayden would only send word in the dead of night for one reason. "Is it over? Is it done?"

"Yes, my lord. Lady Alexia has given birth and—"

"Is she well? Is the child well?"

"Yes, my lord. We waited to see if you would return last night. When you did not, I told Phippen here that we should try to find you since you have been waiting for this news and—my apologies, but I guessed that you might be here."

"Good man. Phippen, come up here. Help Isabella prepare baths. Miller, go to Hayden's house and tell him I will be there forthwith."

He turned from the window to find Leona sitting up in bed. She wore a puzzled frown.

"Why are you shouting out the window?"

"I was not shouting."

"You were at the end. All of the neighbors probably heard. You probably woke them. You certainly woke me." She crawled off the bed and walked over, oblivious to her nakedness or his. She peered down. "Who was out there?"

"My manservant and my valet."

"Is that customary? For your servants to follow you to the houses of your lovers?"

"They came on a special mission." He told her the good news about his new nephew. "Phippen will help Isabella with baths and such. We must hurry though. I want to leave within the hour."

"We?"

"I want to introduce you to Alexia. You will like her."

She looked at him as if he were mad. Or at least half so. "She just *gave birth,* Easterbrook. She does not want social calls from strangers."

"I am not a stranger. As for you, she will not mind. She will be happy to meet you. I am sure of it." A scratch on the door drew his attention to both of their naked states. He grabbed his garments and pulled on his trousers. "I trust there is another chamber for Phippen and me to use. Tell Isabella to make haste."

He gave her a quick kiss, then threw open the door. Isabella startled at his sudden appearance, then lowered her eyes from his naked chest. He pushed past her and went looking for Phippen.

A new lover and a new nephew. It had been a splendid night.

Leona liked to think that she had acquired a worldly sophistication over the years. She knew that she had a talent for adapting to the varied mores found in other lands.

She covered her hair and face when in countries where women were shrouded. She ate whatever food was served her at dinners even if she could not identify its exotic ingredients. She had negotiated with men of every color and religion, but had never tried to be other than a woman to them. The profits she offered bridged any chasms her sex might create, as long as she did not treat their customs and beliefs with scorn.

London was not Macao. There were nuances of propriety that differed from home, even if both were European in essential ways. She had spotted those variances quickly, and done her best to respect the English way of doing things.

All of which meant that as she and Easterbrook rolled down Hill Street in his coach, she was very, very certain that his bringing her along had been a bad idea. She did not look forward to what promised to be an extremely awkward introduction.

She could not reason with him. He was all Easterbrook this morning, sure of his privileges and judgments, impatient with rules that applied only to lesser men. He had fairly dragged her into the carriage when she demurred.

The servant at the door took his hat and gloves and the mantlet she had worn against the morning damp. Phippen and Miller had brought fresh garments to her house, so Easterbrook looked his lordly best as they were escorted to the drawing room.

He paced while they waited, absorbed in thought, so oblivious to her presence that she wondered why he had brought her. Finally a man joined them. Lord Hayden Rothwell, no doubt. He resembled his older brother in many ways, only his face possessed subtle differences that made it even more severe. Stern, actually.

His gaze swept the room and settled on her for a long moment. Her stomach kicked. She braced herself for withering politeness at best.

Then he smiled. It was a very small smile, but it transformed his countenance. She suspected it was not really a smile for her, but the joy of a new father simply having its way.

"I am sorry I was not at home," Christian said after greeting his brother. "I would have sat it out with you if I had known."

"It happened very fast. By the time I could send word, it was over." Hayden looked at Leona, directing his brother's attention.

Introductions were made. Lord Hayden was too good to ask what in the name of heaven she was doing there. She tried to smile in a way that conveyed her apologies.

"Is Alexia awake?" Christian asked.

"She is. She insisted that I bring you up."

"I will wait here," Leona rushed to say. "Please give her my best wishes on the happy news."

"You may give them yourself. When Alexia learned my brother had brought you with him, she insisted on getting a look at you."

It was perhaps not the best turn of phrase, but probably an accurate one.

"So, let us go," Christian said. "I am impatient to see my nephew."

Lord Hayden had taken one step. He stopped and cocked his head. "Were you not told?"

"Told what?"

"It is a girl."

Christian cocked his head in turn. "A girl?"

"A girl."

"Are you sure?"

"There can be no mistake in these matters." He watched his brother with amusement. "Are you disappointed?"

"No. Of course not. It is just—there have been no girls. None of us were girls. Father had no sisters. His father had none either. I just assumed . . ."

"That is something that you are apt to do on occasion, Christian. But I assure you, it is a girl." He held out his arm toward the door, suggesting they go through it.

Leona walked beside a very surprised Marquess of Easterbrook as they went up to the family chambers. When they passed a study, she saw Lord Elliot in conversation with another man, one with very blue eyes and dark hair.

"The odds are about even," she whispered. "You do know that, don't you?" She could not believe she was asking a grown man such a question, but his astonishment was real.

"Of course I know that. I was certain it would be a son, however."

"How could you be certain when no one else can be?"

"I just *knew*. Do you never just *know* something?"

"Not as securely as you seem to. I think that is for the best. Otherwise I might just *know* something as well as you just *knew* this, and end up as wrong in my knowing as you have been."

He scowled, but his expression cleared when they arrived at the door of Lady Alexia'a apartment.

Only women were in Lady Alexia's chamber. They all appeared busy with the kind of aid reserved for sickrooms, but the happy chatter as the door opened was that of friends passing the time. All talk and activity stopped when Lord Hayden ushered in his brother.

Leona held back at the doorway, ready to slip away completely once Christian was distracted. The attention of the women centered on him, but Lady Phaedra smiled a welcome in her direction and another woman, a stunning blonde, gave her a long glance.

On the bed, tucked beneath a clean sheet, lay the new mother. She had dark hair and a kind face and eyes that appeared almost purple in the morning light filtering through the transparent drapes.

A transformation occurred as the room's occupants accommodated the arrival of the marquess. Even among family intimates he was Easterbrook. His station and his title, his authority as head of the family, introduced a note of formality into the way they greeted him. Even Lady Phaedra retreated into herself, in reaction or in deference to how he commanded the room.

Lady Alexia alone did not appear impressed. Her sleepy smile held a private warmth, and her eyes lit up in ways that suggested a secret sympathy with her husband's brother.

He went to her bedside and bent to kiss her forehead. "You are looking well, Alexia. This is a great day for our family."

"Do you want to see her?"

"Of course."

"Rose, please bring Estella."

The blond woman walked to a little crib adorned with drapery and skirts. She carried over a bundle and laid it in Lady Alexia's arms.

Easterbrook looked down a long while on the child's face. Then, without asking, he gently took the bundle into his own arms so he could peer closer.

Leona watched his expression as he cradled that tiny baby. She recognized that deep, serious gaze, and sensed his dark energy seeking something. There was no threat in it, but he looked at the child so long that awkwardness settled among the others in the chamber.

"Hayden, I trust that you will be keeping a good eye on her sixteen years hence," he finally said. "I don't want to have to kill too many young bloods on her behalf."

The ladies giggled. Easterbrook returned the child to Alexia's arms, and ran one fingertip down the infant's tiny cheek. "Well done, dear sister."

Lady Alexia's eyes misted. Leona's did too. That reminded her that she was intruding on a most private event. She took one step back, to make her escape.

It was too late. Easterbrook turned and noticed her. He beckoned her forward. Everyone's attention turned on her then. She had no choice except to go to him.

His blessing given and received, he was determined to ruin the moment by displaying the arrogance that only he would dare. "I have brought someone to meet you, Alexia. You have probably heard about her, and I knew you would be curious."

Lady Alexia's eyes met Leona's with a woman's sympathy for his lack of tact. "Phaedra of course told me about her new friend, Easterbrook. And I have read Leona's letter in *Minerva's Banquet*. It was kind of you to realize that I would be quickly bored in this bed, and to guess that meeting the fascinating Miss Montgomery would be a welcomed diversion."

And with that thoughtful, smooth speech, Lady Alexia swept away the scandalous implications in the coincidence that an early morning search for the marquess had resulted in Leona's presence at this house.

Lord Hayden drew his brother out of the room. Leona sat in a chair beside Lady Alexia's bed. Those violet eyes gave the closing door one long, thoughtful look, then they settled on Leona, most curiously.

Hayden brought Christian to the library, bypassing the study where Elliot sat with Kyle Bradwell, the husband of Alexia's cousin Rose.

"She is very lovely, isn't she?" Christian asked.

"Very. Unusually so. Her eyes in particular," Hayden agreed.

"I have heard they often change colors in the early years. Do you think they will become violet like Alexia's?"

Hayden appeared perplexed, then smiled. "Ah. You are speaking of my daughter. I thought that you were asking my opinion of Miss Montgomery."

"I already know that Miss Montgomery is lovely. I have less experience with babies not one day old."

Although Hayden's enveloping joy did not actually dim, another emotion sounded. Caution. Hesitation.

"I was happy to meet Miss Montgomery, Christian. Somewhat reassured."

"An odd word. Reassured. I do not know whether to be charmed or insulted by your concern."

"Neither, I'd advise. The public attentions you have been paying her are all the talk. It has never happened before in my memory. I was reassured to see she is not another Mrs. Napier, that is all."

"Afraid you might end up with a practiced courtesan as a sister-in-law, were you?"

"Something like that. As it is . . ."

Christian waited for the rest. His brother wanted to say something, but his better judgment was advising silence.

"Is your new child making you feel fatherly toward Leona too, Hayden? Perhaps all that talk troubles you, and you are concerned that I am playing loose with her reputation?"

"If that is the first thing you assume, maybe you only express your own concerns. As it is, I have cause to believe Miss Montgomery is well equipped to take care of herself, however she sees fit to do so."

So much for better judgment. Christian waited for the explanation that was certain to come.

It took some time. Hayden called for coffee. He described the madness of the last few days. He praised Alexia's cousin Rose for her untiring devotion and help. He settled them both in chairs to drink the coffee and finally, when almost an hour had passed, he got down to it.

"I have been making some inquiries on Miss Montgomery's behalf, as you requested."

"That was good of you, considering your wife's condition."

"Alexia ordered me from the house a few times during the last week. I was becoming a nuisance. So this gave me something to do." He set down his cup. "Miss Montgomery is known, it turns out. I have the names of some traders who will be happy to make her acquaintance. However . . ."

Christian just waited some more.

"Do you really know what you have in her, Christian? Seven years is a long time in a person's life."

It was an interesting question. Christian knew that he still had the Leona of the past, but she was not exactly the same person. Those seven years had matured her in many ways, and deepened her depths and brightened her heights. Her essence, however, had been immediately familiar to him.

"What is it you think I should know, Hayden?"

"I said she was known. I should explain further. She took up the reins of that trading house personally, herself, and found ways to keep it alive. She sailed the seas with her captains, and took risks some men would fear, both in the deals she struck and with her own safety. She is famous among shippers who work the East. Even infamous to some."

"You are not telling me anything that I do not know, or have not surmised. I appreciate your efforts on my behalf, and hers. Now, who are these traders who might benefit her? The ones eager to meet her for her purposes, and not just to satisfy their curiosity about the woman trader who sailed the Eastern seas."

Hayden appeared relieved he had not borne any true revelations. And he had not. Christian admitted, however, that in his determined pursuit of Leona, he had not given much weight to those seven years, and to how her experiences might affect her own view of destiny. Hayden's instincts about that were not to be discounted entirely.

Hayden gave him two names. "I think that you should contact St. John first," he said. "One of his captains has already had some dealings with Miss Montgomery, and he will be the most approachable and the most useful. However, he asked to speak with you first, alone."

"Why?"

"Perhaps he wants to be certain that a marquess does not get annoyed if he forges the alliances that Miss Montgomery seeks."

"Or perhaps he wants to make sure that a marquess feels in his debt for doing so."

"In either case, it is for you to decide how the accounting will work."

In other words, St. John, and probably any others, would appease a marquess any way a marquess chose to be appeased. In return, the lord in question would owe those men, with payment due in the currency of favors that influenced government and finance.

One word from him and Leona would have her alliance with St. John, and others too.

A different word and she would not have those alliances. Not soon and perhaps not ever.

Hayden suggested that they join Elliot and Kyle. As he walked to the study, Christian weighed the implications of this conversation with Hayden. It appeared that his patronage of Leona's mission could bear fruit quickly.

Unfortunately, if it did, Leona might conclude she had no reason to remain in England.

CHAPTER
TWELVE

L eona fell asleep in the carriage while Easterbrook brought her home. She only woke as they neared Bury Street.

She opened her eyes to find him in the depths of meditation. Eyes closed, unmoving, he faced her like a statue of peace. She tried very hard to make no sound that might disturb him, but soon his lids rose anyway.

"You appeared to be sleeping deeply," he said. "I trusted you would not mind."

"You probably are more refreshed than I am." She had not been sleeping deeply. Her mind had raced the entire time, summoning images from last night, from the past, from her home in Macao. Her brother had invaded the vivid dream, his face so clear and real that she thought she was with him in fact.

"Lady Alexia was very kind," she said. "Despite her exhaustion, she rallied to entertain me when you left me with her. She spoke very well of you. I think that you have a true sister's affection from her."

Leona had also had a private chat with Lady Phaedra,

a very useful one regarding the writer of her father's death notice, but she would not tell Christian about that. It would only revive their row from yesterday.

"Alexia has my admiration and affection in turn. There are few truly good people in the world, but I knew she was one of them the first time I met her."

She almost teased him about his presumptuous claims to know the hearts of others, but this was one opinion of which she would never want to disabuse him. She too had sensed an essential goodness in Lady Alexia, and a forthright honesty in her character.

"Her cousin Rose is a beautiful woman, and not at all proud," she said. "Was that man in the study with your brother her husband?"

"It was. Roselyn Longworth and Kyle Bradwell married at the beginning of this year. A good deal of scandal surrounds her. You will probably hear of it. I am told the gossip is fading, but in truth it will never die."

"Actually, the only gossip that I have heard about your family, other than that regarding you, concerned your brother Hayden and Alexia."

"He did the right thing in marrying her, but it is a love match now. I am surprised that there is still gossip. Only dim-witted people would find such a tiny scandal interesting."

He dismissed it much as he had when he spoke of Elliot and Phaedra. Scandals of this nature did not impress him at all. Perhaps he believed that they could never truly affect his family. He was Easterbrook, after all.

He accompanied her to her door when they arrived at her house. As was his growing habit, he entered with her as if he had a right to. She was beyond objecting to-day. It was hard to demand strict etiquette from a man who had seen and touched parts of one's body that one never saw and rarely touched oneself.

He would be impossible now. He had presumed much before, and it would be worse. Her disadvantage had increased enormously. Even if she tried to limit his rights, he would most likely ignore her efforts.

Perhaps he also did not want to end the idyll that had begun last night. Maybe he stayed close because he also suspected that the best of that intimacy would burn away with the sun if they did not stand shoulder to shoulder to protect the memory of it from too much illumination.

"I want to talk to you, Leona. About last night. And future nights," he said as they went up to the library together.

"I hope that you are not going to ask me to move to your house again. If so, please do not."

"I will accept your decision on that. However, I would like to ensure that I am welcome in this house instead."

She stopped at the top of the stairs. "You already enter this house as if you own it. As for being welcomed, and for what happens once you are here—I need to think about that, don't I? Despite the scandal in Macao, I am actually new to being a fallen woman."

She meant it as a joke. He did not hear it with humor. "I do not see it that way. I do not believe you do either."

"How I saw it had little to do with your pursuit. You knew your power and you used it and I put up very little resistance. I am not in a mood of regret, Christian. Far from it. That is not the same as agreeing that there should be more such nights, or that I will be your mistress." She touched his mouth, which had assumed a very hard line. "That is what you were about to propose, isn't it?"

"You are determined to make me miserable."

She almost laughed at his pique, it charmed her so. "If you wanted someone who only considered your pleasure, you knew where to find her I am sure. I must live my life as I see is best for me, not you. I know that in your heart you understand that, even if you scowl."

The scowl softened enough to indicate he did understand. Perhaps too well. "So you want to weigh matters. Make lists of income and costs in all their forms before deciding if I am welcomed in your bed again."

"Well, I am a trader's daughter, Christian. Our sort likes to keep tidy books." She gave him a playful kiss and opened the library doors.

As soon as she entered the chamber she halted in her tracks. She peered around, looking for she knew not what. Something was amiss.

"What is it?" he asked.

"I do not know. It is odd, but—" Her gaze swept the bookcases, then settled on the desk. She strode over and looked at its surface. Everything was just as it should be. The inkwell sat in its nook, with the wax lined up beside it. The lamp . . .

In her mind she saw this desk before she left the house yesterday. She remembered writing a note, then pondering her copy of the death notice. She had moved the lamp forward to hold the paper's edge. When Tong

Wei told her of Lady Lynsworth's call, she had opened the drawer and shoved in her papers, then—

An eerie sensation crawled up her spine. She pulled the drawer open. "Someone has been here. I am almost certain. In this room, and at this desk."

Easterbrook strode away. She heard him calling for Isabella.

Isabella arrived, trembling from the lord's tone of anger. She clutched some cloth in one hand and a needle in the other. She had obeyed the summons so quickly that she had not even put aside the mending that occupied her.

"Has anyone been here?" Easterbrook demanded.

She shook her head.

"Please, do not frighten her so," Leona said. "Isabella, have you heard anyone in the house or garden this morning? After Lord Easterbrook's servants departed?"

"No. No one."

"Where have you been during these hours?"

"In your chamber. There were some tears in your chemise and dress and I . . ." Her expression fell in distress. "Should I have remained here? Or near the door? I did not know. Normally Tong Wei—"

"You did nothing wrong. No one thinks that you did. Isn't that correct, Lord Easterbrook? We only wanted to know if you heard anything."

"I did not mean to suggest you had erred. You can leave now," Easterbrook said.

Isabella scurried away. Leona turned to the drawer, to see if anything was missing.

"It was bold of them, to enter this house," Easterbrook said. "Too bold."

"I could be wrong. Nothing appears to be gone. Perhaps I only thought it. I have nothing more than a feeling as proof."

"Feelings can often tell you more than sights and sounds. So can a memory of this chamber and that desk when you last were here. I do not doubt that your suspicions are accurate, even if there is no proof."

"I *do* doubt it, however. More with every minute. Already this library appears very normal to me. I am feeling silly to have raised an alarm over nothing."

He pulled her into his arms. "Leona, in the natural world most creatures, if their environment is threatened, if they are disturbed, will protect themselves. Some will flee. Others will attack. They will react. You have disturbed someone's environment. You must stop probing. You do not even know the nature of the beast you may be wakening with your prods."

"Do not try to command me. And do not try to say I am in danger just because of the strangeness I felt on entering here. The entire world appears a little different to me today. Maybe this chamber did not change at all. Perhaps I did."

He did not try to command, although she saw that he wanted to. Her allusion to her perceptions, and to the other reason for their changing, checked him. He took her face in his hands, much as he had yesterday at the beginning of it all, and kissed her.

"I will go now, so we do not argue about this on to-day of all days." He released her. "Tong Wei's absence has left you without protection. I will send men here, so that you and Isabella are not alone. Expect a footman by day and my secretary, Mr. Miller, by night. Do not think to object, Leona. And do not leave this house without one of them by your side."

He took her hand, bowed, and kissed it. "As for last night and future nights, I will wait for a sign from you."

Leona alighted from her carriage. She glanced askance at Mr. Owens, the footman who held the door. She had come to think of him as a gaoler the last two days.

Lord Easterbrook must have given stern commands about this duty. Owens never left her side when she departed the house, even if she only planned to stroll around St. James's Square with Isabella.

Right now his relentless attendance would be useful. As it happened, she had need of a man.

He shadowed her across the street and along the store fronts to the entrance of the Three Bells tavern.

She opened her reticule and retrieved five pounds. "Please go inside and ask for Mr. Charles Nichols. If he is there, say this note is his if he comes out here to speak with me."

"I cannot do that, Miss Montgomery. It would mean leaving you out here alone."

"Do you fear I will be abducted in the brief time you are gone, with my coachman less than thirty yards away? I remind you that the only time I was ever attacked on a London street, you were one of the men responsible."

He flushed a deep red.

"You will be able to see me through the window so I

will not be out of your sight at all. There will be five pounds for you too if you are successful. If you refuse to help me, I will march in there and seek Mr. Nichols on my own."

He knew he had been cornered. The chance to be five pounds richer made the view from that spot a fairly pleasant prospect, but she knew he saw a big shadow too.

"Lord Easterbrook will never know, I am sure."

Resigned more than swayed, he entered the tavern. Leona stood on her toes to get a good view through the window. Discussion ensued with the proprietor, then her footman approached a corner. It appeared that Phaedra's information, that scribes for the press collected here, had borne fruit.

Owens led a man to the door. Mr. Nichols had what she considered a country type of English appearance, pale and sandy-haired, with a blunt thickness to his features. His eyes revealed the liquid, red-rimmed evidence that he enjoyed the Three Bells tavern more than was healthy.

He gave her a good examination. "You want something from me for that five pounds, I assume."

"Only information. The answer to a question, to satisfy my curiosity about one of your paragraphs in *The Times*."

"The answer is yours if I have it. You are paying more than they ever will for so few words."

"Let us take a turn, then." She glared at the footman, to warn him not to walk too closely.

Mr. Nichols sauntered beside her with a loose, casual gait. She slowed her own pace so they could converse.

"Are you employed by the newspaper?"

He chuckled at that. "I sit in the trials and scribble the drama. I am a playwright, so I have a knack for it. If I make a trial funny enough, one of the papers gives me a few shillings."

"I am familiar with your colorful reports of the trials."

"Are you now?" He beamed, very pleased by that.

"I am interested in some scribbling of a different nature, however." She removed the death notice from her reticule and handed it to him.

He frowned as if he had never seen the words before. "Did a few of these over time. M.P.'s and such."

"This one was written six years ago, and the man lived on the other side of the world. Why did you believe his death would be of interest in London, and where did you find the facts on his life?"

Mr. Nichols truly seemed perplexed. Then enlightenment struck. "I remember now. Goodness, that was long ago. I was commissioned to write this. Families often pay for death notices, and that was how this was done."

"That man's family did not pay you. Someone else did. I know this for certain, because that man whose good name you impugned was my father."

Her accusation made him flush. "I was only given the information, that is all. Told to write it up proper and I'd be paid and my name would be in *The Times*. I was told straight out it was opium, but I thought it better not to be so pointed." He held the page to his eyes and read it again. "Thought I was very clever in how I phrased it, I remember. He thought so too."

"Who is this he? Who paid you to do this?"

"I am sorry if you were hurt, or if secrets were let out. I cannot tell you who hired me, though. He was not an ordinary man. He was the sort you don't say no to easy, if you know what I mean." He walked a few more steps, then added. "The sort you know it's best not to cross, if you understand me."

He described a man like Easterbrook.

"Mr. Nichols, I do not want to compel you to speak. However, that death notice leaves me no choice. It is a lie, you see. He died of a bad heart. You have committed libel. If you do not reveal who hired you, I will have a brief filed to that effect."

The threat alarmed him. "Hardly fair to try to ruin me when it wasn't really my doing."

"I will direct my anger more fairly if you permit it."

Mr. Nichols plodded along, his face screwed in thought. Pained by the decision, he held out his hand for the five pounds. "Viscount Guilford, he was then. Now he is the Earl of Denningham."

It was the first evidence that her father had been right all the time. The man who paid for that death notice was indeed a peer, just as her father claimed some of his unseen oppressors were. Unfortunately, that meant this was not someone she could confront easily.

The problem absorbed her while she walked back to her carriage. She needed to find a way to meet this man. The obvious path was through Easterbrook. He could probably arrange to have her received.

It would mean asking him for a favor. Which meant seeing him before she had decided what to do about him.

For two days her good sense had warred with her

instincts. The latter wanted to throw caution and reputation to the winds. They lined up many arguments for
grabbing whatever excitement and passion were waiting, no matter how hopeless and brief it might be.
Hadn't she regretted not doing so before?

The problem was she no longer was nineteen, and
continued capitulation had implications for many
things, including the reason she wanted this introduction so badly.

She worked it over in her mind. It distracted her so
much that she barely felt the stones beneath her feet.

Suddenly the world crashed into her daze. Sounds
thundered. Views of buildings and sky and street
flashed in quick succession while her body was yanked
to one side so hard that she flew.

The world righted itself. She saw her coachman
standing, waving his whip at a man cantering down the
street on a brown horse.

The danger had passed but its echo made her shake.
This brush with serious injury, or worse, chilled her.

"My apologies, Miss Montgomery." Owens's breath
came hard and his face was flushed from excitement
and alarm. "The fellow almost rode right over us. He
did not even look when he came around the crossroad."

He still grasped her by her arm. They both noticed and
he quickly removed his hand. "Are you hurt? Perhaps we
should return to your house so your maid can—"

Alert now, too alert, she cobbled together her composure. "I am not hurt. Thank you for being more careful than I was. We will return to my house soon. First,
however, I have a visit to make."

CHAPTER THIRTEEN

C hristian sat in his favorite chair in his chamber. The drapes had been pulled to the day's sun. His eyes were closed too. He was not meditating, much as he would like to be. Instead he debated what to do about Leona.

The conundrum had occupied his mind since parting from her two days ago. It even intruded on his sleep. Worse, until he settled an ill ease that had entered him in Hayden's house, he did not trust himself to see her again.

It was one thing to plan the seduction of a woman, and another matter to succeed in seducing *the* woman. And she had always been that, *the* woman, against whom he judged all others and measured even his levels of desire.

Seduction was driven by impulses and needs that have no logic, no concern for consequences. Normally there were no implications for him other than a temporary affair of mutual erotic satisfaction with an experienced woman like Mrs. Napier. Which meant that he had no recent experience with his current situation.

He could not deny that despite his indifference to notions of sin, guilt, and propriety, despite his firm belief that social rules strangled more than civilized, a night in Leona's bed had led to some unexpected moral considerations once the sated bliss passed. Her own hesitation to repeat the sin had only pricked at his conscience all the more.

He had been ruthless with her. That was all there was to it. He had been determined to have her, and he had succeeded. He had used pleasure to conquer her own good sense and her own care for her reputation.

The primitive man did not mind at all, and even preened with contentment. The civilized man knew it was time to make an accounting of the damage.

He was supposed to offer marriage now. That the notion did not send him into the depths of melancholy was a wonder in itself.

It probably had something to do with seeing that baby. The visit to Alexia had reminded him of nature's cycle, of time passing, of the life unlived. Alexia and Hayden's joy had been almost painful to see, and his own soul felt like a void in comparison. With his desire at low tide, his seduction of Leona had appeared selfish while he was in that house on Hill Street.

Then there was the baby herself. A perfectly normal child, from what he could tell. If the heightened sensibility had been in the child, his own sensibility should have felt it. Surely he would have sensed *something*. Maybe it did not have to be inherited by the next generation. Perhaps . . .

If he proposed, would Leona accept? She had all but warned him off that notion when she said in Pennington's garden that he was not her true destiny. Hayden's reports of her fame among Eastern traders indicated that the destiny she anticipated was not one of growing old sitting in a Mayfair drawing room.

The horrible truth was that marrying her would be even more selfish than seducing her. He had accommodated his affliction. He could overcome it for brief periods of time. He doubted any woman could constantly live with its effects without eventually hating how it affected her life and how it ruled him, however. Marriage to a madman would be preferable. She could lock a madman away, or petition to be freed of him.

He opened his eyes to the shadows. He got up and walked into an anteroom to his bedchamber. He lifted a half-written note lying on his writing desk. Addressed to Daniel St. John, it had been a noble but halfhearted attempt to procure Leona the connection she wanted.

If he finished this letter, she might be gone in a week or two.

He reacted badly whenever he contemplated that. Fury gripped him, but something else drenched him too. Something akin to fear.

When she left he would not only lose the rarity of normal pleasure with a woman. He would also be alone again.

He would be left with only the dark center and its cousin escapes, where all perceptions of human nature had to be severed in order to avoid the insidious curse of knowing more than was decent or fair.

He would never again experience the less invasive

but ultimately deeper knowing that was growing with Leona, or explore the nuances of her character that fascinated him—

Mumbles broke through his concentration. They came from his dressing room. Someone was in there with Phippen, engaging in an argument.

He strode back to the bedchamber and opened the dressing room door. Phippen's eyes widened in dismay at his sudden appearance. He pointed an accusatory finger at a footman.

"I *told* him that you do not like being disturbed during your quiet hours. I said that nothing short of torture would induce me to bring the card in." He grew three inches and scowled at the footman. "Now see what you have done?"

"My quiet hours? Phippen, that is the sort of thing one might say about an infirm person. Someone who has gone mad, for example."

"My lord! I would never—"

"Give me the card."

Tight-lipped and red-faced, like a man holding his breath, the footman gave it over.

Christian read it. Leona had called. What a pleasant surprise.

Perhaps she had come to thank him for the carriage full of flowers he had sent to her house yesterday. Maybe she would even scold him for not visiting himself.

His imagination allowed that scold to occur, then moved on to his response, which did not involve any words.

"Bring her to the drawing room. Then tell my aunt

and cousin that I require their attendance in the library. Once they are in there, lock the doors so they cannot get out."

The footman smiled weakly, testing to see if the last command was a joke. His face fell when no one else laughed.

"And see that someone brings Miss Montgomery refreshment."

The footman left to obey. Christian turned to Phippen. "In ten minutes I am going down to the drawing room. I expect to appear fit for the queen when I do."

Phippen gazed down his length, from his unshaven face to his bare feet. With an expression of eternal suffering, Phippen opened the drawer that held the razor.

She appeared beautiful in the light of the north window. Her dark expressive eyes gazed at something in the garden but also something inside her soul.

The newer fashions, with their lower waists, complimented her voluptuous form. His mind saw her body stripped of the dark rose silk and her hair free of the cream hat and her eyes smoky with desire.

He noted the tray and cup that said refreshment had been brought. He assumed that his aunt and cousin had been locked away, but he secured the drawing room doors anyway.

She did not hear the sound of that, or notice his presence. What occupied her thoughts so thoroughly?

He just watched her for a while from the other side of the chamber. He could see all of her in that wash of cool light. His body stirred at once, but so did an inde-scribable contentment. She had always incited that peace. The world was only normal, livable, in the oasis that formed around her person.

His body reacted as if he had been starved for years. Even the desire felt different with her. Wondrous. Mysterious. Clean. He did not fight it, but instead savored the tightening and the rising, pleasurable drive.

She subtly tightened too. Her back flexed and straightened. She looked over her shoulder, then turned to face him.

She knew. Her light flush said as much. A glimmer of dismay flickered in her eyes, but the lights of passion burned brighter. Desire was in the light and in the air, and in her.

The great conundrum suddenly did not matter very much.

Good heavens.

It had been a mistake to come here.

She should have swallowed her impatience to ask this favor and gone home and written a letter. She should have just waited until he called on her again. Now he thought—

He was at his worst right now. His dangerous, com-pelling, delicious worst. It was diabolical, really, how he could excite the most wicked titillations just by looking at her. He might actually be fondling her breasts and kissing her neck or stroking that—

"I came to ask a favor of you." It came out a weak

stammer, as if her breath would not support an entire sentence.

"That is not the only reason why you are here."

"It certainly is."

"No, it is not. And the favor can wait." He strode across the room and pulled her into his arms.

Heat. Insanity. There was nothing gentle in the way he kissed her and nothing ladylike in the way she gripped him. Suddenly she was against his body, imprisoned by his arms, accepting his passion and returning her own.

"This is not why I came here," she muttered between fevered, biting kisses.

"Of course it was."

Was it? It did not matter.

Incredible sensations distracted her. A ravenous sensuality obliterated caution and shame.

She savored the taste of him. She relished his caress. Her body grew impatient for that pressing, claiming touch to venture further. She silently urged more boldness and he responded as if she spoke the words aloud. She wished he would tear off her clothes so she was naked in the abandon she felt, naked to his scorching kisses and dangerous gaze.

Her arousal became unbearable. Furious. Anticipation made her crazed. Impulsively she reached down and closed her fingers around his erection. His breath caught, then he responded with a savage kiss while she stroked him.

Her feet left the ground. The room whirled. Softness beneath her face now. A ledge beneath her stomach. The storm cleared slightly. She opened her eyes. The ledge was the upholstered arm of a sofa. He had bent her over it and her face and arms hugged the cushion.

She felt him behind her, then his hands on her bottom, caressing the silk to her form. Her skirt and petticoat rose slowly. It took forever. She pressed her fist to her mouth to silence moans that wanted to escape.

She could not bear the anticipation. The awareness of what he would do and how badly she wanted it excited her more. Even the vulnerability of her position tortured her with the most wicked licks of pleasure.

Skin on skin now, as his hands smoothed over her bare bottom and down her thighs. The driving pulse so near his hands made her squirm. He responded with one sure, devastating touch.

"I think this is why you came here today." Another touch defeated her and she cried out. "Was it, Leona?"

Too far gone to think or argue, too desperate to care, she nodded.

He caressed more purposefully, until she thought she would weep. She gasped when she felt the pressure that she waited for. Then he was in her, filling her so completely that she trembled around him.

He withdrew slowly, then entered again. "You will cry for me again, darling. You will admit that you want me as much as I want you."

She cried for him. He made sure that she could not stop herself. He took her slowly, deliberately, so her need would just grow. Finally she lost all control. Her sounds would have rung off the walls if she did not smother them in the cushion.

Her submissive position gave his drive a primitive edge. Her bottom, round and raised and erotic, framed by the froth of her petticoat, rocked a little higher whenever he withdrew.

He watched himself enter her and his senses reeled from the way she surrounded and held him. It was too perfect, almost unendurable.

She climaxed first. Her wetness flowed and she tightened around him and she clawed at the cushion. A throaty cry accompanied her beautiful convulsion.

He grasped her hips and thrust harder, losing himself, relinquishing the restraint he had forced on himself. Darkness absorbed him until he knew only sublime sensation and a tightening force and the shuddering of a woman still frenzied even in her fulfillment.

He felt her peak again while his own climax burst in his head and loins. Her soft deep moans spoke in his head when the cataclysm tore sanity to shreds.

He floated in limbo for an exquisite time before his head cleared. When it mostly had, he opened his eyes. His hands gripped the armrest on either side of her hips while he found himself.

He fixed her garments and his own. When he lifted her she sagged limp in his arms. He settled them both on the sofa.

He did not hurry into conversation. In truth she had not come to him for pleasure, no matter what he had forced her to say. He did not expect to like the reason that she *had* come.

"You have need of a favor, I believe," he finally said.

"Do I?" she muttered against his coat. She nodded, as if remembering now. "I need an introduction."

"To whom?"

"To Lord Denningham."

"Why do you want to meet him? He is not a trader. He isn't much of anything besides a lord."

She stretched for her reticule, which had been discarded on the floor. She pulled it open and removed a piece of paper. "This was in *The Times* after my father died. Lord Denningham paid the writer to compose it."

The death notice was brief, but alluded to the cause of death in a way that implied opium addiction. Leona would be incensed by that.

"Denningham had nothing to do with this. You are aiming at the wrong man. I know him very well, since we were both boys. If he were in any way complicit in anything even slightly secret, I would know."

"Mr. Nichols told me Lord Denningham paid him when I spoke with him this afternoon. So whatever you know about Lord Denningham, it is incomplete."

Hardly. There were no hidden corners at all in Denningham's soul, let alone dark ones. "Mr. Nichols lied to you. If you confronted him about this, he would want to be free of you and your accusations. He could have chosen any name. He could have chosen mine."

She glanced sharply at him. He realized the notion had entered her mind. She was not completely sure about him yet. That was part of the conundrum waiting to occupy him again, once his present contentment passed.

"I will not know if he lied unless I meet Lord Denningham, will I? Are you going to help me, or must I find another way?"

He imagined the other ways. All of them promised

embarrassment to Denningham and notoriety to Leona. "I will speak with him first. I am sure that he will be happy to see you. When he does you will understand immediately what I mean about how impossible this accusation is."

She leaned close to him. Their noses almost touched. "Will you do it soon? Or will you put it off, so I continue to be within arm's reach of your scandalous designs for me?"

She was within reach now. He smoothed his hand over her breast so she would not think to move away. Her eyes darkened and desire rose in her.

He was reaching for her dress's fastenings when a commotion distracted him. Somewhere, not far away, loud thumps and thuds shook the house.

Leona stiffened. "What is that?"

A woman's voice punctuated the thuds. Furious yells sounded in the hallway. Anxiety and indignation flowed through the walls.

"That," he said, "is Aunt Hen."

He doubted the servants would stand against Hen if she made such a scene. Seeing Leona naked again would have to wait.

He went and unlatched the doors, then moved himself to a chair. Mumbles and shouts got louder. The drawing room doors flew open. Henrietta stood there in high dudgeon, with Caroline cowering in her wake.

"I was locked in!"

"That is terrible," he said. "No doubt a servant accidentally threw the bolt, or a loose nail made it slide."

"You were supposed to join us in the library," she accused. "I was told to wait for you there."

"Which you have not done, I see."

"Did you expect me to wait for hours? If I had, I would have perished in that locked room if the house caught fire."

"I was delayed because Miss Montgomery came to call. You remember Miss Montgomery, don't you, Caroline?"

Caroline greeted Leona with a curtsy. Aunt Hen cast a suspicious look and all but sniffed the air. Then abruptly she turned her full attention on Christian.

"Thank heavens you are dressed. We don't have much time. What a disaster if he had come and you were in that robe and we were locked in the library . . ." She fretted while she paced into the room and inspected it. She called for a servant and told him to remove the tray with Leona's refreshments.

She eyed Leona again. Her gaze paused on one slightly skewed sleeve.

"If who had come, Aunt Hen? Are we expecting a visit from your very dear friend, M'sieur Lacroix?"

Mention of her lover made her blush. She snapped her attention away from Leona. "Someone else entirely. Caroline's admirer. I told you last night at supper. Do you never hear me?"

Not if he could help it. He vaguely remembered Hen chattering on, exuding anxiety, while he turned the conundrum over in his head.

Leona grabbed her reticule. "I must take my leave. It was a pleasure to see you, Lady Wallingford."

Christian stepped to the door so Leona would have to pass closely while she left. There was much to say, but with Hen's dramatic intrusion all of that would have to wait now.

"It was good of you to visit. I hope to see you again very soon, Miss Montgomery."

"Thank you for agreeing to look into that matter for me, Lord Easterbrook."

She made good her escape. He was not to be so fortunate. Hen turned and nailed him with a glare. "I would think that with Caroline in the house that you would . . . would . . . ."

"Would behave as well as you do, Aunt Hen?" He trusted she did not want a row about their modes of indiscretion regarding their lovers with her daughter standing here.

She recovered admirably. "I think that you would want the best for her future. I hope that you will not do anything odd when he comes."

"I have a finite amount of oddness. If I waste it on him, I would not have enough left for you. To ensure I do not squander it, I will retire to my chambers now."

"You cannot do that! You must stay down here where I can be sure you are available. Good heavens, a fine thing it would be if a man came to ask for permission to propose to Caroline and you sent down one of those rude notes saying you are not in the mood for callers. Most people at least pretend they are not at home, but you make the insult explicit. Do that today and we will never see him again and her future will be ruined all due to your fault."

Within her rambling scold he heard only one enlightening word. Propose. He looked at Caroline. She blushed.

"Henrietta, I would like to speak with Caroline before he comes." Whoever the hell *he* was.

"I assure you that he is perfectly presentable and well thought of. He may not have a title, but with over nine thousand a year he is an excellent catch."

"All the same, I require privacy with Caroline. Perhaps you would wait in the library."

"The library! I should say not. The locks are enchanted."

"Then outside this door." He took her arm and escorted her thence.

Her vexation turned to desperation as he pushed her through the doorway. "You must not ruin this, Easterbrook. She is already in her second season. For once, please, just pretend you are like other men and conduct the formalities without any of your eccentric elaborations. If you scare him off I will never—"

He closed the door on her hysteria. He faced his cousin. "Caroline, when he comes, do you want me to give permission?"

"Yes, I think that I do."

"You think? It is as I feared. You will accept the first proposal just because the world says you must marry, and because you want to get away from . . . well, away from current company."

To his surprise she stretched up and kissed his cheek. "You are much like Hayden. Not nearly as stern as you appear. Do not fear that I will marry only to get away from Mama. I only said I think because I am a little frightened and my heart is jumping every which way. He is very good, and treats me with great care.

And he knows about last summer and does not think the worse of me for it."

She referred to a different *he* and a different pursuit with less honorable motives, an experience that broke her young heart when her male cousins interfered.

She frowned a little. "Would you prefer if we wait for Hayden? Mama thought to strike while the iron is hot, as she put it. With Hayden occupied with the child and Alexia, we thought you would not mind. But if you dislike the idea, I can tell him to wait."

He had not been the best cousin. He was an indifferent guardian at best. He was out of his depths in these domestic matters, but he could probably execute the duty better than most men if he chose to.

"Do you love him, Caroline?"

She looked at him as if he were a charming, quaint cottage. "Mama says any woman can love a man with nine thousand a year."

"I expect most can find a way." Only love, whatever incited it, was not really enough. "Do you want him as a lover?"

She turned very red. She glanced to the door, as if expecting her mother to sail through it to decry the scandalous question.

"It does matter, you know," he said. "Indelicate though the question may be, it is one that should be considered by girls when they face this decision. Since I am sure your mother did not bother to ask, I must."

She lowered her eyes. "I think so, yes."

He did not need her response. The echo of a stirring spoke in her more clearly than any words.

"I will be in the library. Send him to me. If I

conclude that he deserves your love, he will have my permission to propose."

He opened the door. Aunt Hen almost fell into his arms from where she had bent her ear to the keyhole. He stepped around her, to go and wait for whoever *he* was.

CHAPTER
FOURTEEN

The full moon cast a beautiful light in Leona's bed-chamber. She could see well enough to read if she wanted to.

That might be wise. It would be better to occupy her mind with another's words than to lie abed like this, half dreaming and half awake, plagued by images and thoughts that would not allow her to rest.

She looked down her body to the little writing table not far from the foot of her bed. The quill pen stood at attention, casting a large feather shadow on the wall. Near it, prominently visible in the way it reflected that moonlight, lay her last letter for *Minerva's Banquet*.

She had been remiss in her duty. Easterbrook had distracted her badly, and now she had no great revelations to report. Fate had handed her this opportunity to expose the men who quietly profited from opium smugglers, and she had squandered it. Her lessons about the opium trade would have less impact now. They would be remote and abstract problems.

Composing this final letter had been difficult. When

she had completed it, she felt as though she had written "The End" on her visit here. She should complete her family's business, and go home.

Easterbrook did not want that yet. Their love affair was still new and fresh. When his attention had turned to some other woman and he no longer wanted to ravish Leona Montgomery on sight—only then would he be agreeable to her embarking for China. Probably very agreeable.

She opened her eyes and watched the pattern of shadows on the wall. She endured a moment of cruel realism. Her heart hurt from the truth of it.

Would he insult her by giving her jewels, the way he obviously had done with that woman in the park? That necklace must have cost a fortune. One could probably buy a good-sized ship with the money it cost.

A woman knew exactly what could and could not be if she had an affair with a man like Easterbrook. There could be a degree of romantic dissembling. One might lose oneself in the excitement. Ultimately, however, a love affair that would end with a necklace was his intention from the start.

She had been weak with him, especially in his drawing room yesterday. The carnality of the encounter had shocked her once she left that house. However, even in her amazement, an arousal had begun again while she remembered it.

The absence of remorse was another point she pondered tonight. A fallen woman should have at least a little regret, or some anger at her seducer. She could not bring herself to feel either way. She had spent seven years wondering what might have been. Now she knew.

She tried to push images of him out of her head, because they only produced an odd mixture of emotions. Excitement to be certain. A tad of perplexity, because there was still much about him, in him, that she did not comprehend. Sorrow colored all the other reactions, however. Clouds of nostalgia waited on the edges of her heart, ready to drench her.

That pending sorrow would only increase with every encounter. She should explain to him, in a letter if necessary, why it would be unwise for her to allow this affair to continue. If she did that, the rest of her missions might be expedited. He would no longer put off helping her due to his desire to have her nearby for a while.

The feather beckoned. Now would be a good time, while the truth kept girlish flutters at bay. She would write to him and—

Her chamber door opened abruptly. A ghost suddenly appeared. Not a ghost. Isabella. Her long hair flowed and her white nightdress hung in diaphanous pleats.

"You must come," she whispered with urgency. "He is hurt and someone is here and I do not know what to do."

"Who is hurt?"

"Mr. Miller. You come now. I do not know what to do!"

Leona jumped out of bed. She grabbed a shawl and hurried after Isabella.

"What do you mean someone is here? Stay with me. Do not go on your own!"

"Hurry. I will show you." Isabella flew down the stairs.

Leona's bare feet hardly felt the carpet beneath them as she rushed to keep up. Panic beat in her chest and she did not try to be quiet. If someone had intruded, she trusted that knowing the whole house had been roused would urge him to flee.

"Here he is." Isabella stopped at the doorway of the library.

Leona drew up beside her. A chilled breeze billowed the drapes at one window, allowing enough light to see Mr. Miller's form on the floor. Deeper darkness outlined his head and formed a blotch on the back of his blond hair.

She bent down and felt Mr. Miller's pulse. "Light a lamp, Isabella. Bring some water and rags, then run to the carriage house and wake Mr. Hubson. Tell him to go to Easterbrook's house and ask for help."

Isabella tended to the lamp, then ran away. As soon as she returned with a basin of water, Leona knelt beside Mr. Miller. She pressed a damp compress to the wound on his head where someone had hit him hard.

She glanced around the chamber again. A drawer of the desk stood open. She got up and ran over and saw that the few pounds she tucked there were gone.

Then she saw the object on the floor.

Its wrapped base stuck out from beneath one of the drapes. She pulled the fabric back and lifted a crudely formed torch about a foot and a half long. The straw was damp along most of its length, but not at its end. Charred edges indicated it had been lit.

The intruder must have used this to see what he was

about. She knew a moment of paralyzing relief that it had gone out when he dropped it in his escape, before it set the drapes on fire.

A muffled groan broke into her attention. She dropped the torch on the hearthstone and went to Mr. Miller again. "Do not move, please. You are badly hurt and help is on the way."

She gently pressed the damp rag to the wound. He nodded subtly and closed his eyes again.

Easterbrook arrived with three footmen. As he strode up the stairs to the library, he ordered his servants to search the house and property.

Leona had never been so relieved to see anyone in her life. He joined her by Mr. Miller's side and examined the wound with amazingly gentle hands.

"Are you awake, Miller? If so I am going to sit you up against this chair here."

Mr. Miller proved both awake and angry. He allowed his lord to help him to sit, then scowled at the blood pooled five inches from his legs.

"I'd noticed that window could be reached from the small tree in the garden my first night here. I did not expect a thief to attack me if I found he'd taken advantage of it, though."

Easterbrook turned to Leona with a question in his eyes.

"A few pounds are missing from the desk," she said.

"I do not think that they came for a few pounds. A second intrusion, Leona. It does not bode well."

"We do not know for certain that there was a prior intrusion."

"We do now." He turned to Miller. "What brought you here?"

Miller's face found some color. "I heard something, I thought. I came to investigate and next thing I knew I was out."

Easterbrook gazed at him long and hard. Mr. Miller's face turned to stone. Easterbrook's attention shifted to the wall against which Isabella stood.

"You found him. Did you hear or see anything?"

Isabella's gaze remained fixed on the floor. "I thought that I heard a movement when I opened the door. Then something falling. I could be wrong. I am not sure. I saw him on the floor and became very afraid and confused."

"So a sound did not bring you here to begin with? It was only once you were in the chamber that you thought someone was in the house?"

Her head lowered more. "I—it is all confused now—perhaps I heard something before—I am not sure now."

The three footmen entered the library to report that no one was hiding in the house or in the garden.

"Help Miller back to Grosvenor Square. You will let them support you, Miller. Do not leave your chamber until a surgeon has seen that wound and given permission for you to be up and about. Take the carriage, then send it back to me in the morning."

After the servants left with Miller, Easterbrook spoke to Isabella. "It was fortunate that you raised the alarm. I must speak with your mistress now."

Isabella hurried away. Easterbrook paced the edges of the library, containing his anger with difficulty.

The hardness that he normally buried was having its way, and anyone who entered this chamber would feel it. He was thoroughly Easterbrook now, to an extent he had never allowed her to see before.

"It might have just been a thief looking for a few pounds," she said.

"Unlikely. If you doubted your instincts about the first intrusion, there is every reason to trust them now. The money was only taken to give others a reason to think that you were wrong if you claimed there was more to it. Which there was."

His pacing took him near the fireplace. He stopped and scowled at the object near his boot. "What the hell is this?"

"A torch, I think. I found it near the open window. Fortunately it went out."

He picked it up. He strode to the window and flipped the drape's fabric. There, on the inner surface, one could see soot.

Leona's nape prickled. Images invaded her head, of Miller being a bit longer in arriving here, and of drapery aflame, and fire spreading . . .

She walked over to inspect the drape. Fear struck deeper. Miller's intrusion might not have stopped it. Perhaps only Isabella's arrival had kept that torch from being held longer to the drape.

She and Isabella might have been trapped above while the flames fed on all the books and furniture. They might have remained ignorant of the conflagration until it was too late.

A hot fury broke in her, conquering her icy terror. "They must be very afraid if they would try to kill me."

"If the intention was to light the room on fire, they would have made a pile of books to burn. Look at the soot on the fabric. See the five dark spots. A hand extinguished the embers with the cloth, then deliberately left the torch to be found. The intention was not to burn down the house, Leona, but to frighten you with the evidence they could do it if they chose to."

They had succeeded. Fear clutched her again, and the anger could not hold it back. Chills vibrated through her. She hated how afraid she felt, and how vulnerable.

"You seem to surmise their intentions very quickly," she said.

He did not miss the thinly veiled accusation. He met her petulant tone with his own, tight, angry one. "As you would have surmised them once you were calm and considered the evidence. All the same, the risk of a fire was real, no matter their intentions. The torch could have easily set these drapes aflame."

She knew what this had been. She had seen it before. She had spent most of her youth battling the insidious insecurity and worry that it created.

Coercion. A sly threat intended to plant anxiety and fear and make her hesitant and careful. An outright attack would not eat at one's confidence as badly as the terror that some unknown person stalked and waited.

A man had been hurt tonight. Would it be Isabella next time, or Tong Wei when he returned? Or her? Would the house truly be set on fire next time?

A memory screamed, of being yanked through the

air as a horse clamored by. A brown horse. Tong Wei had spoken of a brown horse following them. . . .

"This is not their first gesture," she said. "It is only the most dangerous."

"What do you mean?"

She told him about the brown horse. And Tong Wei's conviction that someone watched her movements and her house.

Christian's face hardened to the firmest angles and his mouth to its tightest line. "I should have insisted that you move to Grosvenor Square."

"Your invitation had nothing to do with my safety. Do not imply that my refusal led to this night, as if it were my own fault."

He raised one hand in an impatient gesture. "You would have been protected. So far you have not been harmed, but—I will visit that house across the way when the carriage and footmen return." It sounded more like a threat than a plan. "Our intruder may have taken refuge there when Isabella raised the alarm."

"If so, he will be long gone before the carriage comes. I do not think you will find him, but if you want to go and look I will be safe until you return."

He hesitated, clearly torn. She could tell that he wanted to take some action, whether useful or not.

"Are you certain that you will not be distressed to be alone? The culprit is long gone, but you are unsettled."

"I am not as unsettled as you think," she lied. "Nor am I alone. Isabella is here. I would prefer that you go and see now. Perhaps you will learn something to ease my mind."

He peered at her as if he tried to determine if he

dared believe her. Or, perhaps, to check just how badly her mind needed easing.

"Go," she urged. "I would like to be reassured that I am not living across from my tormentors."

"You are admirably brave, Leona. Most women would refuse to be alone for a week."

He took his leave, with a promise to return in five minutes. She walked over to the hearth.

It was much easier to be brave when one held an iron poker in one's hands.

Christian barely contained his fury while he sought the garden gate and the back door of the house across the way. It was just as well that he had not taken one of the pistols from the carriage. If he had, any intruder lurking in this dark building would have fared far worse than Miller.

As soon as he entered the kitchen, he knew that the building now held two apartments. The kitchen had been obviously arranged to accommodate two cooks.

He assumed that the families were above. He was now the intruder in the night. All the same, he climbed the stairs to the ground floor and eased open a room in the front.

The moonlight allowed him to assess its contents quickly. Lightly patterned chairs surrounded a table that held a sewing basket. A delicate settee hugged the far wall. The evidence of feminine occupants reassured him. It was possible that the man of the house had been the one that Tong Wei saw watching, but the room almost appeared too domestic for nefarious purposes.

He climbed the stairs, passing the next level that would hold the private chambers of this first apartment, and went on to the next. Doors stood open here, revealing little furniture. He entered the chamber facing the street, and walked to the windows.

Across the way he could easily see the window to Leona's drawing room down below. He pictured Tong Wei standing sentry there, gazing up. The emptiness of this apartment all but screamed at him. There were no souls up here, sleeping or otherwise.

He walked to the fireplace and used the flint to light a lamp on a nearby table. He carried the lamp around the chamber, illuminating it better. Back near the windows he paused.

The lamp's glow revealed dark shadows on the floor. He bent and touched them. Ashes. Some of them still formed little mounds. He smelled his fingers. Someone had stood here a long while, perhaps often, smoking cigars.

He would find out if the family below let out these upper floors, or if an estate agent managed the whole premise for someone else. In the meantime—

He felt his coat. His palm landed on a flat, small object. How like Phippen to remember such a thing, even when his master was roused in the middle of the night for an emergency.

He removed the case from his coat, and thumbed out one of his calling cards. He set it on the sill of the center window.

Leona knew it was Easterbrook when she heard the steps on the stairs. She gripped the poker tighter anyway.

He did not stop in the library. Instead she saw him continue up to the next level. Perhaps he did not trust his servants to have searched well enough.

He finally joined her five minutes later. He was not as angry now, but she doubted his face would find softness for a long while. Still, taking some action, any action, had blunted the worst of the danger sharpening in him.

He paused when he saw her. Then he walked over and gently pried the poker from her hand. He set it back by the fireplace.

"You cannot stay here," he said. "Short of sending a small army of servants to live here with you, day and night, I cannot be confident of your safety. You must vacate this house."

She looked around the library. It was not really her home, but it had become familiar now, and served as a refuge. She did not feel so much the foreigner here. She guessed that the independence of this house meant even more to Isabella and Tong Wei.

"Please do not expect me to join you at Grosvenor Square. None of us belong there."

"If I say you belong there, you do. No one will treat you otherwise."

"You know what I mean."

He offered his hand to help her to rise. "Go back to your bed and try to sleep. I will be here until dawn, and make all arrangements. I have already told Isabella to pack for both of you."

Frightened though she was, she did not care for the

presumptions in his plans to protect her. "When I said do not ask me to go to Grosvenor Square, I did not mean that you should skip the request and just assume the result. I appreciate your help and concern, but the decision must still be mine."

"I can see that your spirit is returning. That is a good sign. However, you will depart this house tomorrow, in my carriage, with your lady's maid. You will leave London completely, and we will make sure it is known that you did."

"I do not want to leave London. I have matters to attend—"

"You will leave London, Leona. One way or another, you will. I will brook no argument on this."

No, he wouldn't. She still sensed a dangerous anger that he barely controlled. She doubted he would hear reason once he made a decision tonight.

"If I am leaving London, where am I going?"

"To my country estate. You will find it very pleasant."

"I think that I will find it an inconvenient interlude in performing my duty."

He strolled over, lamp in hand. He moved it slowly, so that its golden glow bathed her. "You look lovely in that modest nightdress, Leona." He reached out and touched one of her long curls. "Much like a girl I knew once in Macao. I am thinking that I should escort you upstairs, to make very sure that no one lurks up there."

Even the remnants of the night's fear could not stand against the way he stirred her with this sudden shift in attention. His mood added to the excitement. It enhanced his mystery and inserted a note of thrilling fear.

She stepped away. "You are guarding us tonight, remember? You must avoid distractions."

"I suppose so. Especially since I am certain that a similar distraction is why Miller ended up on the floor."

CHAPTER
FIFTEEN

Christian made short work of packing Leona off to the country soon after dawn. As soon as the coach rolled, he mounted his horse to return home. Once there, he climbed five flights of stairs and opened the door of a chamber on the first servant's level.

A pretty blond maid bent over a bed while she pressed a rag to Miller's head. From what Christian could see, the invalid was too aware that the ministrations brought the maid's round breast within tantalizing range of both his hand and mouth. The most primitive masculine heat filled the chamber, and the maid recklessly stoked the fire.

"Mending quickly, I see," Christian said. "It would not be wise to overdo it, though."

The maid startled badly. She blushed, dropped her rag, picked it up, curtsied, and rushed away.

Miller made a movement to stand. Christian gestured for him to stay put.

"Is Miss Montgomery well, sir?" Miller asked. "I

feared the shock was affecting her right before you arrived."

"Miss Montgomery is well, and safe, and on her way to Oxfordshire. With her maid." He settled his boot on the edge of Miller's bed and propped his crossed arms on his knee while he bent and hovered. "I need you to think very hard about what happened, Miller."

Miller pondered the matter. "I entered the library and noticed the window had been left open. Then I was hit from behind. It was as I told you before."

"You misunderstand me. I know the events. I am not hoping that you will remember more. I am telling you to think about what happened, and why."

Miller managed to appear perplexed despite the spiking caution leaking out of him. But then Miller was very good at dissembling.

"I was caught unawares."

"You were caught unawares because your thoughts were elsewhere. You went to the library to meet someone. A pretty someone with long, dark hair, in a white nightdress."

Miller's eyes bulged in shock. "Sir, I would never presume to—You accuse me of the worst disloyalty. I am most grieved, however, that you would cast aspersions on Miss Montgomery."

Oh, yes, young Miller was very good. "You are trying my patience. We both know Miss Montgomery was not the only pretty someone with long dark hair in a white nightdress last night. Nor was she the one who found you."

Miller touched his bandaged head and dramatically grimaced from the pain. He arranged to lose some color in his face. "She heard something and came to investigate."

"We will not argue our differing versions of the night's events. You are of no use to me if you are not beyond distraction when you serve me. If harm had come to Miss Montgomery, I would have seen to it that you held no more trysts, ever again, due to incapacity."

Miller truly blanched this time. "It will not happen again, sir."

"Good. I expect that you will be up and about in a day or so. I will have some matters for you to address then. I will leave instructions on your desk in the study for when you are ready."

He left Miller and went down to his apartments. He told Phippen to send for coffee, then made his way to the dressing room off the fencing chamber. He threw open the trunk, retrieved the leather half folio at its bottom, and carried it back to his chambers.

He settled in his favorite chair. It was time to read this, much as he would rather not. Despite last night, Leona had indicated that she was still determined to expose whoever could be exposed.

If there were any whoevers, and the evidence now suggested there really were, something might be found in these notes that would identify them, even if Leona's father had not realized it.

Three hours later he closed the folio. The anger of the night returned, only now it aimed in new directions, including those far into the past.

Reginald Montgomery had amassed an impressive amount of evidence to support his accusation that a secret company, based in London and owned by men of power, contracted ships for smuggling opium into China. By interviewing captains and bribing sailors, by obtaining records of ships' movements, he had created a chain to support his theory that lacked only the final links.

Worse, his investigations indicated that this company did not only operate in the East and transport opium, but also smuggled goods that avoided tariffs in the West Indies and around Europe and even into England itself.

That explained these bald threats against Leona. Her persecutors thought she knew more than she did. It was not only the exposure of opium smuggling into China that they feared, but the revelations of crimes closer to home, revelations that would cost them more than a few stained reputations.

Montgomery had been methodical and thorough. He provided lists of names, of captains who conspired for certain and others he only suspected, of customs officials being bribed, of merchants who accepted the goods.

Regarding the owners of the company, however, Leona's father only posited one name with any secure belief that he was correct. Indeed, he speculated that this man was the founder of the whole enterprise.

The Marquess of Easterbrook.

Leona kept eyeing Isabella. Isabella kept avoiding looking back. That alone made Leona think that Easterbrook's allusion to Mr. Miller's distraction might have been correct.

She said nothing about it the whole of their first day in the carriage. The coachman made a very leisurely pace, and they stayed the night at an inn outside the county border of Oxfordshire. When they resumed their journey the next day, she debated whether she should quiz Isabella about Mr. Miller.

It did not help that she was in no position to scold. Isabella knew what happened the night that Easterbrook stayed in their house. If the mistress dallied with a lord, the maid might think it fine to dally with a manservant. Yet the costs were different for the maid, and higher in the game of survival.

"Isabella, Lord Easterbrook said something that worries me. About you and Mr. Miller."

Isabella turned her gaze from the passing country-side. She looked over with an expression as bold as she had ever shown.

"Has Mr. Miller importuned you?"

"No."

That did not answer the bigger question. Isabella's eyes dared her mistress to be a hypocrite.

"I think that Mr. Miller is a very handsome man," Leona offered. "Perhaps not an especially kind one, though. I sense that he is somewhat ruthless, and too inclined to just take what he wants and not consider the consequences to others."

"He is kind when he wants to be, I believe. As for the rest, you describe most men. You describe my father. And the marquess, for example. At least Mr. Miller does not frighten me the way the marquess does."

"Perhaps you should be frightened. It is different here. You need to remember that. There are no concubines in

Europe. There are no rights for a woman who gives herself to a man outside of marriage, and a man can have only one wife. Her children have no rights either. Your father was European and that is why your mother had no security."

"Tong Wei reminded me of all of that already."

Leona frowned. "He did? When?"

"When I was excited that Edmund had visited you that day. He told me that you were not suitable to be such a man's wife, and that there was no other place for you that was respectable." She looked out the window again. "It is better in China. A woman can still have a place even if she is not suitable to be an important man's first wife."

Leona did not know what to say. This conversation had begun as a warning for Isabella, but was turning around and aiming elsewhere.

"Isabella—"

"He is kind to me. He speaks gently," she whispered. "He is a servant too." She blinked hard and licked her lips. "He notices me. I am not the scorned girl of impure blood to him."

The coach entered a little town just then. Leona joined Isabella at the window. Shoulder to shoulder, they peered out at the cottages and the lane of shops.

There was no use in warning Isabella to be wise. No matter what had happened between her and Mr. Miller in the past or what would happen in the future, no matter whether his motives were affectionate or ruthless, that handsome blond man was going to break Isabella's heart. It was already too late to stop that.

"Oh, my goodness."

Leona muttered her astonishment while she watched Aylesbury Abbey come into view.

"I do not think I have ever seen a house so big. I have heard of such palaces in China," Isabella said.

The house was massive. Nor did it look at all like an abbey. A fine-boned classicism governed its style, giving its extended height and wings an unexpected lightness and elegance.

Nothing thus far, not Easterbrook's huge house at Grosvenor Square, not the army of footmen in their antiquated livery, had prepared her for this.

Amidst her wonder, her conversation with Isabella echoed inside her. *Not suitable for such a man.*

She already knew that. She was not ignorant of status and what it meant in the world. It was just that this estate, and this "house" that loomed larger the closer they got, encapsulated and explained so much.

I am Easterbrook.

A little ritual attended their arrival. More footmen emerged from the house. One who accompanied her handed over a letter that was rushed inside. A man appeared. His air of authority marked him as someone of importance. He introduced himself as the house steward, Mr. Thurston, welcomed her, and escorted her inside.

A housekeeper waited to take her in hand. Isabella was herded away. After a gentle flurry of activity and commands, Leona found herself in an apartment with three rooms overlooking an extensive garden. The furnishings dazzled her so much that she barely heard the housekeeper explain the household routine.

The woman seemed to surmise the dismay underneath the amazement. "I would be happy to show you the property if you like. I find that visitors are more comfortable once the house is familiar to them."

Leona quickly refreshed herself, then joined the housekeeper for the tour. Her trader's mind calculated costs for the appointments and fabrics, only to reach sums so high that she entered a state of disbelief. The rooms themselves possessed perfect proportions that helped create an effect of calm grandeur.

She especially liked the library. Despite its large size and its soaring ceiling, it managed to appear an intimate, warm space. The warmth of the jewel-toned fabrics probably helped, as did the many mahogany cases filled with books. A variety of upholstered sofas and chairs and reading tables kept it from appearing as vast as it truly was. Handsome landscape paintings decorated the walls.

"The marquess prefers this room," the housekeeper confided. "When he visits he will sit here of an evening. His mother was a writer. She used to spend her days at the writing table over there. Lost to the world, she was, as she wrote those poems."

Leona pictured Easterbrook in dishabille, by the fire, oblivious to the way his appearance spoke of his indifference to his wealth and position, and also his utter security in both.

"Does he visit often?"

The housekeeper shook her head. "He did come down for a wedding last January. The cousin of Lord

Hayden's wife was married in Watlington nearby. A real country wedding it was, and the marquess condescended to attend, which was all the talk in the county. Not like him to accept such invitations. A very private man, the master is."

When the tour ended, Leona asked to return to the library. "How do I have a letter posted?"

"Give it to the butler and it will be done. There is paper in all the writing tables and secretaires. Will you be taking supper in your chambers or the dining room?"

Leona pictured herself alone at the banquet table that seated forty, sipping soup with six footmen in attendance. "My chambers, thank you."

The housekeeper left her and she sat down at the writing desk to compose a letter to Lady Lynsworth. She needed to find out if Tong Wei would return to London soon. Aylesbury Abbey was a palace with every comfort and luxury to be imagined, but she did not want to visit longer than she had to.

Isabella arrived to prepare Leona for the evening. She reported that she had been given a fine room up above, on the same level as the most important servants.

"The housekeeper told me to inform her if anyone treats me with disrespect," she said with wonder. "She said the marquess specifically instructed her to help me."

Leona thought that remarkable. Despite the danger still coiling out of him when he sent them off in his coach, he had taken the time to add instructions about Isabella in his letter to the steward and the housekeeper.

He had been sensitive to the ways Isabella's mixed race might make her an outcast in the other servants' eyes.

It was the kind of act that made Easterbrook impossible to understand. He could cut society right and left, he could be ruthless in his pursuits and arrogant in his assumptions, he could be self-absorbed to the point of rudeness, but he had these unexpected impulses of endearing thoughtfulness.

A fine meal arrived. The servants set a little table in the apartment's sitting room, near the window overlooking the garden.

"You may join me if you like, Isabella."

"There is a large table for us below. I will go there if I may. One of the maids is going to show me some of this palace's many chambers and buildings. You do not think that is wrong, do you? It is permitted, I hope."

"I suspect that none of the servants here enters places that are forbidden. You do not have to come back tonight. I will manage myself, or call for help if I need it."

She sent Isabella off to explore the servants' world. She imagined the extensive staff sitting at that table below, and all the talk and laughter. Isabella would have many new experiences here and meet many new people.

Her mistress, however, would take her meals alone, while she gazed out at a spectacular but empty garden.

By the time the servant cleared away the remains of the supper, dark had fallen. Leona had also made a few decisions.

She would write to Easterbrook and explain that being sequestered at this house did not suit her. In the least she would demand to know how long he expected her to remain here. The latter point had never been discussed. In his haste to send her away, and with her emotions still jumbled from the night's events, she had never even asked about it.

Now, however, she concluded this flight had been too precipitous, and a mistake. She might as well have published a notice, telling these men that they had won.

She went down to the library. She would write a firm letter to the marquess, give it to the butler, and lay plans for an escape should her demands be ignored. It might be wise to choose a few books to occupy her useless hours until she learned which course she would be taking.

On her way down, she passed an upstairs sitting room. No one occupied it, but a low fire burned and three lamps had been lit. She imagined the servants going around every evening, year in and year out, preparing the home for a family that never came.

It was the same in the library. She opened the door to the glow from the fireplace. High-backed upholstered chairs angled toward it, creating an appealing but empty domestic vignette. A lamp sat on one of the writing tables, as if anticipating her intentions.

She walked toward it, then stopped when a movement caught her eye. A long leg encased in a tall black boot stretched out from one of the chairs near the fireplace. She walked around the chair to investigate.

Easterbrook sat there in a lazy, relaxed sprawl. If he had appeared a pirate at their reunion, he looked like a highwayman now. A black riding coat matched the rest of his garments, except the white shirt open at the neck. His hair still showed the effects of fast riding, and tumbled around his face in reckless waves.

He brooded over something while he watched the low flames that fought the spring night's chill. The golden light made him dangerously attractive, and his eyes deeply mysterious.

He noticed her but displayed no surprise. His gaze drifted over her in a line much like the sinuous, seductive lock that fell on his temple.

Trembling thrills followed similar serpentine paths inside her. He knew how she reacted when he looked at her like this. She did not doubt that. He had named her desire from the start and used it shamelessly.

She had been very stupid. She should have assumed he would join her here. In her fear after the attack on Mr. Miller, she had not been very clever, or nearly skeptical enough. Now it entered her mind that the intrusion into her house had suited Easterbrook's purposes all too well.

"I did not realize that you would be visiting the country too," she said.

"Did I neglect to mention that? I suppose that I did. You cannot be too surprised, however."

No, not too surprised. Nor had he schemed to trap her here deliberately, where they would be alone together for heavens knew how long. He had merely taken advantage of the emergency that brought him to her house two nights ago, and of his resolve to tuck her away somewhere safe.

Her certainty about his motives surprised her. She had no proof he had not been the one to send men stealing into her house to begin with. He might have decided to frighten her so badly that she would allow him to pack her off to where she could ask no more questions.

She did not think he would have allowed Mr. Miller to be harmed, but that detail was not the real reason that she believed he had not schemed so ignobly.

The truth was that her heart trusted him even if her mind still weighed and wondered.

She admitted that to herself. She squarely faced what it implied. As she absorbed the significance, a wall of protection that she clung to crumbled, leaving her grasping at nothing. Vulnerability flooded her, and love flowed on its currents.

The poignant emotion did not totally bedazzle her. Another truth whispered too, and she could not deny its voice. Even while she allowed her heart to freely feel what it had yearned to experience for years, she saw the future.

Isabella was not the only woman whose heart would inevitably break.

CHAPTER
SIXTEEN

Leona sat in the other chair near the low fire. "Is Mr. Miller better?"

"Mr. Miller should be mended enough to leave his bed in a day or two. I spoke with him about Isabella, by the way," Easterbrook said.

"So you are certain that he entered that library for an assignation?"

"Very certain."

"Did you warn him off?"

"It is not for me to do so. I did explain that his amorous pursuits must not interfere with his duty."

She could taste Isabella's eventual disappointment now, because it also would be her own. "He was only there several times. They could have spent very little time together, and yet . . . I think that she has lost her heart to him."

"I am sure that she has. If it helps at all, I am also certain that he thinks of her affectionately, which is unusual for Mr. Miller."

"It does ease my worry now, but it will not help in

the end. No matter what his affection, she cannot stay here with him. She does not belong in his world."

"I doubt Mr. Miller had thought about that yet."

"No, but she has. Women always do."

They looked into the fire, neither seeking the other's eyes. The mood grew too pregnant with unspoken words. She sought a way to dispel the heavy air.

"Once more you express complete certainty about your view of people's hearts, Easterbrook," she teased. "I am beginning to think it is not just normal arrogance on your part."

"I am not certain at all about you, Leona. If you were any other woman, I would know if you are glad that I followed you here. With you I either have to ask, or use pleasure to ensure that you are glad enough by morning." He smiled. "I don't even know which of those choices you would prefer I take."

Rather suddenly they were down to very frank talk. Normally she preferred that, but tonight, with her heart fluttering so badly and a girlish excitement threatening to block all sense, she could not think clearly enough to spar with him.

"Nor do I know which I would prefer. I am confused about everything concerning you."

Terribly confused now, sitting within an arm's reach of him. It was wonderful to want him and love him but also distressing to know that it would be a mistake to be glad he had followed her.

They sat like two friends passing an hour. He did nothing to begin a seduction, and yet a low stimulation already hummed in her, flushed now by affection that warmed the arousal in perilous ways.

She was beyond dissembling or being clever. Perhaps in a few hours she would reclaim that part of herself, but here, now, in the dark and silence, basking in his sensual, masculine presence, she could not defeat the way her heart urged her to rashness.

"What would make you less confused, Leona?"

What would make her less confused? The question begged for more analysis than she could muster.

"Answers," she said. "Answers to many questions about you, and about the past and now, and about your mind and your heart."

"I am not accustomed to answering questions, let alone many of them."

"Yes. Of course. You did ask your own question, however. Do not blame me if you do not care for my attempt to answer it."

He smiled at the rebuke. "Do you think we could start with a mere one question tonight? There must be some that confuse you more than others."

"That is true. One in particular should be asked before this night gets much older."

"Then let us start with that."

It required a few moments to work up the courage to put it into words. The answer might be devastating.

"What do you want with me?"

"That is really two questions, depending on how it is interpreted."

She felt her face warm at the boldness of the second meaning he inferred. She had intended to ask why he was bothering with *her*. He had heard another, specific question that emphasized the "what" and all its possible answers.

He turned very serious. She could see no humor in him now. No lightness.

"I never forgot you, Leona. Not your vivid spirit or quick temper or expressive eyes. I always knew we would meet again. If my pursuit has been too insistent, it is because despite all the changes the years brought, some things did not change at all. I had waited too long to experience them again." He reached for her hand and held it in the gap between their chairs. "You asked your question as if any woman would do, as if I trouble myself with you for no purpose. To me, you are unique. You knew me, and understood what you knew, better than anyone. I think that you do now as well."

It touched her that he spoke so openly. It was more of a declaration than she ever expected. But it saddened her that this man who was so contained and confident believed that her incomplete understanding was the best the world had ever offered him.

"Now, as to the other question, *what* do I want with you, I dare not answer with complete honesty because you might run away like you used to." His eyes turned a little devilish. "In bed, I want whatever you will allow. I want you for as long as I can convince you to stay. Would you prefer it if I wanted more?"

The question, asked so casually, stunned her.

"I know that I was the first with you," he said. "I am supposed to offer marriage. I have considered it, but there are reasons why such a match would be ill-advised. However, if you want a proposal—"

"No. I am not expecting anything. Least of all that. I know why it is . . . impossible. Certainly for you. For me as well. I could never abandon my brother like that." She had never allowed herself to consider such a thing. A silent litany of reasons why it could never be shouted and drowned out the mere thought even now.

"Not impossible. Just . . ."

"Ill-advised. I understand. Truly."

"No, you do not. Truly. Perhaps I will try to explain sometime." His hand held hers more firmly. "Are you less confused now?"

"Somewhat."

"Then since I have summoned my better nature this long, I will stay on the honorable path. I will ask instead of act. Are you glad that I followed you here?"

She rather wished he had chosen to be dishonorable. Now the decision was hers. This conversation had done little to encourage a sound one.

"I am still settling that question," she said.

He took it very well. He stood. That brought him closer to her, so close that her heart rose and flipped. He looked down and she sensed that dark power surrounding her. It was a very brief attempt at invasion, but it left her mesmerized and helpless.

He still held her hand. "I will allow you to ponder the question on your own. I will set aside my inclination to tip the argument in my favor the only way I know how."

"That is good of you."

"I doubt that I will be so noble for more than a day. If you conclude I must be warned off, you had better settle in that direction quickly."

He began to let go of her. She tightened her own fingers so he could not.

"It truly is good of you, Christian. Very kind, really.

I have more than proven how weak I am with you already."

"And I have been ruthless as a result. I succumbed to a bad family trait, to make sure I got what I wanted." He kissed her hand, and released it. "Unless I want to succumb again, I must leave you now."

He was an idiot. A fool.

He slammed his fist against the sill of the window where he stood looking out at nothing.

No, not nothing. Above him, out of sight, another window emitted the faintest light. It fell like a faerie glow on the garden. The evidence that Leona was still awake made his jaw clench.

So much for the great conundrum. Hell, when she tallied up the good and the bad, the pleasure and the cost, then added in the potential misery and scandal of an affair with the half-mad marquess, her shrewd mind would settle the question in the way he least wanted.

He had almost killed himself riding cross-country to get here tonight. Even his dislike of this house could not diminish his impatience. It was a miracle that he had not slung her over his shoulder and taken her to bed as soon as he saw her.

Instead, in a fit of sentimentality that came from God knew where, he had all but told her to throw him over. As if she wasn't going to do that soon enough anyway, without his leading her to it.

She had appeared stunned at his reference to marriage. Appalled. If the notion had ever entered her head she had discarded it long ago.

Just as well. Doing the right thing often resulted in living the wrong thing forever. All the luxury in the world would not make that life any easier. That was one calculation on Leona's part that pleasure had not obscured.

He glanced to the valise on the floor, still sitting where he had dropped it upon arriving. The servant who had trailed him upstairs to play valet almost fainted when a snarl greeted his attempts to unpack it. Inside was that damned leather notebook.

The notebook was one excellent reason why a proposal would be ill-advised. If she learned its contents, or if she found her answers some other way, she would be certain he had gone to Macao to betray her father.

There were plenty of other reasons too. Leona had compiled a long list of her own should he want it.

She thought him willful, peculiar, rude, conceited, and arrogant—and those were the opinions she had actually voiced. One could only imagine the ones she politely kept to herself. She did not treat him carefully, as if he were half mad, but she considered his habits unbearable.

I will not join you in that isolation.

The night suddenly got darker. The low light leaking from the window above disappeared. Desire carved through him with a vengeance, mocking the stupid hope that light had given him.

He opened the window to the chilled air. He stripped off his clothes and stood there naked. The cool breeze did not help. He burned from the inside. The fire in his blood and head would not go away.

He strode to the bed, feeling more inner chaos than

he had since he had left Macao. Anger at what he was, fury at his impotence to change it, alarm at how fate had played a cruel joke that would never end—it swept him as he lay beneath the sheet and faced a sleepless night.

With the dark emotions came the insidious craving to escape into paradise. That was what opium seemed to offer, and still did at moments like this. He was in hell but heaven was in the pipe, waiting to provide solace. For a brief time, while in opium's haze, the world was simple and perfect and he was normal and full of potential.

He rarely experienced this craving now. Normally he could seek the dark center and find peace, but that would not work tonight. All the same he controlled his breathing the way Tong Wei had taught him.

It sustained him through the peak of the wave that the hunger formed, through that instant of unbearable physical madness when a man will sell his soul for relief. Then, also as Tong Wei had promised, the worst was over even as it happened. The crest of the craving signaled its retreat.

The breathing had not been enough to break the chains that were forming in Macao. Even meditation had not been enough. True control had required he gaze a long time into the mirror Leona had held up that night.

Accepting the past as irrevocable had been a big part of his victory. Accepting his inheritance in full had been the rest.

This house was the least of it. The title, the wealth— all of that hid the darker legacy. He may have received the estate, but he had also received the worst of his family's blood.

It might have been tolerable without his mother's curse. If he had not sensed the extent of his father's ruthlessness, he could have chosen to ignore his own inclinations in that direction. He could have even pretended that the old man was not as bad as everyone feared.

If he had not watched his mother retreat from everyone and everything, if he had not watched her isolation bring her to the brink of true madness, he might have overcome his fear of his odd gift earlier too.

He saw her sitting at that library desk, lost to them. The rumor started that his father had locked her away. Her eldest son knew differently. She had just withdrawn into the world of her mind where only her own melancholy had to be accommodated.

He knew the temptation to hide the way she had done. Hadn't he tried to run away himself? From the chaos that came from knowing too much, and more than others ever did. From the sense of having no identity after his father died, because he dared not admit that he shared too many similarities with the last marquess.

Whatever you run from is inside you.

The craving subsided, but not the chaos. His thoughts ran wild through past and present, as if he had a fever. He saw Leona in Macao and then in the library below. He experienced again her trembling when he first kissed her years ago, and when he first took her last week.

She would leave. No matter what else happened, she would go.

Maybe she feared he would not allow that. Leona still read his heart better than anyone ever had. She probably sensed in him the temptation to do whatever was necessary to keep her, but she would never understand the reason.

He had spent two years finding his true self, but in reality the man who returned to England had been a feint, a construction designed for survival. Tonight was proving that.

He was only his true self, he only really lived, when he was with her.

CHAPTER
SEVENTEEN

It was astonishing. Amazing in its way. Here she
stood, almost breathless with excitement, but inside
her soul she experienced total calm.

She opened her door. No one was about. She walked
to the stairs and descended. Her bare feet sank into the
deep strip of carpet that silenced her steps.

She knew where Easterbrook's apartment could be
found. She had noted it more specifically than she ought
when the housekeeper gave the tour. The truth hiding
inside her had counted the steps to her own chambers,
and mapped the corridors and memorized the doors
while the housekeeper chatted away.

She pushed at the entry door to his private rooms.
All was dark, but she felt his presence. She peered into
the corners, to see if perhaps he sat in the blanketing
blackness.

She padded across to another door, one that was
ajar. The vaguest light filtered out that crack. She gazed
into his bedchamber. Like her own it faced the gardens,
and the drapes had not been drawn. Moonlight flowed

in, giving form to the bed and its hangings, and the moldings and furniture. And to him.

He was not sleeping. He was in bed, though, almost sitting against the pillows, his naked chest carved by the moonlight and one leg bent atop the white sheet that covered most of his lower body.

He did not move when she entered. He did not even greet her. He just watched while she set her lamp on a table.

The room quaked with what was in him. She recognized the turmoil. She thought Easterbrook had tamed that confusion, but tonight, for some reason, it had triumphed again. She wondered if he would reveal the same sardonic humor that Edmund could employ to mask his soul's disorder.

"I am grateful that you are here," he said.

He sounded sincere. But then a man expecting pleasure would probably be grateful at the proof he would not be denied.

She could not worry about his reasons. She barely knew her own. It had not been her mind that urged her to come to him, after all. It had argued forcefully that she not do this.

A detailed accounting had been taken up in her chamber, listing all the costs. The final sum should have discouraged any woman. Instead her heart had noted the amount, then swept it away in an outpouring of yearning.

She would not pick up the debate again. Yes, this was a mistake. Yes, she would regret it soon enough. Yes, too many questions remained unanswered. Yes, even the memories might not survive after the world demanded its payment.

"I knew I should settle the question differently, but could not." She walked to the side of the bed, and turned down the sheet. "I only ask one promise from you first."

He waited to hear it, with no reaction.

"You must allow me to leave when it is time. You must help me finish what I came to do, then allow me to return to my brother. He needs me. I have duties to my family that are equal to yours."

"I cannot permit you to walk out that door now that you are here. You have your promise, but do not expect me to like it."

"I do not require that you like it. I may not either. It is how it must be, however. I must not forget who I am."

She went to the window, and closed it to the night's chilled breeze.

"You are lovely in the moonlight, Leona. You always were. Stay there a moment so I can see you."

She wondered what he saw. Not the girl who had gone into the garden that night in Macao, even if her hair fell like it did that night, and the white garment was much the same.

He had kissed her then. It had been too long coming, and she had almost wept at the beauty of the intimacy. She had never forgotten that kiss.

"Take off your nightdress."

His command made it clear that she was no longer that girl, and that she had come here for more than one sweet kiss.

She plucked the ribbons of her simple nightdress.

The gap at her neck grew until it sagged on her shoulders. She peeled it down and let it fall to the floor.

She gazed out the window because, for all her boldness tonight, she was not so experienced that she could stand naked like this and not feel embarrassed. The vulnerability contained erotic depths, though. His attention already fanned the low burn that had tortured her since she noticed him in that chair by the fire. Its tongues of anticipation flicked at her without mercy.

"I have imagined you like that more often than you can know. I see you in a moonlit garden, but you are naked like this, and perfectly beautiful."

"You imagined the girl I no longer am."

"You were not really a girl. You always had a woman's manner about you. A woman's way of understanding people."

Whatever stormed in him had calmed, but hardly disappeared. It remained, a distant rumbling that wanted to grow.

"Come here and lie with me."

She padded across the chamber. She climbed onto the bed and lay beside him. He turned and braced his weight on one arm so he could look at her. He caressed down her body.

She closed her eyes and savored the lively reaction of her skin to his firm, warm palm.

"There are things I should tell you. Explain to you," he murmured.

"What things?"

His head dipped and he kissed her. There would be no explanations now.

She expected an explosion of passion like the last

time. She expected to be pulled into a mindless state of hunger and sensation. Instead he caressed her slowly. He purposefully delayed surrendering to the crescendo that drove them in the past.

The pleasure grew beautifully, as if he lowered her into a warm bath of sensuality. Her body responded more thoroughly to this subtle, nuanced seduction, until all her consciousness followed the paths of his hand and mouth.

He moved on top of her, and settled between her spread legs. His arms surrounded her, supported her, and lifted her to his kisses. Slowly, so slowly, his mouth burned and bit and explored.

She clung to him and explored too. She tried her own kisses, tasting him with mouth and tongue. He encouraged her, and seemed pleased with her efforts.

The tide rose languidly but it rose all the same. Her body grew impatient for more, and frustrated from the tense craving twisting ever tighter inside her. She felt his arousal near her thigh, hard and big, so tantalizingly close. It maddened her. She tried to wiggle down just enough, so that he would press her where that needy pulse throbbed.

"You are too impatient," he chided quietly. "Tonight of all nights, it would be better not to encourage me. If I succumb to what is in me, I may be too rough." He removed her arms from his body, and placed them on the bed so they flanked her head. "I want to enjoy you at my leisure tonight anyway."

She took stock of her position. She could not even touch him now. "You want me to just lie here like this? Completely still, without moving?"

She felt his smile against her neck while he nuzzled her. "I do not think you will be still for long. Let us see if you can manage it for a while, though."

She did not manage long at all. When his kisses moved to her breast and his tongue tantalized the tips, she arched. The titillations became a luscious torture. She barely resisted the urge to embrace him so she would not be so helpless to it. He unwound his own embrace and closed his hands on her wrists, removing that option. He demanded that she submit to his control of her pleasure.

She opened her eyes and glanced at her wrists, then at the way her breasts rose full and firm. His soft waves brushed her skin. His teeth closed gently, causing a sharp arrow to penetrate the slyer sensations. It aimed low, increasing the intensity of desire that frustrated her.

The tide rose ever higher, saturating her with need. She could no longer control her reactions. She began sinking into that dark place where sensation ruled, and where pleasure became her whole world. Still he teased at her, luring her deeper, his tongue laving her nipples.

She moved. His weight and hold restrained her but she found a way. She bent her knees and raised them so they flanked his hips. She sought a way to demand relief, completeness. Groans formed in her head, and became impatient, needy, urging sounds. The pleasure kept intensifying, focusing, and collecting low and full.

He released her wrists. She reached to embrace him but it was too late. His shoulders lowered as his kisses moved down her body. He held her hips while his mouth pressed its heat on her stomach and flanks.

Then there was no weight. No hold. She opened her eyes. He braced himself above her on rigid arms flanking her body. He gazed down at her spread thighs and splayed knees and the way her position begged for him.

Her mind chanted pleas and urges. She wanted him to touch her, to caress her, to fill her. She wanted him so badly she could barely stay sane. She moaned her frustration when he moved again, to kneel between her legs. His long caresses on her legs seemed designed to madden her.

The sight of him awed her, though. Kneeling tall, his torso sculpted by the dim light, he looked strong and hard and in command of this night and her. His tousled hair made him appear less than civilized, free of laws and rules, and wonderful in his differences. Her heart filled even more because this pleasure was shared with *him*.

His caresses lightened, softened. His fingertips became feathers on her knees and thighs. The lightest kisses joined his touch. She could not breathe and her gasps sounded louder. She watched that dark head bending, felt those feathers teasing, and her legs spread all the more.

So close. So close. She clutched at the sheets while her skin became more sensitive. Her body wept, and it felt as if those feathers would never stop and she would die from how needful they made her.

The kisses became less random. They moved in a path down her thigh. She knew their destination. Her body knew. The notion shocked her but her legs parted all the more. The first touch, the first kiss, sent her consciousness spinning, spinning, moaning with gratitude and triumph.

A new torture. Pleasure so intense it was unnatural. She could not control her body. She rocked and cried and it seemed as if the sensations only grew and deepened until they encompassed her, surrounded her, and vibrated from their source where gentle fingers and masterful kisses did their wicked worst.

Her climax broke hard. He made it go on and on. He would not let her hide from it, retreat from it. The quake seemed to continue forever.

He took her then. It was hard and rough as he had warned. She absorbed him and let him release the storm. She sensed it in him, felt the turmoil darkening the pleasure, saw the relief spreading with each thrust. She did not accept him passively. Instead her body stirred again, and the shivers of release grew once more until she merged with him in a ferocity of emotion and need.

Everything burst at the same time. The hunger, the pleasure, the darkness. She held onto him during a long moment when everything except their essences ceased to exist.

The darkness dissolved. Her soul found her body. She embraced a physical man again.

It was not a normal kiss that he gave her then. She could not name how it was different, but it moved her so profoundly that her eyes burned.

He moved aside and held her in a silent peace. She lay with her head against his chest while his arms embraced her closely. The heart beneath her ear sounded very familiar, as if she listened to her own life pulse.

His mouth rested in a long, unending kiss on her crown.

There were no questions now. There was no confusion.

They went for a long walk the next morning. They strolled through the formal gardens where an army of men tended to rosebushes and other plantings, and past fields being prepared for a kitchen garden. Finally they reached some woods.

"My cousin Caroline will be getting married. I had to meet with her intended, after you left me that day she and Hen intruded."

It charmed her, how he shared this family news. It fit the morning. Last night a deeper understanding had developed between them. Although born of passion and her decision to go to him, it affected more than their physical intimacy.

"Is he worthy?"

"He appears earnest. My aunt is happy because he has nine thousand a year. Already the house is calmer now that it is settled." He shrugged. "It was not a duty that I wanted. I am not even her guardian. Hayden is absorbed by his family, however, so I agreed to do it."

"Caroline was probably very grateful."

"She kindly offered to spare me, as if she knew my inclinations better than she has cause to."

"I think she may have better cause than you can guess. You touch the world, Christian, even if you do not want it to touch you."

She received a sharp, thoughtful look for that, but

his expression quickly softened. "At least I am confident that it is a good match. He loves her so much that he will not mind when she reveals her true self. She has been hiding that, due to her mother. She is not nearly as vague and unformed as she appears."

"Perhaps she has already revealed herself. Maybe that is why they are in love." She could not resist poking him, literally and otherwise. "You once more are uncommonly sure of your opinions—that they are in love, that Caroline has been hiding. Would that every girl had a cousin so definite about her future happiness."

He reacted more thoughtfully than her playful tease warranted. He strolled on, pensively.

He drew her to a spot where the treetops broke to allow sunlight to filter down. He stopped there and took her in his arms.

"I do not merely think my opinion of that match is accurate. I know it is."

"Just as you knew Alexia would give birth to a boy?"

"This is different. That involved events. This is only about the feelings of two people. I told you last night that I would like to explain some things. This is one of them."

He appeared so serious. So . . . vulnerable. That was an odd thought to have about this man of all men, but it entered her mind despite his stern expression. She dared not make light of whatever it was that he thought he now revealed, even if it was probably nothing more than a man's excuse for his presumptuous arrogance.

"Then explain it, Christian. Right now I understand nothing."

"I will try, although I never have put it into words before." A frown formed. His attention turned inward, as if he sought a means to express something impossible to articulate.

"My perceptions are better than most when it comes to people, Leona. I realized this difference when I was around twelve years old. Until then I assumed everyone could be very sure of another person's intentions and feelings, and I did not understand why people acted as if they were not."

"It could be that others did not assume their perceptions were accurate, as you do."

"You are not hearing me, perhaps because it is too strange a thing to fathom," he muttered. Then he spoke firmly. Almost angrily. "I do not assume. I know. It is just there. I have only to pay attention to be very sure. Even when I don't pay attention, even when I take pains not to know, it is in the air waiting for me to recognize it, like a soundless noise."

He watched to see her reaction. She tried to keep her expression impassive. He described something bizarre, yet it was clear that he truly believed he possessed this ability.

He shook his head in exasperation. "Now you think I am mad too. It was a mistake to speak of it."

"Not mad. Not at all. It is just—are you saying that you read others' minds? You know their thoughts?"

"I know their emotions. My interpretations of the reasons for the emotions, and the thoughts that accompany them, can be in error, although with experience they rarely are now."

He released her from his embrace and took her hand again. They returned to the canopy of treetops.

She knew that he had confided something very important. If he had never voiced it before, there was a reason. His reference to madness distressed her. He always joked about that rumor. Now it appeared that there was something in him that made him wonder if it were true.

"You realized when you were twelve, you say. It must have been frightening, to see a difference in yourself at such a young age."

"It was hell," he snarled. He took a deep breath and controlled whatever memories her question evoked. "However, it was also a relief. It explained many things. I was able to avoid misunderstandings after that. With time I learned that this sensibility is unusual only in its degree. I realized that almost everyone possesses it to some extent. I just do more than most."

"Still—I do not comprehend what you describe, Christian. I would like to, if you are willing to attempt to explain it further."

"I would if I could, Leona. I am at a loss about how to, however. It would be better to forget I spoke about it at all."

They could not do that now. He must know that. "Do you feel what others feel?"

"I do not speak of sympathy, but empathy. Have you ever passed a funeral carriage, and sensed the sorrow of the family inside? You do not share the sorrow, but you know it is there and feel its presence. When Isabella came to you the other night, did you not sense her fear even before she spoke or you saw her expression?"

She began to see what he meant. Sometimes another person's emotions were in the air and one could not avoid recognizing them.

It was that way with him, sometimes. Certainly she possessed a heightened sensibility when it came to his desire. It affected her physically, and was almost tangible between them. Even his darker moods—she did not have to see anger in him to know when the storms gathered. She had sensed them even before she entered his bedchamber last night.

The implications startled her. "If it is always there for you, then whenever you are with someone their emotions are present too."

"Yes."

When he was a child, he would have known his parents' feelings toward him. Not just the loving ones, but the angers and disappointments, and the indifference, if it existed. As a young man, he would have sensed every girl's reaction when he met her, and every friend's truth or falseness.

Even now, with his family, with his peers, he would know more than they might want. More than he might want.

"At first it sounds wonderful, to have such insights. However, I can see how it can be a curse," she said. "There is some usefulness in how people often pretend with each other. I am not sure we could all live together without some dissembling."

She thought about being able to sense anyone else's emotions at any time. It would be horrible if she could not choose to be spared. It was a wonder he had not gone mad after all.

"There is power in it, of course," she said. "Dangerous power, if one was of a mind to use it."

He barely hesitated, but the pause was still there. "Yes."

"There could also be pain, I would think."

The pause stretched longer this time. "Yes."

"Is this why you retreat from the world? To spare yourself? To spare others?"

"In part. I suspect that I would have had a low tolerance for society's games even if I were the most normal of men, however."

Except that he did not entirely withdraw. She could not ignore what that meant.

"Forgive me for now contemplating the extent of my disadvantage, Christian. I am remembering every emotion I have experienced while near you. I am trying not to resent that you did not give me fair warning. I think that a stern scold is in order."

"Some people are immune. More guarded perhaps. You are one such person. I do not intrude on your soul, Leona. I swear that I have never had that ability, or that temptation, with you. Not now. Not in Macao."

It was one of her appeals, she suspected. Perhaps her only appeal. Most people yearned to know the minds of their intimate friends. Easterbrook probably found ignorance a respite and relief.

"Have you ever misused this? I can think of ways one might."

"I confess that it has allowed me to have my way with women very easily."

"I suspect it still does. That was very bad of you. They did not stand a chance."

"I like to think that any sins that resulted from knowing their pleasures too well were forgiven by the pleasure itself." He did not appear the least contrite. "And I will admit that I won more money at gambling than I ought when I was at university."

"As with the last, this was wrong but hardly dangerous."

"The more sinister temptations I managed to thwart for the most part, and now I avoid them."

But they existed. Of course they would. It would be difficult not to exploit such an invasive advantage. The struggle against that lure might be the worst part of this odd aptitude that he professed.

"Mostly now I use it to indulge my curiosity about people. Especially if I feel obligated to make a judgment about them."

"Such as the young man asking for Caroline's hand?"

"I think that I can be excused there. My cousin's future happiness was at stake."

"But you do not have such an advantage with me, you said. Not at all?" Of course he did not. He would have remained silent otherwise. And he had sworn. But . . .

"If I did, I would know if you are thinking I am some unnatural monster right now, Leona. Or worse, pitying me for having an incurable affliction."

His suggestions horrified her. She wished that he could read her emotions just this once, so he would know for certain that she did not harbor such reactions.

"I do not find you unnatural. I know you are not at all mad either. I am glad you told me. I understand

Edmund much better now, and Easterbrook too." She laid her hand on his face and peered up at him. "Nor do I pity you, but I suspect that this was a terrible curse when you were young, and still a bad one even now, when you so admirably accommodate it. I do not think I could live with this."

He held her hand to his face, then turned to kiss it. He closed his eyes and his mouth pressed her palm for a long while. "I trust you to keep this to yourself, Leona."

"Does no one else know? Not even with your brothers?"

"They would not understand."

Yet he had thought she might. He had trusted her with this secret. He had risked that her reaction might be horror, or mockery, or even fear.

She reached up with both her hands and cupped his face. She lowered it so she could kiss him. She made very sure that it was not a kiss of pity.

Desire sent its rivulets down her body. They stayed like that a long time, sharing the mutual fire that needed no special perceptions to recognize in each other.

CHAPTER
EIGHTEEN

L eona never mentioned the conversation in the
woods again. Christian saw her contemplating the
revelations sometimes, however.

A question would enter her eyes and she would try
to guess what he was perceiving. It happened once
when a servant entered a chamber where they sat, but
mostly she checked to make sure that he was not knowing too much about her.

He did not blame her for wondering about him, no
matter which way that wondering went. It moved him
that she had at least tried to believe him, and had not
judged too harshly.

His contentment deepened over the days because of
it. The peace he knew in her presence increased tenfold
now that he had confided in her. He had never realized
how much the secret itself created an isolation even
when he accepted the company of others.

He would have preferred to stay in the house with
her. His bed would have been his particular choice of
location. He knew better than to do that. He was not

such an idiot that he would turn a sojourn of pleasure into a hell of imposition.

He made an effort to keep her from being bored. During the next two days she joined him while he rode through his estate.

He veiled his ignorance of the improvements his land steward had wrought. The tenants that they passed in the fields were not so accomplished at pretending that his inspection was a regular occurrence.

"They are gawking at us," Leona said after an hour of suffering wide-eyed stares.

"That is because you are so beautiful."

They paced their horses past a group of farmers sitting to their morning meal. Leona slyly watched them out of the corner of her eye as she passed.

"It is not my face that astonished those men," she said. "They squinted at you very hard before their mouths fell open."

"It is possible that they first mistook me for Hayden. We look much alike."

"And the gape-mouthed reaction when they realized you were not he? You do not attend to this estate, do you? Not at all."

"Hayden deals with the land steward. He took it on when I traveled, and proved so talented that there was no reason to have him stop."

"I am sure that he executes the duty superbly. However, the land is yours. The lives of these people depend on you. I think it reassures them to see you take at least a tiny interest in the estate today."

Her voice remained sweet, even speculative, as if she voiced a passing thought. He heard a scold anyway.

When they passed the next field, he felt obligated to acknowledge the way work stopped. He made a display of looking over the crop.

A lad no more than twelve grinned and waved in response to the lord's moment of attention. Leona waved back. The boy's father waved now too. Christian felt Leona's rein slap his leg. He lifted his hand.

"See? They are very happy to see you. They will talk about it for days."

He could imagine what they would say. These good people did not populate London's drawing rooms, but their gossip was much the same.

Two days later Leona accompanied him to the village of Watlington. They visited the shops and Leona bought some pins at a mercer's. Christian examined the shelves while she completed her business.

"That shop appeared to interest you," she said when they were out in the lane again.

"I have not been in it since I was a boy. Much has changed."

"You do not visit this village now, do you?"

He could not remember when he had last, except for the Bradwells' wedding. "Not often."

"It is like your attendance at parties and dinners, or going to the park during the fashionable hour. Your normal habits do not include these things." She tugged gently and surreptitiously at his cravat. "Even this. You had little cause to wear one a month ago."

"You are worth a cravat every now and then."

She smiled at him, and her eyes reflected the day's sunshine. "I am flattered that you think so. You honored me with your pursuit, to a degree that I did not understand. All of those crowds—it was unpleasant for you."

Not too unpleasant. Not as much as he expected. Even now, on this market day in Watlington, as bodies jostled by, the curse affected him much less than in the past.

Her presence beside him made the difference. His attention had little time or room for anyone else. Whether they conversed or he daydreamed about the nights past and those to come, she created a place of freedom and calm in which he tasted a normal life.

"I am not sacrificing myself, if that is what you assume," he said.

"If you sacrificed a little, I would not feel bad. You have been teaching me some very wicked things, and you should pay a little something for my shameful compliance."

"Whatever you want is yours, Leona, whether you comply or not."

She blushed prettily at first, then a shadow entered her. She turned her attention to tucking the pins into her reticule. "I may ask you to be true to your word someday, Christian."

Most likely so. He might regret this impulsive offer that was born of a desire to shower her with gifts. Happiness was making him stupid.

She smiled a very private smile that made him more stupid yet. "The compliance has not been without its own rewards. You owe very little on the account."

The flattery pleased him to a ridiculous extent. As they strolled on his mind naturally contemplated what other compliances might be obtained.

She was wrong, of course. He already owed her more than he could ever repay, and it had little to do with pleasure. Worse, she had already warned that when she called in the note, his cost would be the loss of her.

Having abandoned good sense, Leona did not go in search of it for a week. She ruefully acknowledged to herself that Easterbrook kept her in such a sated daze that she could not have found good sense even if she tried.

The erotic lessons grew bolder, but each one seemed the most normal and natural thing to learn. She became accustomed to his quiet voice guiding her. Normally she would be so crazed that the suggestion did not shock her at all. He knew how to ensure she would want what he wanted. He had learned what gave pleasure all too well.

The morning after their sixth night at Aylesbury, they sat to breakfast in his chambers. She wore nothing more than her nightdress and he lounged in hastily donned trousers. The servants served the meal as if both marquess and mistress were dressed for a promenade on Birdcage Walk.

She watched the flourish with which all was made ready. The house had come alive this week. The servants all stepped quickly.

"They are happy that you are here," she said when they sat at the table.

"Who?"

"The household. The servants. Your visit gives them purpose."

He glanced to where a man swept the hearth. "I trust they do not expect it to become a commonplace now."

"You do not care for Aylesbury Abbey?"

"I used to hate it. Now . . ." He shrugged.

She wondered why he hated it, but that shrug discouraged any questions on the matter.

He turned his attention elsewhere, but eventually it returned to her.

"This was not a pleasant home when I was a boy. My mother feared my father, and had cause to."

"Did you fear him too?"

"As a child I did. Later I pitied him and, by the time he died, despised him. Now I just ignore the memory of him." He gestured at the bedchamber. "For years I refused to use these rooms. Then I realized that was a perverse form of sentimentality. So I banished his presence by imposing my own on the spaces he commanded. But, yes, I still dislike Aylesbury, although I have not thought about that this last week."

"The housekeeper said your mother spent much time here, though. Writing poems, she said."

"She retreated here the last few years of her life. The rest of us lived in London. We would visit her, and she would pretend to care. But she rarely left that library, or the chambers of her own mind. There were others who suspected my father of a serious crime. She unfortunately knew it was true." He paused. "She just knew."

The way he said that, so similar to how he described his own curse, made Leona blink. He thought this was inherited.

Was that why he physically withdrew at the end of their passion? Not only to spare her the common consequence of an affair, but also to ensure no child would live what he had lived?

Her heart clenched at the evidence that he assumed he must avoid being a father. She had not dwelled on his revelation the last few days. It did not directly affect her, and no one else shared this time with them. Yet here it was, inserting itself again, affecting her understanding of him and the choices he made.

"Was she correct in her knowing?" she asked. "Were you perceiving the same thing?"

"Guilt saturated him. Hardened him. Frightened him." His jaw squared. "He killed a man over her. Not with any pretense of honor either. Not a duel. He had a man murdered."

The revelation stunned her. She had not imagined that a shadow like this hung over his family.

"Are you certain? Do you just know, as she did, or have you sought the facts?"

"I am certain, but I have chosen not to confirm it with facts."

"Then you could be wrong. She could have been wrong too. Perhaps the guilt came from something else. You said you do not read minds and must interpret what you sense. I would want to confirm such a thing before I damned a person. The truth is you only believe this, Christian. You do not really *know*."

"Perhaps you are right. I count on the chance that you are. If I seek confirmation, that corner of ambiguity ends. I would rather leave the worst parts of his legacy unclaimed."

Mail arrived with the coffee, the bread, and the fish that he favored in the morning. He glanced through the letters.

"My visit to the county has been noted. Invitations are pouring in." He started a stack of them to one side while he flipped through the mail.

One letter received more than a passing glance. He handed it to her, and continued with the rest.

She held the letter, but only looked at him. His expression had cleared. There was absolutely nothing in him that she could see to indicate things were amiss. Yet his displeasure was like a mist escaping his soul.

This is what he meant, she realized. *We all possess this perception with our intimates.* He was only unusual in that he also did with strangers and casual acquaintances.

He was not nearly as odd as he thought. She would explain that to him. It would not change what he experienced, but he might find it good to know just how much in common he had with other people.

"Aren't you going to read it, Leona?"

"Of course." She turned her attention to the letter. The bright day instantly lost its innocence.

Lady Lynsworth had written.

A sad note sounded inside Leona's heart. It so affected her that she could not read the words in front of her eyes. She knew, just knew, that the letter meant the end of this idyll. The man across the table knew it too.

She read the letter. Lady Lynsworth expressed excitement and gratitude. Tong Wei had worked wonders with Brian. So much that Tong Wei would be returning to London in two days. The letter closed with a long paragraph of heartfelt relief and declarations of eternal friendship.

Another letter suddenly appeared on the table in front of her.

"That is an invitation to a county assembly next week," Christian said. "Would you like to go?"

The invitation was to her specifically. He held an identical one in his own hand.

"Is this appropriate? To invite your paramour?"

"They are inviting my houseguest. As for your relationship to me—This house is very big, the servants are very discreet, the gossip cannot be proven, and I am Easterbrook."

She held the two letters. Once more he was allowing her to make a decision. Only there were times when a person could not ignore the world and choose to follow her heart.

The confusion returned, more horrible than her first night in Aylesbury. She resented Lady Lynsworth for writing, even if it had been in response to her own letter sent her first day here. She did not want her obligations interfering with the closeness she experienced with Christian.

She closed her eyes and immediately the intimacy bathed her, just remembering it. The perfect silence as they lay together—the freedom they shared and the way her heart swelled in the best way while she lay in his arms. She had tasted rare emotions here, and she believed that he joined her in them. He could be both Easterbrook and Edmund if he wanted. He did not have to hide the storms in his soul all the time.

She looked up and found him watching her.

He reached and took her hand. He held it for a few moments. Then he tugged gently. Her body rose in response to the silent command. He drew her around the table and settled her on his lap.

He knew how to obscure the confusion. He knew how to seduce her away from all thoughts. She surrendered quickly. She wanted to forget for a while longer that of course this would not last. Except she did not entirely forget. Her throat burned even while her passion soared.

He stripped off her nightdress and turned her so she faced him. Her legs dangled and her thighs flanked his waist. He loosened his trousers, lifted her, and lowered her so they were joined. He teased her breasts until she swayed in a rhythm of desperate need.

It took a long while for her to find fulfillment. The sorrow wanted to intrude. He waited for her, and subdued his own ferocity to the sweet longing that imbued this morning's pleasure.

There was no cataclysm this time. The peace broke in her slowly, releasing a stream of bliss. She held his head and shoulders in a wrapping embrace so his breaths warmed her chest. She accepted everything her heart and soul experienced, even the ache flowing within the beauty and purity of their intimacy.

It occurred to him, as his mind cleared, that he might put off the reckoning forever if his body did not betray him.

God knew he was trying. They were back in bed and the breakfast remained uneaten. He had used pleasure as ruthlessly with her as he ever had, to defeat the reminder of her responsibilities that had intruded with that damned letter.

He still floated between oblivion and the world, entwined with her. It was much like the state achieved in meditation, only his self did not disappear. Instead his consciousness filled the dark peace. And, it appeared, another's self could be there too.

Not only her self, but her essence. Her worries. Her sadness. In these moments of serenity, he knew her better than he had ever known anyone, even himself.

He guessed what was coming even before she withdrew into herself. He sensed her retreat, and knew.

"I need to return to London, Christian." She spoke quietly, right near his ear.

"No, you do not."

"I would be vexed by the commanding way you said that if I were not so sated. I have little will for this argument now. You knew I would not."

She still embraced him. Outside the window he could hear the gardeners toiling away. Had she been correct about that? Did the master's visit give them purpose?

"Nothing is being accomplished here," she said.

"I would say a great deal is being accomplished here. You are learning enough about pleasure to last a lifetime."

"I do not need reminders that it might have to." Her embrace loosened. She rose up on her arms so she could see his face. "Lady Lynsworth writes that Tong Wei will be back in London in two days. I will be safe in town with him there. I no longer have an excuse to dally here."

"You have the best excuse." Except she really didn't. This was not a woman who would let pleasure decide her path. She had made that very clear when she came to him.

He would try a different tack, for all the good it would do. "You should consider why you go back to London and what you plan to do once you are there."

"I do not have to plan it. I already know. I will see the shippers that you told me your brother arranged for me to meet. I will also visit with Denningham, the way you promised."

"I told you already that you will learn nothing of value from him. Your scribe erred, or lied."

"Your certainty carries more weight now, of course. It no longer stands as a mere opinion. However, I still want to meet him so I am certain too."

She was relentless. It was time to distract her again.

He tried to rise to the occasion, as it were. He failed. Damnation.

"I had hoped to put off this conversation today, Leona."

She smiled mischievously. "You succeeded magnificently for hours. However, even the great Easterbrook cannot keep it up forever." Her gentle finger traced down his torso until it skimmed the object of her joke.

That touch was all he needed. It turned out he could keep it up one more time after all.

CHAPTER NINETEEN

~

He managed to delay the conversation, but it waited for them. Its cloud shadowed the day. By nightfall Leona concluded that if she did not force the issue, it might be months before she left Aylesbury.

She thought about Gaspar for the first time in days while she prepared for the evening. She felt guilty for the degree he had dropped from her mind. She saw his confidence in her when they parted. Their business desperately needed the alliances she had come to forge, and he assumed she would be successful. He trusted her judgment more than was reasonable and depended on her more than was wise. She might want to dally at Aylesbury forever, but she would fail him if she did so.

She went down to Christian's apartment earlier than normal that night. She found him still dressed in shirt and trousers, sitting in the dark. His stillness told her that he was meditating.

She wished she had learned how herself. Her heart thickened with dread about the row to come. It would be useful to escape to the peace that Tong Wei said could be found in that loss of self, where one relinquished desires and ambitions.

She set her lamp down as she always did, then sat in a chair. He emerged from his retreat and saw her. The abstraction lifted almost immediately. His attention centered on her.

"I will be leaving tomorrow," she said. "If you will not send me in your coach, I will hire one for Isabella and myself."

She braced herself for lightning. None flashed. No heat. No turmoil. He calmly considered what she had said.

"You must know that you are not going to go anywhere, Leona, in my coach or any other, unless I permit it."

She swallowed hard. "I am trusting that you will permit it."

"You have more faith in me than I do."

"I have faith that you will keep your promise."

"I promised to allow you to return to your brother. Not to London."

"You know that I cannot go back to China until I return to London first."

"That is not true."

"Do you intend to make me a prisoner? To create a new choice, this house or a ship to Macao? I can either stay with you or I can return home having failed in my purpose?"

"Purpos*es*." He emphasized the plural, firmly. Tightly.

Every part of her stilled. This was not about keeping her here. Perhaps it was not even about wanting her. He kept her from the second purpose, and would make her sacrifice the first if necessary in order to do so.

"If you are worried about my safety in London, Christian, the sooner I finish my questions, the quicker I will be safe."

"It is not worth the risk. Even with Tong Wei to protect you, even with me—I have told you to give this up. Now I do again. Even in victory you will gain little, and you risk your safety and your brother's business with those questions."

She hated how he sat there, so damned sure of his judgment. She glared down at him but he still dominated the chamber and her. He did not even have to move to do that. Nor did he have to compromise. He wore his power quietly, but it still cloaked him. He knew he could stop her.

It dismayed her that he wanted to. She walked away from him. Her heart urged her to capitulate, to do anything so this night would not end in sorrow, but she had to know now.

"Christian, our first night here, I said that I had questions. You offered to answer one. I am thinking I chose the wrong one. I forgot who I was after all. I must ask another now."

He did not respond. His silence sapped her courage. The lord waited to hear the petition.

"My father had a notebook. A leather half folio in which he wrote down the patterns he saw and the names he learned in his efforts to expose the smugglers and their masters. I never saw it after the night that you left Macao. I did not find it in his private belongings after he died. Did you take it when you left?"

"Yes."

She closed her eyes so she might contain what his admission did to her. Disappointment so pained her heart that it affected her physically. Her stomach sickened. She feared that if she looked at him again she would see a different man from the one she had been holding. She might suddenly notice all kinds of aspects of face and character that excitement had blinded her to before this.

Her eyes burned. Her better sense had always warned that his interest had ulterior motives, or indifferent ones at best. These last few days, however, she had allowed herself to believe differently.

"Don't you wonder why I took it, Leona?"

His voice, so close, made her startle. She opened her eyes. He had left his chair and now stood right in front of her.

"Think back to that night, Leona. To the danger you saw and felt. You took refuge in anger and action, but I could see your terror. Even your father, who had suffered other attacks and losses, could not believe they had been so bold as to fire that ship right there in Macao."

She let her mind drift back. To the smoke and the vain attempts to stop the blaze. She saw her father, ashen-faced and stunned. He had been on that ship just an hour earlier, showing her brother how to check a bill of lading against a cargo. It was mere luck that they had disembarked earlier than expected.

"They tried to kill him." Her fury from that night flashed through her again now. "They failed, but they broke him just the same. And all the evidence that he had, all the proof, was in that notebook that you stole. *Damn you.* I looked for it. I was going to do what he could no longer do, and end it all. I would have gotten word to the emperor's viceroy in Canton. I would have—"

"You would have gotten yourself killed. And him. And maybe your brother too. I took the notebook so you could not."

"I think that you took it for other reasons."

"There was no other reason. That night proved it was bigger than your father could fight. Bigger than you could fight. I took the notebook to protect you."

She wanted to believe that, but she was beyond believing anything now. "Do you still have it? You do, don't you? I want it."

"No."

Frustration ripped her composure and set her teeth on edge. "I need to *finish this*."

"You will finish nothing. You may prove your father was correct. You may discover the names of men here in England who profit from that trade. You may even expose them to the world's scorn. But even if you are successful, it will not stop. Your family's business will once more be punished, and you will again be in danger. You already are."

She could not believe he was so implacable. So unsympathetic. He wanted to do more than protect her, too. She just knew it. He had had possession of that notebook for years. He had read it. He knew it would help her, but he did not want to allow it for his own reasons.

She looked back at the last week, at the emotions

and the discoveries. This conversation made her doubt everything she had perceived and believed about him.

"I want the notebook, Christian. You said in Watlington that I could have whatever I wanted."

His anger finally showed. His hand sliced the air, in a lord's gesture of finality. "I did not mean *this*."

"No, you meant jewels or silks or gifts. Distractions, so I would not ask any other questions, or make a request that inconvenienced you."

"Most women would be content with jewels and silks, damn it."

"If I were any woman, you would not have wanted me. What will it take for you to give me that notebook? You said you wanted whatever I will permit. If I say I will permit anything at all, will that sway you?"

He considered it. She could tell. He looked at her in a way that made her tremble. Shaking inside, hiding the way his darker mysteries could still lure her, mourning how much he had become a stranger again, she managed to face him down.

"You insult us both, Leona. If I wanted you for my whore, I would have settled the terms at the start. That is the customary practice. I did not realize that your damned mission means more to you than your own pride."

His rebuke served as a slap. The anger parted to allow her to see what she had just done. Her breath caught at the cruelty of her words, and the way she had tainted everything they had shared.

He turned away from her, physically and in every other way. If a door had shut in her face, his disgust could not have been more manifest.

"Often you provoke the best in me, Leona. Right now you are inciting the worst. It would be best if you ran away before I accept the offer you just made."

She held down the tears that wanted to spill. She walked to the door with what dignity she could summon. Once out of the bedchamber, she did run. She flew to her bed, where she wept harder than she had in years.

CHAPTER
TWENTY

The message arrived with a breakfast tray at dawn. The servant explained that Lord Easterbrook had given orders for the coach to be made ready for her by nine o'clock.

Isabella arrived soon after. She also had received a message. She silently set about packing.

Leona could not stomach any food. She stared sightlessly at the garden while Isabella laid out her carriage ensemble. There had been no sleep last night, just a stupor of sorrow that still dulled her senses.

"Did you displease him?" Isabella asked quietly.

"I asked to leave." And she was leaving, even if it felt as if he were sending her away. Because he was sending her away. She did not lie to herself that he merely acceded to her wishes in arranging for the coach.

Isabella frowned while she poured water for washing. She muttered to herself in Chinese.

"What are you saying?" Leona asked.

"Forgive me, but I was saying that Europeans are a stupid people." She helped Leona out of her nightdress.

"Were you calling me stupid? Or him?"

"There may be enough stupidity to share. However, it is not hard to please a man, so it would take a stupid woman to displease one who was so eager to be entranced."

It was easy to be stupid if you were angry and reckless and spoke rashly. She had conjured up a hundred ways to have ended that conversation last night other than the way she had.

She tried to take some consolation that at least she had affected her initial design. He would not stop her. The victory seemed very small this morning, and was not enough to ease the pain in her chest. Her heart believed it had lost more than she gained, and refused to listen to reason.

Isabella set about brushing her hair. "I have a book. My mother gave it to me. I will give it to you."

"A book?"

"A pillow book. It is about pleasure. My mother received it from her first lover. She gave it to me when we left. She dreams that I will become a concubine to a great man here. She hoped it would be different with Europeans if they were not in Macao." She brushed some more. "My father liked this book. It has some pictures."

"Isabella, Lord Easterbrook and I had a row last night, but it was not about *that*."

"My mother says that if there is a row, *that* is the way to end it."

"This is not so simple."

"I see. Of course. Forgive me." Isabella brushed on,

but Leona heard her muttering the same words in Chinese again. *Europeans are a stupid people.*

It did not take long to prepare for departure. A few servants came to say good-bye to Isabella. The house steward performed his duties. Easterbrook was nowhere to be seen.

Leona pictured him sleeping in that big bed. Perhaps he was awake and meditating. Quite likely he was relieved to be done with her. After a life of isolation, it would be unnatural to spend so long in another person's company.

She gazed at the big house while the carriage began its journey. The windows on the third level drew her eyes. An odd sensation entered her. She felt his presence up there, watching her leave.

Ridiculous, of course. His chambers faced the garden, not the front of the house. He was the one with special perceptions, not she. Her subdued mood merely played tricks on her this morning, while she yearned for some sign that she had not completely lost him.

She settled back into her seat. Beside her Isabella was lifting a valise.

"Is that a gift from the housekeeper?" Leona asked.

"I do not know. It was in the carriage when we entered, on the floor here. Do you think it is a gift? Or perhaps there are gifts inside?"

Isabella unfastened the valise, opened it, and peered in. She made a face, shut it, and set it down. "No gifts. It was left here by accident. It contains someone's old, dirty book."

They rode a few hundred yards before Isabella's

words poked through Leona's melancholy. She eyed the valise, then bent over and lifted it onto her lap.

She opened it. The smell of leather wafted over her. She looked inside and saw her father's notebook.

The coach rolled away, disappearing into the last of the morning's mist. Christian watched until there was nothing more to see.

Down below he saw a groom bringing around his horse. His orders had called for his own mount as well as the coach. He would return to London too, only not with Leona.

He had no desire to share the carriage with her while she read that notebook. After last night, she would not entertain any explanations from him regarding what it revealed about his father. That notebook would convince her for certain that he had gone to Macao bent on betrayal to protect the name of Easterbrook.

She was smart enough to comprehend the rest of its revelations, too. The reasons for her danger would be clearer. He did not think that would stop her, though. She had to see it through. Just as well, most likely. The danger would not end if she gave up and went home now anyway. Someone had concluded that she knew too much. Now that she had the notebook, she did.

He walked back to his chambers. It was his imagination, surely, that her scent still lingered here. He opened the windows so the breeze would make quick work of his inclination toward nostalgia.

The gardeners were busy once more, clipping and pruning and mounding soil. There were households where the lord and lady knew every servant's name, but that had not been the style in the manors of Easterbrook. He had as little congress with servants as possible.

You touch the world even if you do not want it to touch you. She had a knack for holding up those mirrors, it seemed.

A low cough broke into the silence. He turned to see the house steward near the door.

"Did the letter to Mr. Miller go with them, Thurston?"

"I handed it to one of the footmen myself, sir."

The letter had ordered Miller to quadruple the guard at Leona's house. She might think Tong Wei was all she required, but Christian wanted more protection of her than one man if she left the sanctuary of Aylesbury Abbey. She would have to suffer the intrusion whether she agreed to it or not, until he returned to London himself, found the men who threatened her, and ended this once and for all.

"I came to say that your horse is ready, my lord."

Christian looked down at the garden where he and Leona had spent many pleasant hours. His gaze swept the bedchamber.

"Tell the grooms that I have changed my mind."

Thurston bowed and began backing out of the room.

"Wait. I will ride after all. I will not be leaving for a few days, however. Send word to the land steward that I will meet him at the footbridge over the stream at ten o'clock. And send up that fellow who has been serving me."

Thurston bowed, and backed off a bit more.

"His name, Thurston. What is it?"

"Who, my lord?"

"That young man serving me."

"That would be Jeremiah. He is a sober and dedicated young man. I have the highest expectations for him."

Christian went to the dressing room, content that he had set his course for the next few days. He would have to remember to ask Thurston for the land steward's name too.

Perhaps one afternoon he would ride over to Watlington and visit the Bradwells.

He imagined Mrs. Bradwell's reaction when she found him at her door. He would send an invitation for them to dine with him instead, so they could avoid him if they chose.

The plans lightened his mood, but he knew it was a feint. Activity would be nothing more than a distraction from the utter certainty that he had lost the joy of the last week.

Still, he would remain at Aylesbury for a while. He would bask in the warm spring that Leona had created here, before returning to the empty winter of his London chambers.

Leona heard the singing chatter outside her chamber door. Isabella and Tong Wei conversed in Chinese. She did not understand more than a few words, but she knew that they talked about her.

She did not care about that, or about anything else. She only wanted to sleep.

Except she never did. Not completely. Hours would pass while her mind hovered on the edge of consciousness. Memories would agitate her, then fly away.

Speculations streamed in undercurrents beneath her deadened spirit.

On the few occasions that she fully woke, the most sickening sorrow shredded her composure. Her heart could not accommodate how very wrong it had been about Christian.

Wrong because it wanted to be wrong. Wrong because it was still a girl's heart, childish and dreamy. She had badly wanted to believe that a young, handsome, mysterious man just happened to show up in Macao, at her father's house, by a caprice of fate.

The evidence it had been otherwise was there from the start. More had been added since she saw him again in London. He had quizzed her on her purpose here that first day. He had kept an eye on her, and distracted her, and seduced her away from learning the truth.

Her heart had mourned while she read that notebook. For her father, whose personality came through in every jotting that mapped his increasing fear and unshaken resolve. For her innocence and her foolish love, when she saw the lines where he linked Easterbrook to the entire matter.

Easterbrook had been the only lord he believed with certainty was among the owners of the secret company that smuggled opium. He had not described why he settled on that one. He had, however, made notations that indicated not only opium was involved.

Instead he described a plot, a long and old one, of smuggling tea and luxuries into England, and its colonies too. If he was right, not only the Chinese emperor's laws had been broken, but also those of England.

Why had Christian put the notebook in the coach

when it linked his father to such crimes? Perhaps he felt obligated, after she had reminded him of his offer to give her anything.

Most likely it had simply been the parting gift that he decided she deserved.

She tried not to picture him. She fought to forget that argument the last night. For all the revelations, her stupid heart still burned when she thought about him. She had nothing to be sorry for, and she hated how the pain would not go away. He had accused her of treating their affair as something base, but he had only pursued her from the very start for the most callous reasons.

A hand touched her shoulder, interrupting her mental raving. She opened her eyes to see Isabella beside her bed. Tong Wei looked down at her too. He held a bowl.

Isabella moved a chair to her bedside, then left. Tong Wei sat. "You will eat now."

"I am not hungry."

"You will eat."

He lifted a spoon to her mouth. She sipped a spicy broth. Her English hired cook had not made this.

She held him off and sat herself up. She took the bowl in her hands. "You should not be serving me like that. I will do it."

He watched her. Whenever she paused, he began to reach for the bowl again. She kept sipping so he would not demean himself on her behalf.

"You have not asked about the brother of Lady Lynsworth," he said. "You sent me away from my duty here, you gave me a task that left you unprotected to the worst danger, but you have not asked if the young man will survive."

She sipped more broth. Some rice lay saturated at the bottom of the bowl. "Will he?"

"No."

"She thinks that he will."

"He is free now. She again sees the brother she knew. However, he is weak. I do not think he wants the freedom as much as she thinks he does. Someday he will succumb again."

"I am sorry to hear that."

"You knew how it would probably be."

"You have been wrong before." She prayed for Lady Lynsworth's sake that Tong Wei was wrong again.

He sat placidly while she ate the rice. He took the bowl and set it aside. "Are you pining?"

"Pining? Goodness, where did you learn that word, Tong Wei?"

"It is in the book I am reading. I also saw it in a poem. English people seem to pine away. I do not know what it means, but I thought perhaps you are doing it."

"I am not the sort of woman to pine away."

"You are not the sort of woman to take to your bed if you are not sick either, but here you are."

Yes, here she was. "I have made a muddle of things, Tong Wei."

"Isabella says that you have fallen out of favor with the marquess."

"He has also fallen out of favor with me. Completely. The worst part is that I do not think Easterbrook will help me now." It was not really the worst part, her heart whispered. Refusing to acknowledge the other pain would not make it go away.

"He still does help, even if we do not want it. There are his men here all the time. Too many. They carry pistols in plain view. I tell them to go away, but they do not."

"Even if his people stay here to protect me, I do not think I will see him again. There were introductions to important traders to be made that I have now lost."

Tong Wei's expression remained bland, but she knew his mind considered the problem. While he did so, Isabella reentered the chamber and opened the drapes.

"If the marquess will not do this, then you must do it yourself," Tong Wei said. "If you know the names of these men, you must go and speak for your brother."

She knew their names. She had broached the subject one night in Aylesbury, briefly, and Christian had told her.

"They may not receive me."

"You can, perhaps, say that the marquess recommended you to them, can you not? It is not a lie."

It was not a lie, but it was an "almost lie." Tong Wei was correct. She needed to do what she could. She had to try at least. They could not sail home until she did.

"I have cause to think one of them knew my father. I will try him first." She had only recently realized this old connection existed. This shipper's name had also appeared in her father's notebook.

"I will make a bath," Isabella said. "You will dress. Tomorrow you will feel yourself and know what to do."

Tong Wei left. Isabella threw back the bedclothes. Leona forced herself to her feet. Pining could wait. She had the rest of her life for that, after all.

CHAPTER
TWENTY-ONE

Daniel St. John did not make regular use of the private offices he kept in London. Leona learned that when her first visit resulted in no response to her rap on the door.

She returned each of the next three days. Finally on the last one she met with success. A clerk opened the office to her, Tong Wei, and three of Easterbrook's footmen. He took her card away.

She rehearsed her "almost lie" while she waited. She hoped that Mr. St. John would not examine it too critically.

Tong Wei took a position near a window, looking out much as he had that day in the drawing room. He was always on alert now, despite the guards who crowded the house and garden.

"What do you see?" she asked.

"He still follows," he said. "The rider on the brown horse. He does not even try to hide his presence now."

She peered over his shoulder. Down below in the street the rider in question, hat brim low over his eyes, boldly sat near the crossroad forty yards behind her carriage.

"He wants me to see him. He wants me to be afraid. That is all this is."

Tong Wei shook his head, but not in disagreement. "Before this is over, I think someone will die. My duty is to make certain that it is not you. Make your alliances quickly, so I can return you to your brother."

The clerk returned then. He ushered her into the back office.

Mr. St. John was gracious enough while he sized her up, and even a touch courtly in his greeting. A man with a rather startling handsome face, there was something uncompromising about him.

He invited her to sit, then lowered his tall, dark self into another chair. He was the sort of man who made one uncomfortable from the start, no matter how polite he might be.

"How did you find me?" he asked.

"The Marquess of Easterbrook suggested I should meet with you."

He smiled. It did not do much to soften what was by nature a fairly cruel mouth. "Perhaps he did, but Easterbrook did not give you this address. He does not even have it himself yet."

Oh, dear. "I visited the Royal Exchange and asked where I might find you. A clerk at the offices of Lloyd's mentioned these chambers."

"How indiscreet of him."

"Please do not hold it against him. I confess that I cajoled shamelessly."

"I expect that there are many men who are susceptible

when you do that." It was not meant as flattery. He put her on notice that he was not such a man, if she were stupid enough to think he might be. He settled more comfortably, however. He was not going to send her away.

"What do you want with me, Miss Montgomery?"

"When Lord Easterbrook mentioned you, I recognized the name. You are known in Asia, of course. I thought you were French, but I was interested at once in meeting you when I learned that you are in London now."

"Miss Montgomery, twice now you have dropped Easterbrook's name with ease. The implication is that he sent you. However, I know that he did not."

"You do?"

"His brother approached me. I was agreeable to seeing you, but I requested a meeting alone with Easterbrook first. That has not occurred."

"You have found me out, sir. Lord Easterbrook's aid has been removed, and I am making my own way once again. I pray that you will hear me anyway, perhaps due to your old acquaintance with my father."

Her reference surprised him. "I did not realize that you knew about that."

"I recently read some of his papers. In one he speculated about the opium smugglers, and listed captains and shippers who might be available to ply that trade. Beside your name he jotted, 'Never. I know him, and it is impossible.' I confess that is one reason why I decided to approach you first."

"My ships do not take cargoes of slaves either. Just so you know, in the event that you—"

"We are of like mind, I assure you. We do not want that trade."

"Perhaps you should explain what you do want."

She described her desire for an alliance that would expand her brother's reach and improve the efficiency of his routes of trade. She suggested that if St. John contracted to make use of the holds of Montgomery and Tavares, he could expand his own business.

"Miss Montgomery, what you describe is of little benefit to me. Currently, that is. In five years, however, the alliance that you propose might prove very profitable."

"We do not want to wait that long." Without an alliance they might not survive that long. "Why would we be of more interest later than now?"

"The remaining monopolies of the East India Company will not survive in its next charter renewal. When trade between England and the East is open to all, your family's connections with the Canton's *hong* merchants will become much more valuable. As will any partnership that I may forge with you."

His vision of the future made a lot of sense, but his last sentence dismayed her. "Partnership? I did not propose a partnership."

"Nothing less would benefit me. I would also require a controlling interest in the resulting company. The relative strengths and sizes of our current situations warrant it."

"If there were a partnership, I think it would have to be equal. That is only fair."

"I doubt that your assets are even one tenth of mine. Aside from that, there are other issues that unbalance matters."

"We are in Canton. That alone tips the scales back in our favor."

He shook his head. "Your brother is in Canton, not *you*. He is still green, and as a woman you are not allowed there. The business is too dependent on you, and admirable though your successes have been, your sex limits your reach. Your father's refusal to ignore the smugglers weakened you and your ships are still vulnerable. If I throw in with you now, I must have a free hand to deal with all of that, to ensure that you do indeed survive for the future."

He spelled out their vulnerabilities rather too well. "It is my brother's company now. I cannot effect the kind of partnership that you describe without his agreement."

"I have a man in India. I will give you a letter when you sail back. If your brother is agreeable, bring that letter to my factor in Calcutta. He will know what to do once he reads it."

Mr. St. John assumed it would only go one way. He knew just how tenuous the solvency of Montgomery and Tavares had been these last years. She had hoped to forge informal alliances that would offer some protection, but it appeared this shipper would accept only a merger, where he swallowed her father's company whole.

"And my brother? What should I tell him about his position in this unequal partnership?"

"Since he holds the Country Trader license, he will be needed as long as the current system remains in place. If he proves to have your abilities, there will always be a place for him. If not, he will share the profits but not the decisions. I will want one of my people in Canton with him as soon as the deal is struck, however."

"I can see that I have much to consider. I do not even know how to present this when I go home, or how to advise him."

"Consider at your leisure and advise as you must. The East India Company's monopoly will not end tomorrow, and, as I said, this partnership is of little benefit to me currently."

It might be of considerable benefit to Montgomery and Tavares, however. She suspected there would be fewer episodes with pirates and port officials if St. John's free hand was at work.

She stood to take her leave. He escorted her to the door and opened it for her.

"If I may ask, Mr. St. John—How did my father know you?"

"We did one small piece of trading together. It was long ago. I was little more than a boy."

"And yet he formed a strong opinion of your character. Would you tell me how you met him? It is rare for me to speak with someone who knew him back then."

She paused at the door, hoping he would indulge her.

"Perhaps you should be content in your memories, Miss Montgomery."

"My memories are of a man fighting to survive. Of a man old before his time."

He examined her critically. "It may be best if I tell you. It could affect your brother's decision, and your influence. I would not want you to later think I had deceived you."

"Deceived me? I do not understand."

He closed the door. "I had one ship back then, and my use of it could be reckless. I was not above a little smuggling into the Eastern kingdoms that forbad normal trade. The Chinese coast is a big one, and very porous. Your father had bought a cargo of bronze pots in India. He paid me to deliver them to the coast, forty leagues north of Canton."

"Bronze pots? He paid you to smuggle bronze pots into *China*?"

"A little like smuggling coal into Newcastle, isn't it? That preyed on my mind as I sailed toward China. One night I went below and opened a crate and examined those urns. They were not empty. They had been packed with opium."

His accusation stunned her. "That is not possible. I do not believe you."

"Believe what you want, but I smuggled for him, and that was the true cargo. It all went into the sea, Miss Montgomery. I delivered the pots as contracted and nothing more, and I never dealt with your father again."

A sentry stood on Grosvenor Square. Christian noticed him as soon as he turned his horse onto the street.

Everyone else noticed Tong Wei too. He might have been a statue, he remained so still. An exotic statue, dressed in shafts of sapphire silk, with his ageless face fixed in resolve.

He moved and blocked the groom from taking

Christian's horse. One second Tong Wei was immobile and the next his face was turned up to Christian's own.

"You should come now," he said. "I think she will talk to you."

Christian handed the reins to the groom. "I am sure that she does not want to. Nor can I say anything to make her less angry."

"She is not angry. That would be normal. Healthy." Tong Wei shook his head. "She has not been herself. It is worse today, not better. You will come and she will talk to you."

Tong Wei walked away. Christian entered his house.

"How long has the Chinaman been outside?" he asked the footman who took his crop and gloves.

"Two days, my lord. He was first there yesterday, early morning. Lady Wallingford demanded we remove him, but he did not seem to understand what we were saying. Lord Elliot called in the afternoon, and told us to leave him be."

"That was wise advice." He would not want Tong Wei insulted by the servants. Nor would he want to see the damage if Tong Wei felt the need to defend himself against them.

Leona had not sent him here. He had come on his own. Tong Wei was not a man to care about lovers' quarrels, and his worry was deep. If he had stood on the street for two days, awaiting acknowledgment, there was a good reason.

"I will need a fresh mount. Tell the grooms to bring my bay around as soon as he is saddled."

———

He found her in the garden, sitting under the small tree that had offered entry to the intruders. She noticed him watching her from ten feet away. A sad half-smile formed, then she looked at the ivy at her feet.

It was not much of a welcome, but he had expected worse. He went over and sat beside her on the stone bench.

"Tong Wei is worried about you."

"Tong Wei can be an old woman sometimes."

"He takes his duty very seriously. You cannot fault him for that. Your behavior concerns him."

She sighed with exasperation. "I do not have to be talkative all the time. I do not have to always be busy. I am allowed periods of reflection too, am I not? Tong Wei reflects all the time. You have wasted half of your life in reflection. Why am I supposed to be devoid of deeper thoughts, even for a day or two?"

He chose to ignore her easy annoyance, but he did not miss her criticism of his habits. "He does not think that this melancholy is caused by any emotion that he understands."

"Did he go to you and tell you to come here?" Her color rose with her embarrassment. "He should not have imposed like that."

"It was no imposition. I would have come anyway." And he would have. He would have found another excuse if Tong Wei had not handed him this one. "I might have washed first, and changed my coats, but I intended to call."

Her gaze darted at him. He read the question in her eyes. Why?

Why indeed? Why bother? Why inconvenience

them both? Why face her suspicions? Why pick up the row again?

He did not know. Because she had not left his thoughts during these days apart, he supposed. Because after activity ceased and he was alone with himself, a new void existed in his isolation. Because he still wanted her.

"I read the notebook," she said. "I know why you took it, and why you did not want to give it to me."

"I did not read it until recently, so you know more now than I did even a fortnight ago. I took it for the reason I said, Leona. No other. Your father was determined to pursue his investigations, no matter what the danger. The fire on that ship said he might pay with his life. Or yours. I took it, but not to protect anyone but you."

"But you guessed what was in it."

He had chosen not to guess. Not to know. There had been too much of that in his life. "Did you never wonder how I arrived at your father's door? Why he accepted me as a guest?"

"You were English. I assumed that you had a letter of introduction."

"I had no letter. I only had a name. I brought him the Marquess of Easterbrook's greetings. I arrived in the East before word of my father's death became known, so he thought I spoke for a living man."

"But why?"

"I had seen my father's accounts and papers. I had the names of men in places like Canton and Macao and India, and I used them like stepping-stones. They gave direction to an aimless journey. Reginald Montgomery of Macao was one of those names. I swear that I did not know how and why our fathers knew each other. And I used a false name because my use of opium shamed me even as it enthralled me."

She remained skeptical. Of course she did. He did not blame her.

"When he told me about his troubles, and his conviction that there were men in England profiting handsomely from the smuggling . . . I suspected the connection then," he admitted. "He was not confiding so much as quizzing. He wanted to learn if I knew anything, or had been sent by the marquess for the reasons you suspect."

"My suspicions, and his, fit the facts better than your story does, Christian."

"There is nothing that I can do about that. I do not expect you to believe me. That would take more trust than you can have and much more than I expect."

Her face fell. He had never seen her look so sad before.

"Do not tell me what trust I am capable of. I trusted for seven years despite my suspicions. I trusted even after I learned you lied about your identity. I trusted against my better sense. I trusted you enough to give myself and my—" She inhaled deeply and fought for her composure. "The truth is, whatever you did has become a very little thing in light of what I learned two days ago."

An odd mix of reactions cascaded in him. Worry at her profound sorrow. Relief that he had not caused it. Dismay that even his betrayal would be no more than a very small thing to her.

"What did you learn? Tell me now."

With a hesitant, miserable voice she described a

visit to the shipper St. John, and the shocking revelation at its end.

"That my father had been a smuggler at all—I could
forgive that. I could swallow that if he had worked with
those men and that secret company to evade tariffs in
the East with cargoes of porcelains and bronzes and
cloth." Her breath caught. "But opium? He hated it. He
despised the men who traded in it. He died fighting it. It
was an unbelievable accusation and I almost did St.
John violence. But—" Again that stricken expression.
"I think he told the truth, Christian."

"Quite likely not. He was bargaining with you. He
thought this would make you more pliable."

She shook her head. "He already has the advantage
in any negotiations. He had no reason to lie, although I
had a passing vexation that you were not with me so
you would know at once if he did."

He sought a way to convince her that this tale was
not true. Her disillusionment pained him and he would
lie outright to spare her if he could. He wished he had
in fact been there with her, so she would believe him if
he discredited St. John's claim.

There was little doubt in her now that it was the
truth. Nor in him. It explained why her father had been
targeted for so much trouble and coercion.

The goal had not been to force Montgomery into
joining the opium smuggling. They sought to coerce
him into silence once he broke away from them. And if
he had once been part of that ring, he would have cause
to know if they worked for nameless men in London,
and whether their activities extended to the West, and
not only China. Reginald Montgomery's crusade had

been even more dangerous than Christian had previously understood.

It also explained the reference to Montgomery that had sent Christian to him in Macao in the first place. His father's correspondence had not established that connection. Rather Montgomery's name had been in a very private account book, with a series of payments noted.

"It changes everything, of course," she said. "What a comical figure I must appear to them, whoever they are. Fighting a moral battle against men who were once my father's partners. Small wonder my father did not want me to involve myself, or hand me what he knew so I could finish his work. He feared what I would learn."

"What have you learned? That many years ago he did this, that is all. He more than made up for it later. He stopped at great cost to himself. He spoke against it, and wrote to the Company and the emperor's officials. He risked everything, and would not bend to their demands that he stop. Perhaps his zeal was twice that of most men because of his past sins."

She looked at him with an incredibly vulnerable expression in her eyes.

Then she crumbled. She covered her face with her hands, bent low over her lap, and began to cry.

Her weeping dismayed him. What had he said? Hell, he was supposed to be here to help, not—Tong Wei had warned that she was not herself.

He took her into his arms and cursed himself.

She released the horrible emotions that had been burning her heart. Slowly she found some calm. Her composure returned.

His kindness both comforted and embarrassed her. She had allowed herself to think the worst of him, to accuse him of deceit, but he had come here today anyway. He had listened to her sad tale with sympathy. Then he had restored her best memories of her father, and painted a portrait of strength, not hypocrisy, in doing so.

She could not face him. She kept her face buried in his coat even after the sobs ceased wracking her. There were things she needed to say, but her courage failed her. She took refuge in the commonplace instead.

"Were you in Oxfordshire all this time?"

"Most of it. I made a short journey to take care of some family matters."

Her throat burned again. She held in the tears. "I am sorry about that row we had. I said things that—"

"You have a temper and I do too, so sometimes we will say things that . . ."

She smiled at the way he left the *that* unspoken. He could be very wise sometimes. She cuddled closer. The emotion-laden peace reminded her of the mood after they made love.

"I am sorry that I wasted these days," she whispered. "I wish that I had asked for silks or jewels after all, and not that notebook."

His kiss pressed her crown. "Then let us make up for the lost time, Leona."

He stood with her in his arms and carried her toward the house.

CHAPTER TWENTY-TWO

Silence. Stillness. The pulse creating utter calm.
Higher consciousness in the loss of all awareness.
Floating now. No loss. No fear. No time. No sound.
A disturbance. The center shattering like dark glass.

Christian opened his eyes. Two men stood ten feet away.

"Hello, Hayden. Elliot."

Hayden sighed. "Damnation, it is like you don't exist when you sit in the dark like this." He strode over and pulled the drapes open to the night's vague light, then used a flint to flame a lamp.

"You did tell the footman to send us up here," he added. "Do not dare object if we intruded on . . . whatever the hell you were doing."

"I did not object. I welcomed you."

"At least he is dressed already, Hayden," Elliot said.

"Of course I am dressed. The dinner tonight celebrates Caroline's engagement. I need to be there."

Hayden crossed his arms. "What did you want us for?"

"Sit."

Hayden glared.

"*Please* sit."

Elliot chuckled and sat. Hayden scowled and did as well.

"I need to speak with both of you about our father."

Elliot's humor left him.

Hayden's expression softened to something more troubled. Old conflicted emotions poured out of them both.

It had never been clear to Christian whether his brothers had been spared or scarred from not knowing their parents as surely as he did.

"Best to leave that alone," Hayden said.

"I thought so too. I was happy to damn him without conclusive proof. I decided to find out if that was unfair."

Elliot appeared curious. Hayden looked resigned.

"I wish that I could say that I have learned that we were all wrong about him. I cannot."

They had expected no less. The conclusion still sobered them.

"You are certain?" Hayden asked.

"Very certain. Last week I met with the man who acted on his behalf in that murder."

"As did I last year," Elliot said. "He denied it."

"You did not believe his denial, however. You admitted as much to me."

Elliot shrugged. "It was just a feeling. He was amiable. He acted innocent and ignorant, but . . ." He shrugged again.

"He also denied it to me. However, he was lying to us both."

"You cannot be sure," Hayden said.

"I am sure." As soon as they were introduced, he knew. As soon as his title was spoken. "He finally admitted it to me."

"Why would he do that?"

"Because I am now Easterbrook, and the last Easterbrook was his partner in crime. He had been paid. I have found the proof of that. He hopes to be paid again now that I know the truth."

"Will he be?" Elliot asked. "You were adamant last year that this secret be kept in the past."

"He will not be paid again, but he will try for it. I sensed him plotting even as we conversed. He will blackmail me. When he does, I will see him in the dock for it. I thought you should both know, so you can prepare for the scandal when it all comes out."

Christian did not explain that he had allowed the scoundrel to think he would be successful in that blackmail. He had lured him into it until he knew the bait was swallowed. He had not exploited his curse so ruthlessly in years.

Silence fell. His brothers privately pondered the implications of a public trial that touched on their father's crime.

"Hell, Christian, what's one more scandal and a pile of gossip to us?" Hayden said. "This family is a damned magnet for it."

Elliot snorted. They both snickered, then laughed so hard that it almost convulsed them.

Elliot wiped his eyes and tried to compose himself. "Oh, no! Not a scandal," he squeaked, imitating Aunt Hen. "Whatever will we do, Hayden?"

That set them off again.

Christian waited while they had their fun. Finally they settled down.

"I am glad to see you make light of scandal. That is heartening. Because there is something else about our father that will probably be known soon too. He was among a group of men who founded a secret company that still smuggles tons of opium into China."

The meeting in his chambers did not last much longer. Christian told his brothers what he knew, then they all headed down to the drawing room to join the other family members.

Hayden fell into step beside him. "The land steward at Aylesbury tells me that you spent several mornings riding through the estate with him while you were there," he said. "I received a letter from him today."

"It was a very interesting tour."

"He said that you asked a hundred questions. He fears that you are suspicious of him, and are investigating his management."

"I merely was curious. It is my property, after all."

"Your curiosity was odd in itself. He did not miss that. He assumed that you did not even know his name, so his concern is not unwarranted."

"Of course I knew his name. Goldenwaddle. Who could forget a name like that?"

"You. And it is Goldentwattle. Not Goldenwaddle."

"Reassure Goldentwattle that I was pleased with what I saw. I have no major criticisms of either his stewardship or your oversight."

Hayden cocked an eyebrow. "No *major* criticisms?"

"I do have a small list of suggestions."

Hayden sighed with strained forbearance.

"They are very minor suggestions. More ideas than commands. You can blame Miss Montgomery. She scolded me for not paying attention. She seems to think that it matters if I do."

They entered the drawing room. Christian cocked his head toward Hayden and spoke confidentially. "Caroline's fiancé is a little dull. It is the unfortunate consequence of his sobriety and goodness, and we should not hold it against him. However, I thought I should warn you, in case you sit near him at dinner."

"I will be spared. I bribed Aunt Hen for a place beside Miss Montgomery, and I expect my conversation with her to be anything but dull."

"I feel very wicked," she whispered.

He certainly hoped so. He kissed her breast while he slid her chemise down. Her dinner dress and stays already formed a feminine puddle on the floor. He sat on the edge of his bed, unveiling her slowly, enjoying the way she gently trembled while she stood before him and submitted to this slow disrobing.

"Your aunt is in the house," she whispered. "And your cousin. They retired early, but they probably know I am still here."

She did not mean wicked, unfortunately. She meant uncomfortable.

"Leona, there must be a hectare of space in this house. Would you have misgivings if my aunt and cousin were in a cottage on a farm that neighbored mine?"

"But your aunt—"

"My aunt is busy with her own lover. By now M'sieur Lacroix has slipped in the kitchen door and made his way to her. Your presence in this house is the furthest thing from her mind."

He eased her leg up, and propped her foot on the bed beside his hip. She glanced down at how her position exposed her. He played at her garter, released it, and slid the stocking down her leg.

She steadied herself by holding his shoulder. She appeared stunning and erotic. He could not decide whether to bother with the other stocking or not.

"It is not really your family that disconcerts me." She did not whisper this time. "It is this bed. This chamber." She looked in his eyes. "This is your true home, in ways Aylesbury was not. These are the chambers where you find privacy. I feel that I am intruding."

"People are in these chambers all the time. Servants. Footmen. Phippen almost never leaves me alone." Best to skip the stocking. He caressed her thigh, trusting his hand's path would distract her.

"Servants are different. Does anyone else come here?"

"My brothers were in the sitting room just today." He cupped her mound. Its soft warmth entranced him. He gently stroked at the flesh below it and within its cleft. He watched ecstasy transform her face.

Her breath caught again and again and her hold on his shoulders tightened. He assumed he had overcome her misgivings in the best way possible.

He was wrong. She could barely breathe but she spoke all the same.

"You do not understand, Christian. I am not speaking of family in your sitting room. That is not the same as my being *here*. Have you allowed your lovers in here before?"

"Hell, no."

"See? I am intruding."

In a way she was. Except he had invited the intrusion. He had plotted it with great care all day.

He kissed a careful path around her nipple. "I want you here. In this bed, in this chamber. I want to take you here, and I want your scent to linger after you leave. I want the memory of our desire to haunt the rooms long after you are gone."

New emotions joined the pleasure and desire in her eyes. He saw lights of resignation and sadness. And surprise, perhaps, that the memories would matter to him.

There was not much talking after that. She abandoned herself to him. She held her breast so he could lick and suck it while his fingers entered her and made her groan.

She held his face to an aggressive kiss while she moved on his fingers, finding her pleasure while she flexed and circled. She pressed the kiss harder and held his shoulders with both her hands so she would not fall.

"Do you know what a Chinese pillow book is?" she asked while her expression reflected every sensation.

"I have heard of them. I have never seen one."

"I thought perhaps you had. Isabella has one, and some of the things that you do are in it. Like this."

"You saw it?" He pictured Leona paging through a book with erotic images. He got so hard that his mind clouded.

"I just peeked. She left it with my bath today while I prepared to dress for the dinner. She is convinced I am too stupid to know how to please you."

"I do not think that it is right that you saw it."

"It was a very small peek."

"I meant it is not right that you have seen it and I have not." She was so hot against his hand now, so wet. He doubted he could wait much longer. He began unfastening his trousers.

Her foot left the bed. She helped him with the garments. She freed his cock and closed her hand on it. She broke the kiss and looked down to watch her two hands move.

She stood naked in front of him, her long, wild curls pouring around her, her face that of a woman lost in pleasure. Her gentle grip pumped and her thumb circled and flicked. He gritted his teeth so he would not lose control.

Her gaze met his. Dark eyes. Erotic eyes. Her tongue's tip slid along the edges of her barely parted teeth.

"I am feeling very wicked," she whispered again. "I want you inside me. Filling me. I want it so much I could faint. But I also—" She looked down at her hands, then back in his eyes.

His jaw clenched. His whole body did. He almost begged. He almost commanded. He did not have to. She lowered herself until her beautiful naked body knelt

submissively. Her tongue laved, then she enclosed him
in unbearable pleasure.

"Stay like that. Do not move."

She turned her head to see him leaving the bed. Her
body reacted with frustration. His caresses had her waiting again. Waiting with aching impatience. Her breasts
tingled against the sheet below her. Her bottom rose a
little without her intending it.

He bent down and kissed the small of her back. "I
will return very quickly. I just realized that I have to
call for the carriage. It will be dawn very soon."

He pulled on a long garment cut much like a great-
coat. Its rich fluid fabric indicated its informal purpose.
He fastened several of the buttons carelessly, and went
over to pull the bell cord.

She had not noticed the hour. The night had seemed
endless just a moment ago. She was sorry it would
soon end.

She could not stay, of course. He had suggested it
again. He wanted her living here, close by, so he need
only pull that bell cord to invite another intrusion on
his isolated habits.

She heard him speaking lowly in the sitting room,
giving his command to a servant. She pictured him returning and seeing her like this, the way he had left her,
naked and vulnerable, her arms stretched above her
head and her legs spread wide. He had gently bound
her wrists together with his cravat, but she felt enough
slackness to know she could get free if she wanted.

There would be one more wicked pleasure before

she left. One more in a night of many. The lessons had left her so sensitive that the most sensual parts of her trembled while she waited.

He returned to the bed but did not rejoin her. He looked down, his hair barbaric in its disarray, his eyes scorching.

"Roll over."

She obeyed. His taut arm stretched and he gently stroked her nipple.

Delicious pleasure streamed down her body at once. Impossible need overpowered her. She arched so her breast rose toward that touch.

"It excites you, this game of submission." He glanced to where her bound wrists lay. "You know that you are not really afraid."

He was correct, but it was not entirely a game. This vulnerability seemed a physical reaction that matched the instinctive one she had always experienced with him. More than her body felt exposed as she lay like this, spread and bound, naked to his gaze and erotic touch. She was helpless to his power unless she worked to get free.

He stroked the other nipple, devastating her until she squirmed.

"What are you going to do?" she asked.

He got on the bed. Both hands teased her breasts while he knelt tall between her thighs. "I am going to watch your delirium grow while you tell me about that pillow book. Then we will try one of its secrets."

Her face warmed. She was not sure she could describe such things without using scandalous language.

His head lowered and his teeth gently nipped her breast. "Tell me. I command it."

He made good on his word to make her delirious. His tongue and mouth, his mere size dominating her, made the excitement frantic. She tried to describe one of the pictures. The mere attempt made it vivid in her mind again. Only she did not see two Chinese people this time, but Christian and herself.

That aroused her in ways she never expected. She described another more freely, giving herself over to the erotic details. Her body responded very specifically to words and images.

"We will try that one." He swung away from her and lay with his back propped on pillows.

She was desperate now, with a sensual craving so intense that she could think of nothing except wanting him. She turned on her side and scrambled to kneel. Her bound wrists interfered and she held them toward him.

"I think we will keep that part," he said.

"It was not in the book."

"The artist lacked imagination."

He helped her to stand. She positioned herself with her feet flanking his hips. She lowered herself down to a crouch that faced him, one so folded that her knees touched her own breasts. He entered her as she settled. He filled her fully, deeply. His hardness pressed high in her and made her lips and passage throb.

She held his shoulder and moved. She sought ways to feel him better, harder as she circled and rocked. Her control brought indescribable pleasure that drove her toward an aggressive completion.

She was still exposed in this position, to his gaze

and then to his touch. He reached between her legs and their bodies and caressed above their joining, carefully playing at that sensitive nub in ways that made her feel him inside her even more.

Ecstasy sent its first rippling trembles through her loins, pooling where she surrounded him. She lost control and circled and tensed and cried with frenzied need. He grasped her hips and lifted her enough that he could take over. She became submissive again, her pose making her vulnerable, her body accepting. He held her firmly to a long, hard ravishment until her scream of fulfillment filled the chamber.

He helped her to dress, then pulled on his trousers and shirt. He escorted her down to the front door. Outside, a carriage waited. Only the coachman was there, but he lifted a pistol when Christian looked his way.

Christian handed her in. "My carriage will be at your house tomorrow at three o'clock," he said through the window.

"Where am I going?"

"I have arranged for you to meet Alfred Howard."

Howard was another shipper, only his company was not as big as St. John's.

The reference to her duty dimmed the night's joy. It was good of him to help her the way he had promised, but they both knew what finishing her mission meant.

She leaned out the window to kiss him. "Thank you."

He laid his fingertips on her lips, as if to stop her expression of gratitude. He brushed them in a feathered caress. "The next day we will call on Denningham together."

He astonished her. She had given up hope of pursuing that other goal. She was not even sure that she wanted to anymore.

She tried to read his expression in the night. She saw only his shadowed face and darker eyes. He stepped back, and gestured for the coachman to drive.

CHAPTER
TWENTY-THREE

Two days after Christian informed her of the meeting, Leona entered the Earl of Denningham's London house on Christian's arm at exactly four o'clock in the afternoon.

The servant escorted them to the library. She trusted that this would be a very brief meeting. She hoped that Denningham would explain about that death notice in a way that required no further speculations.

A portly, tawny-haired man, Denningham greeted Christian warmly and beamed at her during the introductions.

For the first half hour he expressed interest in China and flattered her beauty. He joked with Easterbrook about some sins from their university days. He waxed eloquent about a new rose he was growing.

He impressed her as a simple man, for all his titles and status. She doubted that he had ever done anything mysterious, least of all commission a death notice for a man he did not know. Denningham was Easterbrook's foil, all shallow brightness and happy optimism.

Finally Christian took advantage of a lull in the conversation. "Denningham, Miss Montgomery learned something that troubles her. I suggested that she speak openly to you about it."

Denningham's pliable face directed curiosity at her. "If I can help, I of course will be happy to do so."

She had brought her copy of the death notice with her. She removed it from her reticule. "I discovered that this was published when my father died. It appeared in *The Times*." She read it to him.

He listened politely. When she was done he waited for her to make her request. His perplexed expression implied he could not imagine what that request could be.

"I found the man who wrote this. He said that he was commissioned to do it. He said that you had paid him and supplied the facts regarding my father's life and death."

Denningham reacted with astonishment. He looked at Christian, who shrugged. *I told her,* that shrug said.

"Miss Montgomery, this writer, whoever he is, lied to you. I would not have any reason to do what he claimed. I have never heard of your father." He laughed and flushed. "I am not even sure I could find Macao on a map."

She doubted he could. "It appears that he did lie. He must have plucked a name from society, to appease me. Forgive me. That any notice was published is peculiar. That one like this print distressed me, and I had to ask."

"No need to apologize. None at all. I am almost sorry it was not me, so that you could be done with it." His smile forgave her. He turned to Christian. "What ho, I hear there will be nuptials soon for your lovely cousin. Rumor says the groom has nine thousand a year."

The conversation slid away from her. She tucked the notice back in her reticule.

Christian made movements for departure. The gentlemen stood. Denningham offered his hand to help her rise. "You must come back when the garden is in full bloom, Miss Montgomery. I have one of the best in London, if I do say so myself."

Early evening's golden light bathed the street when she and Christian left the house. He spoke to the coachman, then joined her inside the coach.

"Well?" she asked.

Her question jolted him out of a reflective distraction. "Well?"

"Was he lying?"

"Do you think he was?"

"I worry that he would not know how to lie even if his life were at stake."

"Then there you have it."

"Of course, he may be a very good liar," she said. "Too skilled for me to perceive. You, on the other hand, would be certain one way or the other."

"I have known Denningham for years. His emotions are so predictable, so visible, that I have found him a restful presence compared to most people. Today I perceived nothing besides unwarranted joy in life, delight in his roses, an inappropriate masculine interest in you—"

"Surely not!"

"It is one reaction I would kill to avoid knowing, but it is unmistakable. Let me see, he also exuded confusion about that notice, and genuine sympathy for your distress." He casually pulled the curtains on the windows. "And, unfortunately, he was hurt that I did not dissuade you from accusing him."

She pushed one curtain open a bit, so it would not be so dark. "In other words, he was telling the truth and I was given the wrong name."

He tugged the curtain closed again. "Actually, I think he was lying."

"But you just said—"

"Yes. Interesting, isn't it?"

"How do you explain that?"

He shrugged, but it was obvious that the discovery troubled him. "Either he is slyer than I ever guessed, or my curse is not infallible. I have perhaps been too arrogant in thinking it is. I do not care for the notion, however. To suffer this and not even know if my perceptions are valid will be . . . intolerable."

She could barely see his face in the shadowed space. "It is possible that with him, and others, you do not look too deeply into those perceptions. You would have practice in avoiding those intrusions with intimates."

"Perhaps so. I will have to be more critical in the future, however, and assume less. I will never be completely certain again, will I?"

She sensed more dismay than his bland tone conveyed. She began to open the curtain so she could see his eyes.

"Do not touch that curtain."

His command stopped her fingers on the fabric's edge. "Why not?"

"We are about to reach Hyde Park and it is the fashionable hour."

"The whole purpose of the fashionable hour is to see and be seen. Why suffer it at all if you will remain in a closed coach?"

"I am conducting an experiment. The coach will plow into the thick of it, and I will test whether pleasure silences society's tedious noise."

Already she could hear that noise. The coach slowed to a crawl. A river of humanity soon flowed around them, filling the dark interior with its buzzing chatter.

He knelt on the floor, laid her down on the bench seat, and began lifting her skirt and petticoat. "I will do for you, then you will do for me. Or would you rather switch the order?"

A woman laughed right outside the window. Leona tried to push her skirts down. "It is too daring to consider such a thing. There are carriages and riders all around. Inches from us. And the glass is open! If a breeze catches the curtains—"

"Dowagers will faint, matrons will scream, and we will be immortalized. We are courting ruin and damnation." He bent her right leg, and lifted her left one over his shoulder. "Exciting, isn't it?"

Very exciting. Wickedly so. She looked up to the slit of daylight below one curtain, and imagined what would be seen by anyone peering in. Not so much, perhaps. It was dark in here and maybe—"

"You are unbearably beautiful, Leona."

She gazed down her body. His long fingers reached out to touch what he had exposed. She bit her lip to hold in her moan. Forcing her own silence only intensi-fied what his touches did to her.

He could be a devil sometimes, and he was now. He deliberately teased at her, gently stroking in ways that maddened her but avoided the more direct caresses that she craved.

"Open your pelisse."

She fumbled at the closure. The two halves fell away.

"Now touch yourself the way I showed you in Aylesbury. Pleasure yourself while I pleasure you."

She touched her own breasts, hesitantly. This had made her very shy the first time he requested it, and it still did. Her fingertips found her nipples through the cloth. She rubbed. She became even more sensitive where he caressed her, unbelievably so.

He watched her expression, his dark gaze on her face and her abandon. She held in her cries as best she could but the pleasure was defeating her. Finally one snuck out, low and throaty and loud in the enclosed space.

She pressed one hand to her mouth. He smiled and kissed her leg. His hands cupped her bottom and lifted it just enough. His head bowed and his tongue began its devastating torture.

Christian walked a familiar route through Mayfair. His path took him past two dinner parties that he had de-clined to attend, and ultimately to Rallingport's library.

The Duke of Ashford had come this time. Christian took a position near the second table where Ashford's silver hair rose above all the other heads.

"You haven't been in town much recently, Easterbrook," Ashford said. "Dallying in the country, I hear."

"Diddling is more like it, from what *I* hear," Rallingport muttered. He chuckled at his own joke.

"Gentlemen, I advise you to watch your insinuations. I have met the lovely Miss Montgomery, and she is in every way a lady," Denningham said soberly.

"I have proof positive that the best ladies are known to diddle," Rallingport said.

Meadowsun's mouth became a hard line in his shriveled face. "Your schoolboy quips are tedious. I, for one, am glad to see your recent period of activity, Easterbrook. Very healthy. Very healthy indeed."

"Well, he found a woman good for did—excuse me, *dallying*," Rallingport snickered. "And it is well known that regular *dallying* is beneficial to a man's health, both mental and physical. If Easterbrook's lady fair is particularly helpful on that count, the government should make a contract with her and improve the national health."

Christian set his hand on Rallingport's shoulder. "You have been drinking a good while already, so I will ignore that you just crossed a line. Cross it again, however, and I will have to call you out."

Rallingport had been drinking long enough to take umbrage. "The hell you say. Not likely a mad recluse can best me in a duel, so think hard before any glove falls."

"He will have no choice if you do not apologize," Denningham said. "So apologize."

Rallingport's face reddened.

"Apologize," Ashford said with a pointed glance.

Rallingport mumbled an apology. Ashford lit a cigar, signaling a break in the game. Denningham rose and walked over to the tray holding an array of spirits. Christian followed him.

"I was flattered that you brought Miss Montgomery to call," Denningham said. "You have not visited my house in years."

"But you were less flattered when you realized there were ulterior motives to my visit."

Denningham flushed. "To be expected, I suppose. Not your habit to waste time on such things. I should have known that a petition from a lovely woman was at the bottom of it."

"She would have asked her question whether I brought her or not. Sooner or later she would have made her way to you. I only regret that my presence may have encouraged you to lie to her."

"Lie? You insult me with that suggestion."

Christian released his perception as he had not done with Denningham in years. He honed his attention on the man. Despite the indignant bluster, insult did not cloak Denningham so much as nervous worry. Christian had not been sure of the lie on entering this library, but now he was.

"Why would you place that death notice? How did you know Montgomery?"

Denningham tried to hold a stance of wounded outrage. He could not manage it. His bravado dissolved into dismay.

"I did not even remember what she was talking about at first. I never made the connection between your Miss Montgomery and that damned notice. Hell, I'd clear forgotten about it. I did not know her father. He was just a name. I was told to find a man to write up the notice, then arrange for its publication." He smiled sheepishly. "It seemed a little thing at the time, although I did not care for the detail about the cause of death. Seemed unnecessarily cruel. I was glad the writer fellow dressed that up a bit."

Denningham seemed to speak honestly. Although, having erred at least once, Christian could never be absolutely certain about Denningham again. He was still assessing what that meant for all of his other certainties.

"Who told you to do it?"

"My father. He assumed I would know a young writer looking to make a few pounds. He thought he gave me the chance for a bit of largesse to a friend. Hell, I never knew any writers. What would writers want with me? I just picked a name off the court reports."

They returned to the others. Christian took Denningham's place so Ashford would have a decent chance of making up his losses. They played another few rounds of whist in a game of cards begun generations ago.

It appeared the connection to Montgomery was not with the current Earl of Denningham, but the last one. Just as the connection had been with the last Easterbrook.

Christian studied the cards in his hand, then turned his attention to the other gentlemen gathered in this room.

CHAPTER
TWENTY-FOUR

G riffin Winterside examined himself in the big looking glass. The tailor hovered and smoothed a sleeve.

Winterside turned this way and that. He had feared he'd look foolish in this fashion with its snug waist, but now he decided it flattered him. The stays helped, of course. They were deucedly uncomfortable, but . . . The tailor had not overdone that silly puff at the top of the sleeves either. He eyed the low hem. Did he imagine that his legs looked longer?

He decided the length flattered him too. He gave the tailor his approval to complete the finish work.

Delight in the new garment lightened his mood while he left the shop. That coat was worth every penny. He could not afford to look like an antique. All the peers wore this style now. All the young and fashionable ones, at least.

Thinking of the peers turned his mind to his duties. One in particular troubled him. That business with Miss Montgomery may have turned odd. There was a rumor abroad that one of Easterbrook's servants had been attacked in her house by an intruder.

A thief no doubt. Certainly. And yet, when he had met yesterday with his contact on that matter, he could not shake the sense that the man knew more about that rumor than the Company ever would.

Indeed, the entire matter regarding the woman had become vague and murky. A simple affair had grown complex. Winterside did not care for the feeling that he had been someone's pawn in a game gone awry, especially since Easterbrook had probably been angered.

He would have to consult with his superiors. He debated how to do so without implying that he had lost control of the reins—

A body suddenly blocked his path. A chest blocked his sight. A rather broad chest in a very nice coat.

"Excuse me." He started to step around. The nice coat moved too, blocking him again.

He looked up and saw blond hair and an amiable smile.

"Mr. Griffin Winterside? I do have the right man, don't I?"

"You do."

"Good." The blond man gestured. Two more men appeared. "The coach is here to bring you to the meeting, sir, as promised."

"Coach? I have no meeting today. I checked my diary and—"

"I was told you did. Told to bring you. I dare not fail in my duty. If we discover I erred, I will beg your forgiveness."

This young man did not strike Winterside as one

who ever begged forgiveness. That smile did not fool him. He had not worked Parliament for over a decade without learning a thing or two about judging people.

He stood his ground. Except he actually didn't. Somehow their little knot moved toward a coach fifteen feet away. Its luxury and expense reassured him. It was a lord's coach to be sure. Perhaps he had neglected to note a meeting in his diary after all.

The footmen stood aside. One reached for the door. Winterside spied the escutcheon. Alarm made him dig in his heels. This was *Easterbrook's* coach.

He pivoted to bolt. Too late. Arms lifted him like he weighed nothing and deposited him inside the vehicle.

A half hour later he found himself a prisoner in Easterbrook's house on Grosvenor Square. He mounted the servant stairs with two men in front of him and two behind, like a prisoner going to the noose.

A door opened, and he stepped inside a huge, empty chamber. The door closed. They left him there, alone, without even a chair to sit on.

"He is here. Sweating in the fencing chamber." Miller stuck his head in the dressing room to report his success.

Christian finished tying his cravat. "Did you get that other information that I sent you to obtain?"

"Lord Hayden said he attempted to sell out a company called Four Corners while you were away on your self-indulgent adventures. It had made no payments for over a year, and the company's solicitors did not respond to his queries for accountings. He gave me what he could about it. All the facts are on the table in your sitting room, near that chair you use."

Christian examined the cravat in the looking glass. "Self-indulgent adventures, Miller?"

"Lord Hayden's words, sir. You commanded that I tell you exactly what your brother said."

"Did my brother say whether I still have a partnership in this company?"

"Lord Hayden says it is not clear. His exact words again. There has been no income or correspondence since before your father's death. Lord Hayden said he long ago assumed the partnership had been dissolved."

A fair assumption on Hayden's part. A wrong one, however. The other facts were unassailable. Hayden never forgot numbers. If he said there had been no income, that was how it had been.

"Do you want me with you when you talk to Mr. Winterside?"

"That will not be necessary. He will follow the path that benefits him and his employer. I only need to explain which path does. However, when you are at Miss Montgomery's house tonight, be very alert. If Winterside decides to cover two bets after he leaves here today, there may be trouble."

It was past midnight when Christian rode his horse to Bury Street. As expected, Mr. Winterside had proven shrewd and pliable. He expressed honest dismay on hearing the danger in which Leona had been placed. He was adamant that his only interest lay in sparing the

Company from embarrassment. It had not been difficult to convince him of the best way to do that.

One of Christian's footmen opened the door to Leona's house, but Miller was in the reception hall. Arms crossed and back resting on the wall, he sat on a bench near the bottom of the stairs that led up to the next level.

He stood when Christian entered. "Everything is quiet," he reported. "I check the house every half hour."

"Any new cigar ashes across the way?"

"Not for over a week now."

"Where is Tong Wei?"

"Last I saw, he was in the library. He sits on the floor. Odd, that."

Miller was all serious duty on the surface, but an uncharacteristic emotion flowed deeper. Something similar but softer bathed the stairs. Christian glanced up and saw a bit of white fabric poking around the corner of the wall atop the landing.

He imagined Miller sitting down here stoically, and little Isabella up there, staying as close as she could. Not only desire flowed between them in the silence. A deeper yearning was palpable, and it went both ways.

"I will check the garden now, sir."

"There is a man there. He will raise the alarm if anyone intrudes. Better if you secured the house again. The upper chambers. Take your time and do it carefully. I will take your place here until you return."

Miller began up the stairs, but paused on the fourth one. "When do you think they—When do you think Miss Montgomery will go back to China, sir?"

"Soon, Mr. Miller."
Too soon.

She drifted toward the surface, but did not fully wake. Warmth surrounded her. The rhythm of another's breaths matched her own. Comfort and peace spread, easing her slowly out of her dream.

She touched the arm embracing her and smiled at the heartbeat against her back. Christian was here. She had not expected him.

She did not stir. She just enjoyed the way he held her and relished the contentment he brought to her. He had tried very hard not to wake her, she could tell. For an arrogant, somewhat imperious man, he had his moments of sweet consideration.

She finally reached the surface. She turned on her back, so his breaths tickled her ear. She resettled his embracing arm for her comfort. He in turn moved it again, so his hand could cup her breast. His hold just lay there, not in seduction but in a gesture of possession and unity.

"You are very late," she said.

"I arrived soon after midnight, but allowed Miller a respite from his duties for a while."

She guessed what Mr. Miller had done with this respite, while he was free to roam this house. She should scold Christian for aiding his servant in making free with her own, but she had neither the heart nor the hypocrisy to deny Isabella whatever happiness she could have right now.

"Miller asked me how long you would be staying in

England. He wants to know how much longer he has with her."

The night's poignancy increased with his statement. He was not only talking about Miller and Isabella.

"What did you tell him?"

"I told him that I thought you would be leaving soon. You said that your introduction to Howard the other day was fruitful, so I imagine it won't be long before you go."

"Not too long, but not so soon either. That meeting was perhaps too fruitful. I am faced with an embarrassment of riches. I have a difficult choice to make."

"Is it your choice alone?"

"Actually, it is not mine at all. I meant my brother will have a difficult choice. In the end it will be his decision, of course."

"Of course."

If one could hear a smile, she did in the way he said that. He did not believe Gaspar would make the choice any more than St. John did. It was true what St. John had said, that Gaspar was still green. Her brother would probably follow her counsel in this as in so much else.

"Both St. John and Mr. Howard would be good allies," she explained. "The difference is that St. John wants to swallow Montgomery and Tavares, but Howard will allow us to remain independent. So the two alliances offer very different things."

"Which one resolves the problems that brought you here?"

"St. John would solve the immediate ones. I do not think pirates prey on *his* ships. And his trading network is very big. He said that he does not think the Company's monopolies will be renewed when their charter expires. He wants us for when it ends, for our Chinese base. He has it all planned. Our appeal is that we are so weak he can demand control."

She puzzled it out in ways she had avoided. She did not lie to herself about the reason she kept putting it off. She had met her traders, and she had obtained the potential alliances. Her primary duty in London, her reason for making this journey in the first place, would be over once she settled this question.

"Howard no doubt also sees advantage in your Chinese base," he said. "Since he does not want to swallow you, if the monopoly ends you will be free to reap the rewards yourself, and only share what you choose. Would you prefer that?"

He appeared genuinely interested. He lay on his side, that hand on her breast, and joined her in weighing it all. His questions encouraged her to think it through.

"Five years from now, if we make no serious missteps, we will flourish if we ally ourselves with Howard."

"Then the choice is clear, is it not?"

Perhaps, but that future would happen only if she continued to guide Montgomery and Tavares the way she had the last six years. Gaspar could not steer the company that cleverly yet.

She wished now that Christian had not helped her to clarify the choices. He should have done more with his hands than hold her breast. He should have seduced her to remain indifferent to her duty.

"The other mission can be settled soon too," he said.

"I do not have even one name, Christian. Not a single one, besides your father. Nor have I been vigilant in looking for them. Lady Phaedra asked me about my last letter for *Minerva's Banquet* at Caroline's engagement dinner, and I pretended it would be sent to her soon. Only it has not been written the way I intended. With what I learned about my father and yours, I lack the courage to investigate this now."

He kissed her cheek. "If I thought that you would walk away from it with no regrets or guilt, if I believed you would be safe in retreat, I would urge you once more to put this matter aside."

She turned her face toward his. "It might be better if I did."

"That is different from knowing that you should. I have a name for you, darling. You need to tell me if you want me to finish this my own way, or if you want to face the man your father invisibly fought and write your last letter the way that you planned."

She did not know what to say. Of course she wanted to confront that man. She wanted to see him ruined, along with any other men involved in this. Her belief in their evil had not changed.

Everything else had, however. She could not expose these men without also exposing Christian's father. Christian deserved more loyalty than that.

Nor could she write about this mission in *Minerva's Banquet* without admitting her own father's smuggling. His conversion would add drama to the story and absolve him in most eyes, but he would be forever linked to that evil.

"Once we do this, I will have no excuse to stay," she said.

He rose up on his forearm and looked down at her. He kissed her. He lay down and pulled her on top of him so her body touched his from her head to her toes. His warmth lured her away from the sad future and back to the contented present.

CHAPTER
TWENTY-FIVE

Barnabas Meadowsun was crossing the courtyard of Doctors' Commons when he noticed Christian. Christian took Leona's arm and walked in Meadowsun's direction, leaving Tong Wei near the gate. The cleric had no choice except to acknowledge them.

"Easterbrook. This is unexpected. It is a pleasure to see you, of course." He barely smiled, but then he never allowed his mouth to reflect joy or sorrow. Discretion had bred in him the ability to make his face a mask and his heart a locked vault.

Christian wondered if the man did not only hide emotions, but also eschew them. It was possible to achieve a state where nothing caused ripples in one's spirit, let alone waves. Christian had come close to that himself, after all.

Christian made introductions. Meadowsun made a little bow to Leona, but his manner conveyed that he was a busy man and had little time for social visits.

Meadowsun's mouth formed its bare smile again. "Are you here for the Faculty Office?"

"I am here to see you. The archbishop's clerk at Lambeth Palace said you were here today," Christian said. "Miss Montgomery, perhaps you would like to sit here while I talk to Mr. Meadowsun."

Leona accepted the invitation to perch on the nearby garden bench.

"I have been looking into my affairs," Christian said. "Digging through my father's papers."

"Ah, so that is why you are in the City. I am glad to see you taking up the reins of your position. It is my hope that you will expand your renewed interest in the world to include government duties. The archbishop feels the same way, and just mentioned it to me this morning."

"His concern is generous. Now, regarding those papers. I found references to a company in which my father invested years ago. A trading company. No ships, though. The best I can tell, captains were contracted to move the cargo, and paid per shipment."

"It probably is a common method of arranging trade. Your solicitor could explain it. I confess that most business legalities escape me." Meadowsun managed not to see Leona sitting two feet away. He pretended she was not watching him with great interest and dangerous eyes.

"My solicitor has been very helpful, but I believe you can enlighten me further. I found evidence of this partnership, but I have received no income from it. My brother, who has been managing my investments, says the partnership must have been dissolved before my father passed away, but my solicitor—he has been helpful, as I said—finds no documents to that effect, or even to the partnership's founding."

Meadowsun glanced around the courtyard, seeking someone to save him from this boring conversation.

"Was it dissolved, Meadowsun?"

"How would I know?"

"You are one of the other partners."

The barest frown. "I do not recall such an investment. If there are no documents how can you assume my involvement?"

"Correspondence indicates that at least four men invested. My father, you, Denningham, and Rallingport. Four of the men who met on a regular basis, to choose where and how to throw their united influence to preserve and protect England."

The perplexed frown did not smooth. The face did not react.

"You still cannot remember? Hayden tells me that tracing this company's owners and earnings will not be difficult once we go to court. I thought I should speak with you first, however. A good deal of money has gone missing."

"You are talking nonsense. I am no trader, no shipper. Nor was your father or the others you mention. What possible interest could we have in such things?"

"Profit," Leona interrupted from the bench. "Profit of the worst kind. A good deal of profit. An obscene amount, I would guess, if the primary cargo was opium and the destination was China."

Meadowsun's eyes turned wizened and shrewd. "I doubt you will find much relief in a court with this mythical business, Easterbrook."

"I expect that I will. I certainly will get a hearing regarding your attacks on Miss Montgomery."

"My attacks? You are mad. Completely insane. I will have to speak with the bishops about that, and seek counsel on whether your fellow peers should be made aware of your condition."

"Are you threatening me, Meadowsun?"

"I am concerned for you, that is all."

"You would be wiser to be concerned for yourself. Winterside told me all about your involvement in the attempts to dissuade Miss Montgomery. He described his meetings with you, and your insistence that he approach me to request my help."

"Nonsense. He would not dare such a thing."

"He would not dare to cross you, you mean? He did not like the way you arranged for his to be the visible face in this game. He realized that the finger might point to him if anyone sought a culprit for those—what did he say you called them the other day—episodes regarding Miss Montgomery."

Leona rose from the bench. Her eyes blazed. "Episodes? *Episodes?* You hounded my father to his grave. You nearly ruined him, and we spent years waiting for the next strike, the next fire or scuttled ship. You tried to run me down with a horse here in London and set fire to my house, and you thought of these crimes as *episodes*?"

An expression of disdain twisted Meadowsun's face. He looked at Leona with revulsion.

He turned on his heel. "I will not be insulted by this woman. If you have more to say, come to my chambers, Easterbrook. But leave your whore here."

Christian gestured for Tong Wei to join them.

"Sit here. Wait for me," Christian said to Leona.

"I will not. I am going in there and I am going to claw that man's eyes and—"

"You will sit here and wait." He physically emphasized the command by pressing her shoulders until she was on the bench again. "Tong Wei, do not leave her side."

"You said I could confront him," Leona protested.

"And you have. I will do the rest alone."

"I want him to admit he did it. I want him to pay."

"He will pay, Leona. I promise."

He looked back and checked on her twice while he crossed the courtyard to the building's entry. It would be just like her to follow him.

He made his way to Meadowsun's chambers. He closed the door after he entered. Meadowsun sat near a window, his profile limned by the bright light outside, his face resolute and his eyes mean.

Christian walked over to him. He grabbed him by the coat, stood him up, and smashed a fist into that creased, astonished face. Meadowsun landed back in his chair with a bad fall. He scrambled to right himself, holding his hand against his jaw. Christian hit him again.

"That is for the insults out there to Miss Montgomery, and the way you have endangered her. Be glad you are a cleric or I'd call you out and kill you."

Christian walked away and forced some calm. Meadowsun collected the fear that had crashed out of him and tucked it away.

Christian gazed down at the man. "The opium trade is not illegal under our laws. Nor the secrecy. Even the attacks on Montgomery—they were long ago and far away and I doubt I can prove your hand in it. Recent events in London, however, were neither legal nor distant. And this company smuggles more than opium, and its ships are not only going to China. You will hear what I say and answer my questions or I will see you answer for all of that with your freedom."

"Then have your say. Ask your damned questions."

"My father kept records of the payments he received. I assume as much or more profit was made in the years since he died. I know how much you stole from me. It adds up to a significant fortune that I did not receive. Why would you risk being caught in such a theft?"

Meadowsun carefully touched his jaw and winced. "You could not be trusted."

"And Denningham and Rallingport could be?"

Meadowsun just looked at him.

"Ah, I see. It was not just me. It was them too, after they inherited. You kept it all."

A silence hung while Meadowsun weighed his situation, and his words. "The sons were not the fathers. I could tell as you one by one took your places at the whist table. Denningham was dim-witted. Rallingport was a drunk. You—well, you were too odd to trust. I stole nothing. The initial investments had been repaid many times over."

So Denningham had been ignorant all along. There was some relief in hearing that.

Meadowsun smiled slyly. "You won't accuse me. I do not care what Winterside said. You don't dare air this in any court. The world would know then. Everyone would know that your father started it all. It was all his idea, and the rest of us bought in after it was well underway."

"That might be true. Or not. If it comes to it, though, I will let a judge sort the facts. I cannot allow you to continue these crimes now, not to protect his name or mine."

Meadowsun sneered. "See, this is why I did not trust you. Why your father's share in the partnership was buried with him. There was the danger you did not take after him, but after that madwoman of a mother."

"You must like being thrashed, Meadowsun. You should be careful. You never can be sure how far a madman will go once he starts."

Meadowsun's face fell. He eyed Christian more cautiously.

"Why did you publish that death notice?"

"Her father was a nuisance, just like her. He was one of the early shippers contracted by our man in Calcutta, then he had a change of heart. He turned against the trade completely, like a damned reformer. We didn't care about that. There are always other shippers. But he had to go writing all those letters, and trying to ferret out who we were. He wrote to the Company. He wrote to members of Parliament. He began to talk to captains, and suspect our shipments into England and France. When he died, it was in our interest to make sure all those recipients of his letters knew he was gone."

"You could not resist indicating he died of that which he condemned, though."

"It would call into question his state of mind when he made his accusations."

Satisfied that he had all of Leona's answers for her, and a few he needed for himself, Christian made himself comfortable on a chair. "So, how would you like to pay me this money?"

Meadowsun's face fell in shock. "*What?* You come at me like an angel of justice, and all you really want is your share? This is about *money*?" He cackled. His eyes cleared, relieved at this most ordinary goal.

"I would like to settle it."

"I am certain we can work something out."

"I would like it now."

"You really are mad. You are speaking of years' worth of payments. It isn't just sitting in my library, to be handed over."

"That is unfortunate. That puts you in a bad spot, doesn't it?"

Meadowsun stared at him. Emotions finally burst out of him. Dismay. Panic.

"I could force the matters through the normal means. Both those of the money, and the attacks on Miss Montgomery. Perhaps a less public solution would be better. You remember how it goes. You have sat around that whist table enough in your years, while alternatives to the king's courts were debated and chosen. Our friend in Kent, for example."

"There were nine others at that table, sharing the decisions. Not just one mad marquess."

"Imagine if you will that Mr. Montgomery sits with me, aiding my judgment. Here is what I propose. First, you will resign your position. When this comes out, you do not want to embarrass the archbishop."

"Comes out?"

THE SINS OF LORD EASTERBROOK

"In *Minerva's Banquet*. Miss Montgomery will be explaining this company's opium trade in her last letter. She will name names. She thought to hold back for my sake, but I insisted she go forward. The story will bring her lessons about the opium trade home to her readers as nothing else will." He paused. "If you are very good, and do as I say, it will only be the opium smuggling that will be published. You will face moral accusations for it, but not criminal ones. The rest of the Four Corners smuggling, however, must end too."

"No one gives a damn about the opium trade. They want their tea and they don't care how many Chinamen die for it."

"They will not be able to claim ignorance at least. Second, my brother Hayden will investigate the extent of this business over the years, and you will aid him, so we determine the full amount due. My solicitor will meet with yours to determine the value of your property and financial holdings. You will pay what you can and give me a note for the rest. Whatever I receive will be donated to charities recommended by some good ladies I know."

"You bastard. You want to ruin me."

"You will be left with enough to live modestly, but I will hold a note for whatever I do not take. You will be out of this trade, however. You will be out of the church and out of London. Mr. Winterside has agreed that the Company will be watching for me, to make sure you do not start it up again. If you do, or if any misfortune befalls Miss Montgomery or her brother, I will call the note and leave you beggared."

Ugly anger poured out of Meadowsun. "You are a

fool if you think it matters if I am in or out of it. Montgomery was a fool to think he could stop it. There is profit in opium because people want it. They will kill for it."

"That may be true, but the profit will not be yours. You brought misery to thousands. In order to preserve the flow of money, you destroyed a man and you endangered the woman I love. Be glad I am not killing you for the last crime alone."

His business done, Christian got up and walked to the door.

"I was wrong about you," Meadowsun snarled. "You *are* like him. Just as ruthless. Just as cold. I wish I had known earlier. We might have worked well together. The son is the father after all."

Christian pauscd. He looked back. "Yes."

He almost stumbled over Leona outside the door. She had followed. She had been listening, and Tong Wei stood twenty feet away.

She took Christian's arm and they walked back to the garden.

"No, you are not," she said. "You are not like your father."

"They will leave now?" Tong Wei asked. "I did not fully understand the meaning of their title before these last days. They are called footmen because they are always under one's feet."

Leona laughed. "Even now they await the carriage to bring them back to Grosvenor Square."

Isabella frowned at the announcement. The departure that gave Tong Wei relief obviously saddened her.

"You must admit that it will be good to have some privacy again, Isabella," Leona said. "I welcome that, but I know why you do not."

Even better would be to live without the sense that she must scrutinize every face she passed. The afternoon at Doctors' Commons had relieved her of a caution she had known half her life. Its absence made her a little giddy but also a little lost.

It was odd, how achieving a goal and purpose could empty one out. The smile would not leave her face, but in her heart there was a void where before unbending determination had thrived. Dismay simmered there as well, at how this resolution left her adrift.

"We can sail back now," Tong Wei said. "If the winds are favorable, you can return before the trading season in Canton is very far underway."

How like Tong Wei to remind her that she was not adrift at all. Her crusade was over, but her life and purpose were not.

"Yes, we can sail home." She counted back the months. It took at least five to sail to China in the most favorable conditions. To have any chance of arriving before winter they would have to leave very soon.

Isabella's face fell more. She ran from the room. Tong Wei watched her flee.

"She was foolish to love him," he said.

Leona's throat tightened. She rose, to follow Isabella and offer comfort, and to take some comfort herself. "It is never foolish to love, Tong Wei."

CHAPTER
TWENTY-SIX

Christian was surprised to see his carriage outside the door that night. He had called for his horse. The presence of Mr. Miller explained everything.

"I smell rain." Miller made the excuse as he held open the carriage door.

"Playing footman tonight, Miller?"

"I thought I would accompany you, sir. To make one last check of the property and be sure nothing is amiss."

"You dedication is impressive."

"Thank you, sir."

The dedication was not to duty but to the little servant on Bury Street. No doubt Miller felt much as Christian did as they rolled through the dark streets toward that house. It might still be spring in London, but these love affairs were entering late autumn. This afternoon with Meadowsun had seen to that.

Christian felt the burden of the decision he had made. The man deserved more than exile and reduced circumstances and even the scandal when the Four

Corners opium trade was exposed. People had been destroyed and almost killed. Serious crimes had been committed. The fullness of it would never be aired now, although he suspected that by the time Hayden was done the sons of the last Easterbrook would know more than they wanted about their father.

He wanted to think that he had not chosen his course to protect any criminal, dead or alive, or even to spare the archbishop from learning of Meadowsun's depravity. The mood in the country was not stable. Confidence in the government and especially the peerage was low. A public airing of all of the Four Corners' smuggling would only fan the fires of public discontent.

The carriage stopped at Leona's house. He walked to her door with Miller two steps behind.

He had given Leona a full loaf at least, even if his conscience only accepted half of one. All the same she had appeared subdued this afternoon while he brought her back here. Like Miller beside him and like his own heart, she knew what the victory meant to them. Pending loss had drenched the carriage's small space and dulled any relief or contentment in her mission's denouement.

"It appears very quiet," Miller said. "I see no lamps."

It did appear quiet. An arrow of grief shot through Christian. A moment of irrational dismay said she had left already. She had slipped away, to avoid a painful parting.

It passed quickly, replaced by a wave of apprehension when there was no response to his knock. Miller instantly exuded alertness and worry too.

"Odd, that," Miller mumbled. He knocked louder, then cocked his ear toward the door. "Did you hear that?"

Christian had. He grasped the latch. The door swung wide and revealed a chaos of shadows. The sound repeated. A moan, not ten feet away.

"Get a lamp off the carriage, Miller."

Christian entered the reception hall. His boots poked the dark shadows. Bodies. Two of them. Fighting a surge of panic he bent down and felt the garments. Men, not women. He closed his eyes while relief almost overwhelmed him. He felt their necks and found no pulses.

Suddenly lamplight threw the scene into sharp chiaroscuro, revealing two men who remained in contorted, awkward rest. A third one, however, lifted a hand. The lamp picked out red silk and an embroidered dragon propped against the far wall, then rose to show Tong Wei's face.

Christian strode over to him. A large dark stain on Tong Wei's shoulder showed where he had taken a pistol's ball. Christian bent low to examine the wound.

"I was careless. I thought it was you," Tong Wei rasped. "There were four. I could not kill them all."

Christian looked back at the bodies. Whoever these men were, he doubted they had been warned about what waited on the other side of this door.

Miller set the lamp on the floor. "I am going to see about the ladies."

Tong Wei shook his head. "They are gone. The men spoke not at all. I do not know where they were taken."

"Miller, help me get Tong Wei into the carriage."

Miller came over and they began lifting Tong Wei. He gestured for them to stop. "On my lap. They put something there. See it?"

Christian gazed down through the mottled dimness. He plucked the small, flat card, tucked it away, and inwardly cursed his own stupidity. Together with Miller he carried Tong Wei outside.

Miller climbed into the carriage too, bringing his storm of worry and anger with him. Christian checked Tong Wei. The pain of being moved had rendered him unconscious.

"Once we hand him over to the servants and send for a surgeon and the magistrate, you are to bring down my pistols, sword, and foils, Miller."

"I've a mind to bring down twenty pistols and a dozen swords, sir. And half the footmen, if you do not mind."

"Rouse them all, but they will not be joining us. I have other duties for them. You might do well to arm yourself, however."

They rode through the dark city for a tense few minutes.

"Do you know where she is, sir? Miss Montgomery, that is?"

"Yes, I think so." Christian removed the card that had been left on Tong Wei. "The person who sent those men left his calling card, so I would know."

He held the card to the window. They passed a gas lamp and its glow washed the card. It was not a calling card of the normal kind but a playing card.

The King of Spades.

He would have liked to bring an invading army, but he could not do that here. Leona had been imprisoned in the least assailable site, right in the heart of Mayfair.

Christian looked up the façade of the large house, to the windows at the top. Was she there, looking out? He thought he sensed her worry, then her love.

Miller felt for his pistol beneath his coat. Christian caught his arm, stopping him. "Do not be rash or I will send you away. I believe that they will both be safe before the night is done."

Miller accepted that, grudgingly. "If you are wrong, sir?"

"Then do your worst. It is why you are here. Just be prepared to swing for it."

Their reception was disturbingly normal. It might have been calling hours midweek, and not the dead of night. A butler took Christian's card away. He returned to usher the guest to the drawing room. He glanced askance at Miller.

"My man will accompany me and wait outside the door."

The butler's vague nod suggested that had not been part of the plan. All the same he brought them up. Miller took a position outside the door, against the wall, hand resting beneath his coat on the pistol. Christian entered the drawing room.

"Easterbrook. Good of you to come."

"I had no choice, Ashford. You have taken something that is mine."

The Duke of Ashford smiled lazily from his place

on a settee. "An interesting turn of phrase, your use of 'taken.' The temptation is notable. She is a fetching woman." He gestured to a side table with decanters and glasses. "Port? Brandy?"

"Why don't you tell me what you want? You had men killed to get me here."

"You mean the ruffians and the Chinaman? They are inconsequential." Ashford puffed on his cigar. "I need you to cease your infernal meddling. I am hoping that she means enough to you that you will see the light to protect her."

"If I do, will you let her go?"

"Eventually. Perhaps."

"You cannot keep two women imprisoned here forever."

"It is a very big house, and there are others. I daresay I can keep anyone imprisoned for as long as I choose. A parting letter from Miss Montgomery to your aunt, saying she has sailed back to China, and the world will forget her."

Not the whole world. Not one man. "You showed your hand unnecessarily. I did not know about you. Meadowsun, yes. My father and Denningham's. Not you."

"Yes, well, Meadowsun is a snake. He does not plan to be ruined alone, does he? And some of that money you seek came to me, not him, so he found it doubly unfair to have to pay my share back."

"So he blackmailed you to help him."

"Not really. Ending our little business would be financially inconvenient. Also, I had no choice once he told me what you knew. I can't have you digging into the past. The opium would only be embarrassing, but the rest . . ."

Of course this was about the rest. Christian went over and poured some brandy after all. He carried it to a chair. This night could only end one way. He might as well satisfy his curiosity.

"I do not think it is even all of the rest that concerns you so much. Just a few years' worth of shipments between England and France. You had considerable influence in government during the war, Ashford. The Admiralty, wasn't it? I expect you could learn the deployment of the naval service along the French coast if you wanted to."

Ashford's heavy lids fell half way. "Who would have thought that Easterbrook's strange heir would notice or remember. I always feared that you were more aware of the world than you pretended. You played whist far too well for my comfort too."

"My father drilled me on such things. He took his station very seriously, and expected me to as well. This is why I do not understand that part of this. The wartime smuggling. The risks and disgrace for all of you could not be worth the profit."

"The risks were minimal. That is why smuggling is a national pastime in England. Ask anyone in Kent or on Guernsey. In our case, the profits were . . . massive. Especially during the war."

"So was the dishonor. The people will see it as treason, no matter what your fellow peers decide."

Ashford shook his head and laughed at the memory of it again. "It started out innocently enough. More a schoolboy prank. Our company had seen surprising success in the East. Your father put a wonderfully simple system in place. A contact in the East India Company in Calcutta served as our agent. He hired shippers like Montgomery to take the cargo. It was so damned easy with the opium. Anyway, there we were at the whist table one night during the war, and Denningham bemoaned the loss of French wine. Well, why not try for some? We went to the western coast, to Gascony."

"Wine? You smuggled *wine*?"

"At first. Then it grew. Rather decidedly toward the end. It would not do for the world to know how it grew. Hence my problem with Meadowsun. And you. It would be better all around if no one unraveled the history of the Four Corners during the war years."

Christian stood. He walked over to the windows that looked down on the street below. "You did not abduct Miss Montgomery so we could have this talk. Unless you release her at once, you are forcing my hand. You leave me no choice except to challenge you."

"I suppose so."

"That was your goal, I expect. To settle this privately, and technically over an insult to a woman."

"That would be best."

"Once you are dead, what is to keep me from revealing everything?"

"Your word as a gentleman. Your duty to your name and family. Your participation at the whist judgments. It would not do for the people to know we are mere mortals, no better than them. You know and accept that." He sipped his brandy. "But I am not going to die. You are."

Perhaps so. Ashford's confidence in how this would end charged the chamber.

Christian faced him. "I will not challenge you. However, you may have no choice except to challenge me very soon. Carriages are arriving. Guests are at your door."

Ashford frowned. He came over and peered out the window. A row of carriage lamps dotted the street, and more moved toward them.

"I'll be damned, Ashford. It appears that some bishops and lords are looking for a game of whist."

Ashford turned, his face slack with shock. "You damn your own name with this if you accuse me in front of them. You betray your father and your blood and your station."

Christian looked down at the men filing into the house. "I reclaim my name and accept my station, not betray them. As for my blood, you better than most should have known what you were dealing with."

Doors slammed and women cried out. Commotion rolled down the narrow corridor between the attic chambers.

Isabella looked over, her eyes large in the lamplight. Leona swallowed her own bile.

"Whatever happens, wherever they take us, Easterbrook will follow," she said. "He is a very powerful man."

Isabella did not look convinced. The noise headed toward them. Leona rose and picked up the wooden chair on which she had been sitting. She positioned herself so she could use the chair to good purpose when their gaoler arrived.

She did not think her resistance would save them. This house was as big as Easterbrook's. An important man, perhaps one more powerful than a marquess, owned it. He had hired many men to abduct her. Too many for Tong Wei to stop the invasion.

Her eyes burned while she remembered the bodies in the reception hall. She and Isabella had been pushed past two dead strangers near the door. Only at the last moment, before being dragged into the night, had she seen Tong Wei and the blood that said he had been shot.

The door opened partway. Leona summoned her strength and raised the chair above her head.

"Isabella?"

It was Mr. Miller's voice. Isabella jumped up and ran toward the door. Mr. Miller strode in and pulled her into his arms. Leona let the chair crash to the floor. Her arms and heart groaned with relief.

Their embrace mesmerized her for a moment. Mr. Miller appeared very young, and very grateful and very much in love. He kissed Isabella again and again, gently, carefully, touching her face as if he checked for damage. He appeared as if he had narrowly escaped death himself, and less confident than Leona had ever seen him.

She realized that the three of them were not alone in the chamber. She sensed another presence, on the other side of the door. She looked around its edge. Easterbrook stood there, also watching the two servants, seeing and knowing more than she ever would.

He noticed her, and the chair near her feet. He drew her into his embrace. "I told him not to rush in. I knew that you would attack anyone who did."

She sagged against his strength. After hours of battling to keep terror at bay, relinquishing the fight felt too good to bear. "I knew you would come. I knew—"

His kiss silenced the rest. She luxuriated in the softness of his lips and the support of his arms.

"Tong Wei . . ." she said, her voice catching.

"He is alive. I am sure he will remain so."

Relief made her eyes brim with tears. "Was this Meadowsun's doing?"

"No. Another man. A fifth partner."

"Has he been defeated?"

"Yes. You are safe now. Completely safe."

She peered up at him. She sensed no darkness. No chaos. He was at peace. "Then you can take me home now."

"Miller will bring you home. There is one thing I still must do, then I will come to you." He looked past her. "Miller, we must go now."

"What must you do?" she asked while he led her past other doors from which servants peeked.

He handed her down many stairs without responding. Outside, carriages lined the street. Some had begun to leave and men were entering others.

"Who are these people, Christian? What has happened?"

Miller handed Isabella into the carriage, and held the door for her. The young man seemed very sober, and not at all happy about this rescue.

Christian tried to hand her in, but she refused. "Who are these men? Why were they here?"

"They are a group of other lords. I laid the accusations in front of them. A judgment was held."

"Would not it be better to lay it in front of a magistrate? A judge? What judgment could these men render?"

"One that said it would be better if your abductor was not tried in the House of Lords, which is the only place where he can be tried publicly and officially. A duke owns this house, Leona. A peer with a high reputation and considerable influence and a title that has a glorious history."

"You are saying that he would never see true justice, I think."

"He might, possibly, but at a cost to institutions that hold this country together. Sometimes it is better for justice to be served in quieter ways."

"As you did with Meadowsun?"

"Yes."

Except it would be over now if it had been the same as with the cleric. She watched the last of these men enter their coaches. Their serious purpose filled the air. They did not look at Easterbrook's coach. They did not bid farewell.

They were all going somewhere. Christian would be going there too.

A horrible fear spilled through her. One far worse than what had gripped her on being grabbed in her house.

A new coach came down the street. It stopped thirty feet away.

"You must go now, Leona. Miller—" He gave her hand into Miller's more demanding hold.

She struggled against the way Miller tried to pull her toward the carriage. "Who is that, Christian? In that coach there?"

"My brothers."

She knew then. The truth stole her breath. Everyone and everything ceased to move in that instant of realization. "Did you challenge him, Christian?"

"He challenged me."

"If you lose, is he free of it?"

"Not for the men who matter."

He spoke very calmly. Almost indifferently. She did not like that placid acceptance. He should be afraid, but he was not.

His demeanor frightened her now. This was not arrogance or confidence at work, but something far darker.

She yanked her hand away from Miller and embraced Christian tightly. She kissed him with all the love she could find in her heart, then spoke in his ear.

"It has appeal, does it not? The total peace. The final silence. It is luring you as it did years ago and perhaps often since. But you must want to live now. For your brothers and family. For me. For all that you are and still can be. You must be Easterbrook, and cannot allow yourself to be Edmund again."

He took her face in his hands and looked in her eyes. She let him see and sense whatever he wanted. That invasive power flowed and she did not run and hide this one time. She let it enter her and find its certainty and prayed whatever he discovered would be enough.

"Go now," he said. "I will see you soon."

"He appears confident," Denningham said, looking across the field to where Ashford removed his coats.

Dawn came mistily and the treetops disappeared into films of gray light.

"He anticipates little trouble with me. He would have never made the challenge if he did," Christian said.

The witnesses arrayed themselves on either side of the space between him and Ashford. Only the peers were here. The bishops, although in agreement that this was the better way, would not attend.

Denningham held the foil. He had offered to serve as second, but under these circumstances he had few duties to perform.

Two other witnesses were present. Hayden and Elliot stood behind Christian. He could feel their worry. There had been little talk in the carriage ride here, other than his explanation to them that the challenge involved the honor of Leona. If he failed this morning, Hayden would learn the truth the first time he entered Rallingport's library as the Marquess of Easterbrook.

He watched Ashford stretch and prepare himself. The man was in good humor. If he lost, he would go to his grave with his good name intact. If he won, no one would ever raise the question about the smuggling at the whist table.

That was how it was supposed to work. A clumsy justice and an imperfect one, but a quiet resolution all the same. The others would know, however. Ashford would be diminished both in influence and wealth even if he lived.

They were all sworn to it, but two men here were not. Christian walked back to his brothers.

"His demeanor is an insult," Elliot said, shooting a glare at Ashford.

"His confidence will be his undoing," Christian said.

Hayden smiled, but his eyes held deep concern. Hayden was very good with numbers and odds, and his calculations on this duel had not been happy ones. "I trust you have used the foil at least once or twice in the last ten years."

"On occasion. I am much improved since I fought the pirates that raided the ship I was on near Japan."

"You fought pirates near Japan?" Elliot asked with surprise.

"Did I never mention that? Suffice to say I am more skilled than you know, and I intend to win today. However, Hayden, in the event that you soon find yourself with the title, I suggest that you look into that partnership that I had Mr. Miller ask you about. Look into it very thoroughly. You are not bound by any promises I might have made, but I advise that you do it very quietly until you comprehend where it is going."

Hayden's smile fell. He looked at Ashford with new eyes.

Christian returned to Denningham, whose distress was palpable.

"Hell of a thing," Denningham muttered. "Damned if I'll be playing whist with him again. He can sit in a corner in the library for all I care if he dares show after this."

"Thank you for the vote of confidence, Denningham."

Denningham flushed, mortified.

Christian smiled to reassure him, then spoke. "I am

sorry that I could not keep your father's name out of it, and yours by association."

"I understand. Decent of you to confine it to the men in that small club, but right is right, after all. If we do not stand for that, what good are we?"

His simplicity charmed Christian, as it had since they were boys. He had always rather envied Denningham that quality. "We must have dinner and some good wine when this is over. I think I still belong to some other clubs."

"Wine, hell. I won't be able to drink another French bottle from my cellar without wondering . . . but, yes, I would like that."

Christian held out his hand. "My foil, old friend."

He handed it over. Christian walked down the field to meet Ashford.

You must want to live.

She understood him too well. She was correct that death had lured Edmund, and even Easterbrook every now and then. It did mean total peace and utter silence. It would be like dwelling in the dark center forever. That was what meditation created, after all, a taste of the selfless existence waiting in infinity.

As a result, Christian did not fear death. He had already visited that plane. He was not inclined to go there permanently if he could avoid it, however.

Not if staying alive meant spending even one more day with Leona.

He came to her silently. Darkly. He arrived at ten o'clock in the morning, dressed impeccably in his most lordly way. He entered her house as if he owned it, the way he was inclined to do. He found her in the library, reading a book whose pages had been ruined by her worried tears.

He sat beside her. She embraced him and let her relief spill. No tears now, just a fullness that made it hard to speak.

"Where is Miller?" he asked.

"Above," she muttered into his coat.

"Are you saying he was taking his pleasure with your servant while I was facing my death?"

She laughed. "Your brother brought your note two hours ago. They slipped away once we knew you were unharmed."

"That is better, then."

She rested against him, her ear to his heart and his arm around her. They just sat there, being together, reassuring each other.

"The magistrate was here at dawn, when we returned," she said. "It was trying, to know where you were and what you were doing, while I answered their questions."

"What did you say?"

"That four men invaded and Tong Wei tried to protect us and was shot for his efforts. That we were taken to a house in the city, I know not where, and locked away. That you and Mr. Miller rescued us. He spoke with Mr. Miller a long while alone, then left."

"Miller knew what to say. It will all be explained to the magistrate's satisfaction in a few days. As will the unexpected demise of my fellow lord."

She had not known for certain that the duke was

dead. The note that came had only said that Christian was well and would come to her soon.

"Do you want to talk about it?" she asked.

"No."

"I understand. It must have been difficult for you, no matter how necessary or right."

He pressed a kiss to her crown. "Not as difficult as it should have been. My father's blood serves me too well in such matters. But I can live with it because you are safe. I never would have been certain of that otherwise." He eased her away and stood. He held out his hand. "Let us take a turn around the square. I find that I am unaccountably in the mood for the noise of life."

CHAPTER
TWENTY-SEVEN

He stayed with her that night. They took slow pleasure in her chamber. The entire house and garden remained silent.

She experienced a new peace in their intimacy. A sense of completion. The duty to her father was over. Her anger about his persecution had been sliding away since they left Doctors' Commons, and she finally released all of it while in Christian's arms.

She held Christian closely and let her entire consciousness dwell on him. She memorized his scent and feel, the textures of his hair and skin. She took him into herself deeply when it was time, and allowed no sorrow or fears to interfere with knowing him.

A touching poignancy moved her, and him too, she thought. The kisses, the ecstasy itself, became a conversation between them that she finally voiced with words. First silent words, spoken in her mind and in her heart, then finally into his ear while they gave themselves to each other.

I love you, all that you are. The good and the sins,

the brilliance and the curse, the storms that still plague Edmund and the mastery that is Easterbrook. I love all that you are.

She slipped from the bed without waking him. She donned a simple *qipao,* then looked down on him while he slept. His hair was getting longer again, and it fell on his shoulders in those barbaric locks. Right now, in his sleep, the softening beauty had its way and he appeared like a dark angel.

She left the chamber. She did not want to spoil the memory of their night with the thoughts that had entered her while she lay in the dawn's light. She could not avoid them anymore. He had given her a victory and helped her more than she expected. They both knew what that meant, even if they had ignored it for these hours together.

She went to the garden and sat among the spring flowers. She did not have much time to herself, however. Soon she was not alone.

He entered the garden and saw her. He had put on trousers and boots and his shirt. He looked much like he had that first day when Mr. Miller kidnapped her off the street.

She reacted the same way too. Their affair had not dimmed that. Much the opposite. He could still excite her with nothing more than the gaze he settled on her now.

He sat down with her. He took her hand in his, admired the flowers, and waited.

Her throat tightened, but she spoke anyway. She only could because she knew he guessed what she was thinking. "I need to book passage soon. As soon as Tong Wei can travel."

"Do you want to go?"

"I do not want to, but it is finished now. I cannot put off this parting."

"You said you would have no excuse to stay once it was finished. I expect that is true."

No, she had no excuse.

"However, you do have a reason, Leona. This." He kissed her. "And this." He kissed her again. He held her face to yet another kiss. "You will stay with me."

"You are seducing me away from my duties again, Christian. You are very good at that."

He looked in her eyes. "You will stay with me."

"My brother relies on me. More than you know."

"Your brother must be his own man. It is time. He is of age, but he will lean on you as long as you are there. Send Tong Wei with St. John's offer and advise him to take it. Your brother will learn your father's trade from St. John's factor and agents. He and his business will be protected."

She yearned to grab his reasons. Her heart had always been weak with him.

"Stay with me. Stay so I do not lose myself inside myself. I am not at the mercy of this curse as much anymore, and that is due to you. I no longer assume that it owns me."

His words touched her. It moved her that this man would reveal his fears, and speak of the pain that he still fought to master.

"Stay with me, darling. Stay because I need you. Stay because I love you. I will wear a cravat every day if you want. I will take you to balls three times a week. I will sit and accept callers with Aunt Hen if I must."

She had to laugh, but tears stung her eyes too. "I do not want you to change all your habits for me. You do not need to be other than you are. You can still be half mad and a little eccentric and mostly a recluse. As long as you do not retreat from me too, Christian."

"I could never do that. I am only my true self when I am with you."

He really believed that. She could tell he did. And she knew these words, all of them, did not come easily to him. He was Easterbrook, after all.

"I suppose I could stay for a while. I could send Tong Wei back to my brother with St. John's proposal. I want to see Gaspar, but I do not yearn to return to China yet. I can at least stay until the jade runs out."

"Leona, I am not asking you to stay for a while. I want you to stay forever, as my wife."

The proposal did not surprise as much as it should. Perhaps that was because she was certain he loved her. She just *knew*. "I thought that was ill-advised."

"For you. Not for me. I know it is selfish to bind you to me. If you do not want it, we will find another way. And if you must return to Macao, if you want to sail the China Sea and fight pirates forever, I will come with you. We will do this any way you want, but . . . I would rather we be together in marriage, if you can bear it."

"I can bear it. However, I assumed you believed that your sensibility was inherited and you did not want the next Easterbrook to have it."

"I am seeing this affliction less darkly now. If it is inherited, we will explain it to our child, so he knows what it is and learns how to live in the world with it. We will make sure he is not alone with it."

He appeared so serious. So determined and . . . hopeful.

She allowed herself to picture that child, and others. She imagined life with Christian, and experiencing the love and excitement forever. She saw the difficulties too, but her confidence in their intimacy made her smile at the thought of his habits.

I love all that you are.

"Are you sure that you want to do this, Christian?"

"I am sure about you. You are my only certainty, Leona." He kissed her once more, and used all of his power over her in that kiss. "Say that you will stay with me."

It was not really a request. Nor was it entirely a command. There was only one answer that he would accept, however, and only one that she could give.

Her heart accepted the truth first, as it always had done with him.

"I could not be happy without you either, Christian. We will stay together."

EPILOGUE

I have decided that I should do the right thing."

"It has taken you long enough, Miller."

Miller's face flushed. "Yes. That was cowardly of me."

Christian nodded. It had indeed been cowardice that had prevented Miller from doing the right thing by Isabella for over three years now. An understandable cowardice, perhaps, but still cowardice.

They stood on the terrace of Aylesbury Abbey, looking down at the garden party spread below. Most of the guests were family, gathered here to celebrate the visit of Leona's brother. Gaspar sat with his sister in the sun, looking far more English than she. He played with the next Marquess of Easterbrook while the two of them talked.

"You understand that Isabella has nothing. No fortune," Christian said.

Miller nodded. His gaze remained on the woman in question. Isabella followed her daughter through the garden. She stayed far enough away to allow the child her fun, but close enough to prevent accidents.

"Being brave instead of cowardly will not change the reality. People will still say things. She looks more Chinese than European," Christian said.

"People will say things, but no person will say anything twice."

Miller's jaw tightened. Christian guessed that a few persons had already learned what Miller would and would not accept when it came to Isabella.

"We would like your blessing, and that of Lady Easterbrook."

"You have it, not that it is required."

They walked down to the garden together. Miller went toward his lover and daughter. Christian aimed for Leona and her brother.

"It has gotten worse," Gaspar was saying as Christian drew near. "Big ships full of opium lay anchor at Lintin now. Chinese smugglers go out to them. Everyone knows the Mandarins all along the coast are complicit. Anyone can trade it openly in Macao, and the Chinese officials turn a blind eye. It is pouring into China."

Leona glanced at Christian. It had been pouring in for decades. The only real news here was that Gaspar had developed a better comprehension of Oriental trade.

"Perhaps another series of letters is called for," Christian said. "I am sure the publisher of *Minerva's Banquet* would print them."

That publisher was over at a tree, instructing her husband to pluck a little girl out of it. The child had just learned to walk, but had managed to get as high as her mother's head in a blink. Elliot laughed while he pried the imp loose. Phaedra literally tore at her hair in exasperation. Nature, in a fit of humor, had blessed Phaedra with a daughter as willful as herself.

"I will write them, but they will do no more good than your speeches in the House of Lords, Christian," Leona said. "The devil is busy, and we do not have enough angels."

No, not nearly enough. He would make those speeches, however, even if this would get worse before it ever got better.

The evidence was that the people of England counted on distance and discretion regarding the opium trade. Leona's last letter had suitably soiled the reputations of four dead lords and one living cleric. Society was shocked that people they knew dirtied their hands with this immoral trade. Then, after an appropriate period of gossip and disgrace, everyone had gone back to drinking their China tea. The hole left by sudden absence of the Four Corners ships had quickly been filled by others at Lintin, but that company's demise had caused bigger disruptions in smuggling elsewhere.

In the case of the last Easterbrook, that scandal had only primed the pump for the bigger one. The bait had been swallowed and the blackmail demanded, most indiscreetly. The name of Easterbrook had been forever linked with murder in the trial that just ended, and the blackmailer was on his way to New South Wales.

Gaspar's attention shifted abruptly from his nephew to a young lady walking down a garden path toward them. Blond and dazzling in the summer sun, Irene

Longworth tilted her head to listen to her sister, Rose, who walked with her.

Gaspar clumsily tried to hand over the child. "I think I might—that is, I will take a turn, I think—"

Christian bent down and took his son in his arms so Gaspar could make good his escape.

He settled himself down with Leona while his son squirmed and wrestled. Aiden was beginning to talk, and there could be no mistaking he had emotions. Specific ones. Varied ones. There was no indication that he had inherited any curse, however.

Christian could not tell if his awareness of the child's feelings was at all unusual. Leona seemed to know Aiden's moods as well as he did. Much like Denningham, little Aiden was an open book.

That would probably change as Aiden got older, but it appeared that no special sensibility was needed when it came to one's own child. Or rather, nature instilled that sensibility in every parent when it came to that child. One only had to choose to pay attention.

Leona watched her brother hail Irene and Rose. "He has been spending a lot of time with her," she said. "The Bradwells do not seem to mind."

"Mrs. Bradwell is delighted, and hopeful that a proposal is imminent."

"You are certain about that?"

"Most certain. Alexia says so."

"So Irene's sister is hopeful and my brother is hopeful. What of Irene herself?"

"She appears agreeable. Look at how she smiles at him."

"I do not want your opinion of how she appears. I

can see that, and it might just be politeness. I need you to *know*."

Aiden squirmed down. He ran off to Hayden and Alexia's two girls, who played with Elliot's son. Aiden barged in, did some pushing, got pushed back, swung his little fist, and found himself under a pile of legs and arms and ringlets and squeals.

"Are you asking me to intrude, Leona? To direct unseemly attention to her emotional state? These things take their own course and it would be unwise and unfair for me to—"

"Oh, *please,* Easterbrook. What good is it to be married to a man with your gift if I cannot even learn if my brother's intentions will be welcomed? Now, go over there and—and—well, do whatever it is you do to know these things."

He laughed and reached for her hand. He kissed it. "I have reason to believe that your brother will be successful. Even the mention of moving to the other side of the world does not dim Irene Longworth's love."

Leona smiled with contentment. "I knew I could count on you, Christian. You have made great strides in controlling that ability. I know that you choose to avoid it, but on a question as important as this, a little slipping can be excused."

He *had* made great strides in controlling it. He liked to think he used it sparingly now, by his own will, and only for the best reasons. The truth was there were times when he still could not block the perceptions.

Still, a more public life had become tolerable, and most people almost so. He did not isolate himself so much now. He only had to retreat to Leona's oasis if the world exhausted him.

"Speaking of pending nuptials, Miller is going to propose to Isabella," he said.

"I am relieved, and surprised. She brings him nothing."

"She brings him her love and herself, which is what you brought me."

"You had no need of a fortune from me. Miller is not so well off that a settlement can be ignored."

"We will settle something on her, darling, but he did not make his decision in hopes of it. I am sure of this."

She smiled. "A little more slipping, Christian?"

"A very small slip."

She laughed in the way that always brought memories of Macao, and of a dark-eyed girl in a night garden who had soothed his soul. He still wanted her as much as he had ten years ago, and still loved her as much as he had during a week of bliss in Aylesbury Abbey.

The various groups in the garden had converged. They created a thick knot of adults surrounded by a whirlwind of children. The din of grown-up chatter and childish screams rose and fell on the breeze.

Leona stood, with her hand still in his. "Shall we join the others, Christian?"

The real question showed in her eyes. *Are you ready? Can you bear it?*

"Of course," he said.

He stood, and together they walked toward the joyful noise.

AUTHOR'S NOTE

The Charter Act of 1833 abolished the remaining trade monopolies of the English East India Company and essentially ended its commercial activities. It continued functioning in a political and administrative capacity until its dissolution in 1874.

After 1833, the established Country Traders in the East expanded and grew restless with China's closed borders. The trade in opium also flourished until 1839, when the incorruptible Chinese official Lin Zexu (Lin Tse-hsu) was sent by the emperor to end it. Under his direction, 2.6 million pounds of opium were confiscated in Canton and destroyed.

There followed a series of diplomatic and commercial crises that ultimately led to the First Opium War of 1839. China was defeated by the British and forced to open its five ports to foreign trade and cede the territory of Hong Kong. The British people were not unified behind this war. Considerable moral outrage was expressed, with the protection of opium trafficking being the main point of criticism. The goal of forcing China's borders open to foreign trade had been achieved, however.

Throughout the novel, I have used the transcriptions of Chinese names that were common in English texts published in the first half of the nineteenth century, during the period when the story takes place.

The process of transcribing Chinese language characters into the Latin alphabet is called Romanization. Today the standard system of Romanization is Hanyu Pinyin, commonly called pinyin. It was first introduced in China in 1956 and widely adopted internationally by the 1980s.

The old anglicized transcription "Canton" is written in pinyin as Guangzhou and that of "Macao" as Macau.

ABOUT
THE AUTHOR

MADELINE HUNTER is the *New York Times* best-
selling author of seventeen historical romances. More
than two million copies of her books are in print in the
United States and her books have also been translated
into nine languages. She is a six-time RITA finalist,
and won RITAs twice for historical romance. Sixteen
of her books have been on the *USA Today* bestseller
list, and she has also had titles on the bestseller lists of
the *New York Times* and *Publishers Weekly*. Madeline
has a Ph.D. in art history, and she teaches at the college
level. She lives in Pennsylvania with her husband and
two sons.